Thomas Barlow has been a research fellow at Oxford University and at the Massachusetts Institute of Technology, a columnist with the Financial Times in London, and a respected adviser on research strategy to a range of organizations in the USA, Australia, and East Asia.

A THEORY OF NOTHING

A NOVEL

THOMAS BARLOW

IVORY LEAGUE
PUBLISHING

Copyright © 2016 Thomas Barlow

Paperback edition ISBN 978–0–9924159–3–8
Digital (epub) edition ISBN 978–0–9924159–4–5
Digital (kindle) edition ISBN 978–0–9924159–5–2

Cover design by Josh Durham, Design by Committee
Typesetting by Kirby Jones

AUTHOR'S NOTE

The dominant incentives in the world of the intellect have tended for hundreds, if not thousands of years to encourage intelligent people to complicate their communications. When any intellectual argument seems abstract and difficult to comprehend, it is customary in the academic milieu to presume that its exponent must necessarily be brilliant. On the other hand, when an intellectual argument seems simple and easily understood, it is usually assumed to be facile. This is why intellectual authors tend to write books that nobody will understand and why intellectual readers tend to read books that nobody enjoys reading. However, an incomprehensible book serves little purpose no matter how profound its underlying ideas, and in this respect *A Theory of Nothing* represents something unusual. My goal has been to create a story so thoroughly incomprehensible, so completely baffling and outlandish, and so utterly devoid of meaning, that it actually makes sense.

For Jeremiah and Cassandra,
both long dead, if they ever existed,
but still the greatest friends a scientist could have.

CHAPTER I

THE FALL

The Cambridge police declared it a suicide, but of course, it was nothing of the sort. I was there when it happened. It was a perfect morning in early summer. An eastern sea breeze was blowing across the campus, gently caressing the leaves of the elms and hackberry trees. The sun was making a bold ascent, its sharp rays segmented and dispatched in a frenzy of Rayleigh scattering, for the sky was clear blue.

My normal routine was to traverse the campus only at its barest moments, in the diffuse light of dawn and in the lengthening shadows of the night, but I had worked particularly late the previous evening and slept longer than usual. I remember thinking how pleasant it was to see the university in broad daylight, when the campus was properly occupied. Indeed, I remember thinking how well populated Harvard felt, even at that very instant when fate reduced its population by one.

The incident occurred while I was walking among the cluster of buildings that constitute the Harvard Law School. It happened without warning, directly behind me. I was on a path next to the brown brick edifice known as Griswold Hall. There was a heavy thud, followed by a high scream, an anguished shout, and the urgent scuffling of running feet. I turned and saw a body on the ground.

It was a woman's frame, white-haired and middle-aged, and it struck me that had I finished my breakfast a mere ten seconds earlier I might have seen the whole thing, as it happened, including the acceleration of a human being at thirty-two feet per second per second. I shuddered.

A man and a woman knelt beside the body, and the man felt for a pulse. Somebody said to call an ambulance. A crowd began to gather. I noticed a woman with a hand clamped over her mouth, the half-turned heads, the murmurs of distress and disbelief, the unwillingness to look – but the irresistible desire to do so. It was clear that nothing could be done.

"She's dead," someone said, and an awe-stricken whimper rippled through the crowd.

Numbly, I raised my eyes and carefully surveyed the side of Griswold Hall. On the fourth floor, there was an open window. Beyond it, I could see only a motionless shadow and the corner of an empty ceiling. I sensed that the room behind lay vacant, and a shiver passed along my spine. Then the campus police and an ambulance shattered the morbid hush with the blare of their shrieking sirens, the sudden screech of brakes, the slamming of car doors, and the dissonance of urgent shouting and running. Two paramedics scurried to the body. Several police officers took up sentinel positions around the scene. A tall young woman in plain clothes, with some apparent authority, spoke in a clipped voice to the onlookers. She asked for any witnesses to remain, but for the rest of us to disperse.

I could not move, however, for at this same instant a paramedic brushed the hair from the victim's face. I gave an involuntary gasp of recognition. The woman lying before us was one of Harvard's most celebrated scholars:

a distinguished professor in natural law, an eminent legal philosopher, public intellectual, freethinker, minority rights activist, and role model for young women. She was the Chair of the National Council for the Humanities, and a winner of the Presidential Medal of Honor for legal scholarship and services to higher education – a fierce and powerful woman, a person unlikely to acquiesce to anything, least of all her own death. Her name was Sandra Hidecock.

I turned away from the awful spectacle and continued on to my laboratory. I had not known her well, but we had been personally acquainted – a fact that played upon my mind. I had a vague recollection that we'd spoken at some point about her work, that she had been a standard bearer for avant-garde culture, and that this had been a source of disagreement between us. In those days, there was a view among many intellectuals operating at the cutting edge of the humanities that all truth is relative; that one should repudiate established knowledge, seek one's own reality, and aggressively question the scientific worldview. My passing memory was that Sandra Hidecock had been of this mind, and I was not surprised, therefore, to discover the following statement pinned to a noticeboard in our department later that day:

> All men and women have a moral obligation to
> achieve the highest state of autonomy possible. I
> am opposed to the soulless and frigid constraints
> imposed upon us all by the laws of science. I
> object to the disempowering and disenfranchising
> consequences of mathematical representations
> of life, energy, matter, and our universe. There
> is but one power to which I can yield a heart-felt

obedience: the decision of my own understanding,
the dictate of my own conscience.

This was extracted from a short article published by the deceased in the *Journal of Semiotic Justice*. Within an hour of her death, these rousing words had been disseminated throughout the university; declaimed, deconstructed and analyzed from a thousand different angles. Perhaps inevitably, rumors began at Harvard that Sandra Hidecock's ultimate plunge was not a deliberate attempt at self-destruction but a courageous act of intellectual rebellion and self-expression. It was observed that, true to the logic of her own personal philosophy, she had simply rejected all pre-conceived notions about mass, proportionality, distance, and force, and that she had stepped from the fourth-story window of her office not so much with an intention to die, but from a deeper and more significant desire to oppose the law of gravity.

The idea began to circulate that this was not a suicide at all, but something entirely different: a profoundly symbolic act; a purposeful attempt to challenge the laws of nature. Several members of the Harvard faculty, especially those in the liberal arts disciplines, began to speak of Sandra Hidecock as an inspirational figure. They spoke of her intellectual integrity, of her courage, and of the injustice of her fate. She was, they said, Harvard's only true insurrectionary.

I will never forget the distinctive crunch as Sandra Hidecock's body collided with the ground and experienced the full brunt of an equal and opposite force, consistent with Newton's third law. My presence at that tragic moment of impact was significant. In many ways, it was the genesis of all that followed, for it prompted me to attend her funeral some days later. I wanted to express my sorrow but I was also curious to know more about her strange, self-destructive deed, which although officially declared a suicide, seemed at Harvard, at any rate, to signify something more.

CHAPTER II

THE WAKE

The funeral was held at the St Crispin Crematorium in Cambridge, Massachusetts, almost in sight of the office from which Sandra Hidecock so comprehensively carried her life's work to its logical conclusion. The building was squat and nondescript. Inside, it was tiled with slabs of faux-marble: off-white and uneven, unpolished in parts, and slightly sticky. It was a backdrop to make the living seem lively indeed. Yet we were more thoughtful than lively that day. Those of us who had known Sandra Hidecock were mostly intellectuals, researchers, and writers of serious non-fiction. The crowd that converged on the crematorium to watch as her body was burned and poured into a jar was highly credentialed. It was perhaps the largest convocation of human intelligence since the Manhattan Project.

We were seated in the Hall of Remembrance, a facility with the acoustic properties of an anechoic chamber. Here, we shuffled onto long oak benches that were dark and battered. I perched at the end of a row, beside a young woman, who was clutching a pink handkerchief.

There was no order of service. The proceedings were unplanned, free and open – an arrangement that seemed appropriate for the woman in question, and for the vast number of literary theorists, artists, and other humanities scholars in attendance. A microphone was provided for anyone who wished to speak, and a great many felt compelled to offer their theories about the tragedy that had brought us together so unexpectedly, and in such emotional circumstances.

Marcia Ortez, the famed transsexual professor of Sociology at Duke University, and former husband of the deceased, delivered a memorable oration. She placed the blame for Hidecock's death firmly with the scientific community. "Only where there is no science, is there no injustice," she said, rivulets of mascara cascading down her cheeks. "Science is the absolute tyrant that obstructs absolute liberty. Its henchmen are the impertinent scientists whose business it is to establish a vast body of laws that require our conformity. Sandra was ashamed of this body of laws. Sadly, she died fighting them."

Others were more temperate in their views. Martin Krupp, Dean of the Law School in which Hidecock had been such an active and inspirational colleague said, "She was a woman of immense courage, of wit, and integrity. I have known few people as independent-minded or as free spirited as she was. But nature is unforgiving, for which reason even the fiercest and most rebellious of dispositions must acquiesce to its will, or face the consequences."

The President of Harvard, the gleaming Emmanuel Porphyrin, was there too, in the front row. He wore a Harvard tie, a lint-free peppercorn suit and a rich purple shirt that somehow diverted attention from the effect of his prodigious eyes. Porphyrin was widely admired within the Harvard community, a rarity for Harvard presidents. He worked long hours and was known for his decisiveness and attention to administrative detail. When it was his turn to speak, he rose majestically before us, lifting one hand in supplication, as if balancing Sandra Hidecock's soul in his palm. The woman next to me dabbed her nose and trembled slightly, while our gazes were drawn to the top of Porphyrin's famous cranium, which shone like a beacon of light.

I can't remember much of what he said. Emmanuel Porphyrin was far too gifted in the art of academic communication to be memorable. But one small segment stands out. "There are few things more keenly felt in our community than the deplorable waste of a great mind," he mused. "But the tragedy we face today is twofold: there is the calamity that we have lost one of our finest scholars, and there is also the fact that this calamity might have been prevented. Sandra worked in the greatest institution of higher learning there has ever been. She has been surrounded by the most refined minds of her generation, yet not one of us was able to save her."

Attributing collective culpability in situations of personal tragedy is one of the main priorities of modern scholarship. Obviously the idea that I personally shared responsibility for Sandra Hidecock's death was implausible, since I hardly knew the woman. But I could see that Porphyrin was only trying to bring us together in difficult circumstances, and to some extent his words had the desired effect, for just as he uttered them, the young woman beside me started to sob. All thoughts of academic propriety forgotten, I put my arm around her and she dowsed my shoulder in tears.

After the ceremony, my embarrassed companion unpeeled herself. At the time, I did not appreciate the significance of this woman. Still clutching her pink handkerchief, she murmured something about not wanting to talk right now, and we went our separate ways.

Leaving the crematorium, I drifted with the crowd back onto campus. No doubt the incineration of any person's body at the St Crispin Crematorium is a moving occasion, but rubbing shoulders with my colleagues and reflecting upon the distraught young woman who'd sat beside me, I was suddenly aware of the essential ordinariness and humanity of these people, and I felt a deep and unexpected empathy. It seemed to me that Sandra Hidecock's particularly tragic exit from the Harvard faculty in some way encapsulated the struggle in which all people contend: to get above and beyond themselves and to break free from the cruel limitations of their world.

Yet these feelings of solidarity dissipated quickly upon my arrival at the Harvard Faculty Club, which was the location for the wake. To my surprise, the mood at the reception was neither convivial nor welcoming. As I joined the party, I nodded sympathetically at a young lady with tear-stained cheeks, who frowned and turned her back on me. I decided to forge a path across the room to Marcia Ortez to convey my condolences. Along the way, I passed a man in a russet sweater expounding grimly upon the hazards of academic life, and wondering who among his faculty might be the next to leap off a building. He, too, glowered at me as I passed. Then I was jostled into the side of a woman who looked, in her expansive patchwork garment, like a hybrid of the Arts and Crafts movement and a Mongolian yurt. She cursed me under her breath and turned away when I apologized, clutching a sodden and crumpled napkin to her mouth as if afraid that she might contract some foul, airborne virus.

In every direction, surrounded as I was by sobbing sociologists, red and itchy-eyed lawyers, trembling literary

9

theorists, and weeping anthropologists, I was struck by an undercurrent of extreme antipathy, and I was unnerved by the realization that at least some of this was directed at me.

Eventually, I saw a historian who I knew vaguely, a British exile called Neville Keegan. He was a creature of university committees, a collegial type who would go anywhere on campus for a free sandwich, and who was famous in the Harvard community for continually nodding, as if locked in a state of permanent agreement with the world. I waved and made my way toward him.

"Hello, Neville," I said.

He looked up and raised his eyebrows, and for the first time in my experience I saw his head freeze. It was as if the bouncing rubber in the back of his neck had been dipped in liquid nitrogen or transmuted to titanium. He leaned toward me, eyes horrified.

"God, Duronimus," he said, "you've got a deal of courage showing your face here."

"What do you mean?"

"Well, most of them hold you responsible."

Such a notion was plainly absurd. I laughed awkwardly as Neville gestured out across the clubroom. To my right, there was a coterie of thin, blood-drained characters with luminous eyes: the comparative literature crowd. On my left, bearded criminologists wore mostly leather jackets. Behind me, there was a cabal of sweaty old men with forests of eyebrows and unwashed collars. Were they the anthropologists? What was astonishing though, and what made me feel distinctly ill at ease, were the unfriendly glances being extended in my direction from all sides.

Then it struck me that I hadn't yet seen any scientists or engineers present. I recalled the convoluted enquiries

I'd had to make in order to discover the time and location of the wake, for I had no real personal or professional relationship with the deceased. I had known Sandra Hidecock only remotely through the Harvard Squash Club, of which she was patron. We'd spoken on a few occasions, but our acquaintance was slight. I had come to this jamboree more from a sense of duty than from affection, and because I had witnessed the fall. Not for a moment had I expected such a hostile reception.

Yet reflecting now upon the content of Marcia Ortez's earlier remarks – "Only where there is no science, is there no injustice" – I began to wonder whether there wasn't some truth in Neville Keegan's observation. I realized the strange possibility that I was a lightning rod for their hatred and grief, and that I was probably as ghastly to them on this occasion as a vivisectionist at an animal rights convention.

I became aware that Neville's head had started nodding again, which reassured me slightly. He suggested that I be sensitive to the "intemperate emotional reactions" of his arts colleagues, that I try to show some "humility, understanding, and diplomacy" in light of the circumstances, and that I watch my back as I depart.

He paused to drain the last droplet of wine from his glass. "Time for a fill up – sorry," he said, waving his empty glass at me and turning on his heel.

He left me feeling rather dazed. I decided to avoid Marcia Ortez, who was still some way off talking fervently to Emmanuel Porphyrin. I began searching the crowd instead, hoping to find at least one friendly face. I needed an ally, someone who might understand what I was doing there, and it was at this moment that I saw the same young woman who had wept on my shoulder at the crematorium. She was standing alone, not four feet away, gazing at me inquisitively.

"Is everything alright?" I asked.

"No," she replied. "How could it be?"

Her eyes were still swollen from weeping. Her face was rather plain, but now that she'd taken off her jacket, there was also something appealingly curvaceous about her. She wore a dark dress with shining green shoes, as if she had a secret wish to be Dorothy in a new, politically charged and environmentally friendly adaptation of *The Wizard of Oz*.

"I'm sorry," I said. "I just meant to ask whether things were any better now than they were back then."

I pointed vaguely in the direction of the door, thinking that this was the simplest way to refer to the crematorium. Then I smiled clumsily and she didn't exactly smile back at me, but she at least stopped looking so furious. Vulnerable and emotionally disoriented, I found myself overwhelmed by the desire to take her by the elbow, steer her to a quiet corner, sit down very close to her, and put a hand on her knee.

Her name was Amelia Middleshot. She was a dentist's daughter from Cheyenne, Wyoming. She'd come to Harvard because, like so many other Harvard students, she believed in equality and had a passion for social justice. Until the tragic events of the previous week, she had been Sandra Hidecock's sole doctoral student. She said that losing Sandra was the worst thing that had ever happened to her and that she abhorred scientists and deemed them all to be personally responsible.

"But I am a scientist," I said.

She looked up at me with her pale green eyes and blinked. "Then you are responsible."

"Why?"

"Because you're someone who invents these laws, these irrefutable laws of nature."

"Not invent – discover!" I exclaimed.

"And by discovering, you constrain us."

I did my best to present a robust defense of the scientific position. I explained that mankind is naturally born free from all subjugation, except for those all-powerful constraints imposed by the natural laws. I made it clear that nature is infinite and man finite, that natural laws are strong and eternal, while we are mortal and weak. I suggested that scientists discover laws not to constrain people, but to find ways around them, and that our overriding goal is to pit one law against another in order to minimize the extent of nature's power over us. I agreed how tragic, unjust, and futile it was that the hardest laws to accept should be those that are impossible to break; and I acknowledged that, when faced with the destruction of a brilliant though flawed mind, these ideas offered very little comfort indeed. Then I gently recommended to Amelia that her worldview was misinformed, that Sandra's tragic demise was really no one's fault but her own, and that the only salvation for any of us lay in the acceptance of reality.

Amelia merely narrowed her eyes and tossed her hair back in defiance. It was clear that she was determined to counter with her own defense of Sandra Hidecock's futile life. She adjusted her legs and thrust out her chest a little. Then she studied me, with her nose pointing off to one side and her lips curled in disdain. I was evidently the contradiction of everything she prized: a man, a scientist, and an empiricist. I could also see that she intended to teach me how little I knew of all the latest, intellectually stimulating breakthroughs taking place in the metaphysical, epistemic, and semantic aspects of European and North American legal studies as applied to scientific philosophy. She put her head on one side and took a deep breath. Then she smirked, condescendingly.

"Okay. So what's your name then?" she said.

"Duronimus," I replied, and this was the strangest thing: suddenly, everything changed. Her mind jammed, like a slot machine. The lecture she'd been about to deliver was instantly forgotten. The venom was gone. Her stiff poise collapsed. Her face relaxed and was eager and excited, joyously youthful for the first time in our acquaintance.

"Duronimus who?" she asked, her eyes widening.

"Duronimus Karlof."

"Oh!" She sank back into her chair and hoisted a black leather satchel onto her lap. "You're Professor Karlof – I can hardly believe it!" She reached into the bag and rummaged about, then extracted an envelope. "I really have no idea who you are but I found this on Sandra's desk. My guess is it was the last thing she wrote," she said, thrusting it at me.

It was a plain white envelope with "Professor Duronimus Karlof" inscribed on the front. A shiver passed through my fingers as I took it. I felt consumed by a macabre curiosity. I looked around at all the demographers, archaeologists, ethicists, Sanskrit readers, metaphysicians, multimedia studies experts, and so on. *Why did she write to me?* I wondered. *Why not write to someone in her own sphere?*

Logic told me that the note must be of minor consequence; a short memo about some innocuous administrative matter. Perhaps the Harvard Squash Club

14

needed someone with mathematical ability to draw up the annual round robin? Perhaps the Law School needed a scientific expert on its advisory board? I trembled. Call it a premonition if you will, but as I ran my thumb across the texture of that flimsy envelope, I sensed I was holding something dangerous.

"Hey, are you going to open it?" Amelia asked.

"I guess so," I said, and broke the seal.

Inside was a small slip of paper, with a note of three short paragraphs. I'd never seen Sandra Hidecock's handwriting before. In keeping with the established convention among some humanities professors, she eschewed the traditional blue or black. She wrote in orange ink. I noted at once though, and with some fascination, that she had neither the fine, rounded, self-consciously elegant style of an art history professor, nor the stiff, chopping technique of a research engineer, nor the careless, devil-may-care, illegible scrawl of a scientist. On the contrary, she wrote with grace. There was a polish and poise to her lettering that was completely at odds with that final, insane act that ended her existence.

I still have the letter. It was dated the day before she died. This is what it said:

My Dear Duronimus,
If you are reading this, then you will know what has become of me. After a lifetime advocating a more liberal interpretation of the natural laws, I have decided to put my money where my mouth is.

I hardly know you, except as a passable squash player. I am aware however that you are widely considered the brightest scientific mind of your generation. If I fail tomorrow, I will have proved only that my abilities do not match my aspirations. This does not mean, though, that your intellect could not succeed where I have failed.

The gravest problem facing humanity today is the constraint placed upon our liberty by the rigid and immutable laws of nature. Discovering a way around these abominable laws is the greatest service any person of intellect can provide to our society. I know you will be skeptical, but I beg you to look over my papers. Perhaps, as a scientist, you will discover something that I have overlooked.

Yours with the greatest regret,
Sandra Hidecock.

Now, I am no champion of natural anarchy, but in support of Sandra Hidecock, and even the unpleasant Marcia Ortez, I have always cherished a humanitarian belief in liberty. As a child, I ardently opposed unreasonable authority, and whereas most people eventually come to tolerate and even crave regulations and conventions, I never succumbed to this way of thinking.

This may seem odd for a scientist, which title I own unabashedly. After all, what use is science to the true freedom-seeker? Science is merely the art of describing nature, so that we may find better ways to obey it. Where nature enchains us, science can perhaps loosen our chains a fraction, but it can never cast those chains aside altogether. Neither the hot air balloon, nor the rocket, nor the airplane can defy gravity; they merely give a semblance of emancipation from that malicious law. We can dream all we like about unfettering ourselves, but every appearance of success is really just a mirage that further shackles us.

I knew it was completely futile. I knew there was no point to any of this. But the wishes of the dead deserve our respect. In a strange way, I felt a moral obligation. Besides, there was something here that attracted my spirit of inquiry. I insisted that Amelia take me immediately to Sandra Hidecock's office.

CHAPTER III

HIDECOCK'S OFFICE

felt like an undergraduate as Amelia led me across the darkening campus to Griswold Hall. She placidly swiped her card to gain access, and then took me up in the elevator to the fourth floor. The corridors were harrowingly empty, like a government research laboratory in the dormant, gloomy hours straight after lunch.

I'd never been in Sandra's office, but it seemed no different from any other humanities professor's place of work. There was an oversized desk with a hideous sculpture on it, made of twisted chicken wire. There were two leather chairs, low and faded watermelon-red, either side of a glass-topped coffee table. There was no room for pictures, as the walls were shelved with books from floor to ceiling.

I took a random volume from a shelf: *Deconstructing the Erection: An Eco-Feminist Interpretation of the Meta-History of Twentieth-Century Representations of the Penis* by Frances Tichel. I made a mental note of this, then reached for another. I found myself holding *Rapeseed, the Boobook, and the Titmouse: Global Cultural Narratives in Scientific Stimulation* by Ruth Veil. Frowning, I wandered over to Sandra's desk where a thin paperback lay open: *The Vulva, the Hermeneutic Circle and the Death of Science* by Arvinder Purdah and Leila

Hijab. It was open on page 67, and I could see a sentence underlined in red – perhaps the last words that Sandra ever read:

> The concepts of mass, energy, light, charge,
> and gravity are nothing more than organizing
> constructs. They are not reality itself and should
> not be misconstrued as real objects. They are the
> symbols and signs by which science establishes its
> primacy in the world, but they are not the world.

What bumptious weeds these philosophers were growing in the garden of the intellect, I thought, but said nothing to Amelia. I sat down at the desk, pushed *The Vulva, the Hermeneutic Circle and the Death of Science* to one side, and began flicking through Sandra's papers. There were not many by a scientist's standards, but they were arranged neatly into little stacks, like a schoolgirl's examination notes. Each page was filled with quotes, references, and interesting observations, all written in that same beautiful hand I'd observed in her letter, and thankfully not all in orange.

Making a valiant effort to restrain her sorrow, Amelia sank down into one of the watermelon chairs and watched me through a slow trickle of tears. I've never liked being stared at while I work, but I put this from my mind. I was operating well outside my own field of experience and I needed to concentrate. Fortunately this was not difficult, for the material in front of me was surprising, fascinating – and very disturbing.

I had long been aware that there existed within the wider community of researchers a fringe element that was opposed, like Sandra Hidecock, to the strictures of natural law. I'd heard that there were thinkers working in the area of gender studies to whom the laws of friction were morally offensive. I was vaguely conscious, too, of a mounting culture of irritation among researchers working in the fine arts toward those scientists who persisted in regarding reality as an objective entity. Having said that, nothing could have prepared me for the intense hatred I discovered in Sandra Hidecock's papers.

I will not describe in detail all of the anti-scientific rationalizations I digested that night, but I will share some examples that deserve special mention. There was a folder marked "Principles". In it, I learned that Isaac Newton's monumental work *Philosophiae Naturalis Principia Mathematica* (otherwise known as "the Principia") had been the subject of extensive criticism by an army of radical feminist and environmental intellectuals, who described it variously as "too mathematical", "boring", a "rape manual for the defilement of nature", "the epitome of all masculinist lunacy", a "handbook to gynocide", and, perhaps most acutely of all, as "a nasty, bitter tract by a depraved, impotent, woman-hating anorexic cannibal whose fetish for numbers has confined women to sexual slavery while their masters ravage the earth's ecology". I had never read the whole of the Principia myself. These days no busy scientist has the time. But I had always assumed it was just a regular book of equations describing the motion of the planets. I'd never imagined it could galvanize such fervor and vitriol.

Another folder entitled "Fact is Mere Consensus" contained several critiques of the history of science. To my mind, the most unexpected was a diatribe against Amedeo Avogadro. In the early eighteenth century, this great Italian chemist postulated that the volume of a gas at fixed temperature and pressure is proportional to the number of molecules in the gas. This was a new, if basic, concept for scientists in his day, and a useful one that a century later led to the designation of Avogadro's number, one of chemistry's key constants. Yet here in a pasteboard binder on Sandra Hidecock's desk, I found a report from a prestigious cross-disciplinary meeting funded by the National Science Foundation, in which a French philosopher by the name of Michel Foucet was quoted as likening Avogadro to a "testicular-shaped avocado", concluding that "all our categories, our science, and our language are mere sexual vehicles for imposing rational, masculinist explanations on an 'arrational' reality".

Foucet, I noted with solemn disquiet, was the Trojan Professor of Sexual Orientation Studies at Princeton and the author of a book apparently well respected in the humanities community with the title, *From Peaches to Petrarch – An analysis of orientation and displacement in vegetables and people.* In her notes, Sandra had photocopied several pages and twice underlined the following passage:

> Avogadro's ideas were nothing but an arbitrary
> imposition on the thinkers of later centuries. In the
> construction of scientific knowledge, the role of
> nature is negligible.

It was lunacy, clearly, that informed these disconcerting ideas. And yet on page after page of those notes, I discovered the same overwrought analyses, the same debilitating skepticism about scientific explanations, and the same shrill anger vented at nearly all the great people in the history of science.

Of course, on one level, such unenlightened and peculiar views about science were hardly new. Ideas like this go back to the time of the Scientific Revolution itself, to the sixteenth and seventeenth centuries when the great pioneers of scientific exploration – men like Kepler, Vesalius, Galileo, and Newton – first began to subvert the prevailing doctrines of their age.

Since that tumultuous period, there have always been those who oppose the strict and all-encompassing scientific interpretation of the universe: of a reality governed by laws without loopholes, of a philosophy that strives for universality and for rules without exceptions. Such naysayers have always existed. Yet it alarmed me to discover that such warped ideas had become ubiquitous across so many fields of enquiry. I had not realized how pervasive this thinking was. It was terrifying to grasp that so many intelligent people were now so actively engaged in undermining the institution of modern science.

At some point I stopped reading and looked up at Amelia. Her sobbing had subsided. She was watching me, sleepily, half smiling now with that mixture of lazy self-assurance and insecurity so common among those studying the humanities.

"So, do you believe all this?" I asked, gesturing at Sandra Hidecock's notes.

"Well, yes," she said, and then paused momentarily as if she knew instinctively that every statement needed qualification, that truth was impossible, and that universal words like "yes" and "no" should never be left to stand on their own. "I guess you could say I'm kind of conflicted about science," she continued.

I winced at her use of the words "kind of" and "conflicted". These are shamefully overused expressions among modern humanities students – a hallmark of their chronic inability to discriminate, which is one of the main deficiencies in their education.

"Conflicted in what way?" I asked.

"I like my car and my dishwasher and my television. Scientific knowledge obviously brings benefits, but it also sabotages the way we see and act in the world."

I looked at her blankly. It was like suggesting that an airplane undermines our ability to walk.

"I detest the totalizing control of the scientific paradigm," she went on. "The scientific worldview destroys spontaneity, spirituality, and the transcendent. I object to a world that is reduced purely to the rational."

I raised a finger toward Amelia, gesturing for silence. There is a lexicon of academic pomposity and in those days, I believed we should limit its use. The fundamental problem, it seemed to me, was that these people were so much better at criticizing than creating, so much more adept at pointing their stick at problems than they were at proposing solutions, and so much more focused on the past than the future. They look backward. This has always been the great flaw of the humanities. These fields rarely attract go-getters or practical people, and their exponents never could resist lambasting those other disciplines that do.

I was weary with the jealousy and incoherence of it all. It was late. I was demoralized from the excess of sociological theory in Sandra's papers, bewildered at the thought of all the Hidecocks and Amelias of this world, whittling their lives away with these utterly pointless, anti-scientific enquiries. I was bemused too by my own macabre curiosity, and by the ease with which Sandra Hidecock's letter had brought me here. The excitement I'd felt when we first stepped into the elevator had dissipated now. I was beginning to feel a little annoyed at wasting so many minutes on this exercise, but I wasn't ready to let go of the problem yet. I just needed some practical measures, I thought.

I signaled for Amelia to stay sitting quietly in her chair, and began to search Sandra's notes for any idea that did more than simply fulminate against science or advocate resistance to "the totalizing control of the scientific paradigm". With a new sense of purpose, I sought Sandra's solutions and her "action" items – her suggestions not about *why* we should object to the laws in theory but about *how* to transgress them in practice.

It wasn't easy, but I got there in the end. I found a monograph composed by Professor Shanka Gumji, Distinguished Professor of Cultural Studies at Yale University. She argued passionately that "the laws of electromagnetism must be denounced in their coarse insensitivity to ethnic minorities", and in particular for being "so transparently in flagrant opposition to all international standards on human rights". Attached to this document was a copy of a letter, co-signed by Sandra Hidecock herself and addressed to the Secretary-General of the United Nations, seeking revisions to the electromagnetic spectrum, specifically in the ultraviolet range and the way it was applied to refugees. "Vulnerable people fleeing persecution and forced to live without shelter in some of the hottest climates on earth should be protected from the dangers of ultraviolet radiation," they asserted.

This struck me as something practical, at least in intent, if not in reality. I made a note of it under a one-word heading: "Regulation?"

Next I stumbled upon an unpublished essay by Professor Rodney Bricolage, an educational anthropologist from the University of Essex. He chronicled a twenty-six-year research project "deconstructing" the relationship between the teaching of mathematics and the self-esteem and worldview of American and European school students.

Professor Bricolage claimed to have shown that "the laws of trigonometry are neo-fascistic in their intolerance of dissent" and called for the implementation of "a more democratic paradigm of scientific discourse that would actively promote self-respect for all students, regardless of socio-economic handicap". He concluded that "the supposed apolitical nature of mathematics is an institutional frame that functions to sustain specific power structures in our society" and that "every mathematics teacher is an ideologue" and that "the only way to counteract their ideology is to ensure that the teaching of this subject be confined to non-mathematicians only".

It struck me that this too was a practical suggestion, even though it would actually reduce the capacity of students to understand mathematics, and I duly noted this example as well, using a different heading this time: "Education?"

Finally, I discovered a copy of a lecture delivered by Professor Brigitte L'Escroc, from the Department of Contemporary Economics at the Université Saint-Arnac in France. She decried the cozy relationship between the "malveillant" transnational petroleum corporations and the "hégémonique" first law of thermodynamics and advocated that "a culture of dissent" be directed not only against the multinational petroleum firms, but also against physicists. In her transcript (my translation), she wrote:

If we oppose petroleum profits, then we must oppose also the law of conservation of energy. Socially enriching community-based energy technologies will only be made cost-competitive with incumbent energy systems when science can balance community desire for a sustainable and ecologically appropriate future with the disappointing obligations imposed by thermodynamics.

Professor L'Escroc's concluding injunction was that all governments must protest against the law of conservation of energy by legislating so that a fixed proportion of the energy used in all societies is derived from technologies operating with very low rates of efficiency. Here too was a practical dimension, so long as one allowed the practical to entail some degree of financial impracticality. I duly noted the facts of this case under a new heading: "Technology?"

For many hours I read on, discovering other similar examples. The situation seemed clear. All of Hidecock's ideas could be categorized by one of three words: Regulation, Education, or Technology. These were the means by which she'd hoped to transform our place in the world, to liberate us from the constraints of the natural laws.

I gazed for a moment at the frail sculpture sitting on the desk to my right. Its little colored stones, those clichéd ornaments, and the ordinariness of its thin, steel wires irritated me. The twists and turns of its structure said nothing new that hadn't been said a million times before by artists and designers and trinket-makers trying to capture idiosyncrasy and whimsy in physical form; and I saw in this a metaphor for everything that was wrong with research outside the sciences.

The unequivocal fact was that all of Sandra Hidecock's ideas for changing the world were based upon an understanding of the world as it already is, not as it might be. So utterly typical of a humanities professor, she and her colleagues had sought merely to constrain the laws by operating within the world that they already knew. They had advocated change via obvious, but limited, social and technical forces when clearly what was required was not change or control, but transcendence. I leaned back in the chair, reflecting for a moment, then shifted forward and scribbled a new heading on my notepad: "Discovery!"

Sandra Hidecock's great wish was no more than a childish daydream. Despite all the papers and articles and lectures, despite the many luminous researchers from high-profile institutions who had supported her views, and indeed despite all the barbed cleverness with which so many of these distinguished professors presented their arguments, it was obvious that science was under no immediate threat. The laws of nature stood as little chance of being perturbed by all her scholarship as the sun or the moon would have of being perturbed by a change in my morning routine.

I glanced at Amelia, who had kicked off her green shoes and fallen asleep. Here was the problem, I thought. The people most passionate about transcending the laws of nature were those least equipped to do it. I stood up. Light was starting to break through the window and I realized that I had worked through the night.

I bent down to wake Amelia, touching her shoulder lightly. "Time for me to go," I said.

She blinked several times, as if I was blurred and she needed to adjust her focal length. "You don't want to stay? Coffee?" she said.

"No."

"Did you find anything?"

A moment of painful silence followed.

"I'm sorry," I said. "Sandra was an interesting woman, but she wasn't a scientist and her views about science are misguided."

Amelia sat up. "I shouldn't have brought you here," she said.

I held out my hand. "Thank you. I'm sorry but I can't help."

She blinked again, her hair falling awkwardly across her face. She looked up at me sadly through her fringe. It seemed we weren't going to shake hands. "I'm sorry too," she said. And that's how we left it.

"Bye then," I said, and let myself out.

However, there must have been some latent germ of rebellion buried deep inside me. In the corridor, as I waited for the elevator, watching the downward triangle light up, I experienced a sudden and disquieting affinity for Sandra Hidecock and her perplexing views. It was an affinity that I could not shake as I left the building.

CHAPTER IV

VORSOGEPRINZIP FOR BREAKFAST

In the world of science, we love to deride the capacities of our colleagues in the humanities, and we particularly love to parody the opinions of intellectually vainglorious academics like Foucet and Bricolage. I'll openly admit to being an offender. But what if Sandra Hidecock had discovered something unique, something genuinely original; perhaps not an answer, but a question? What if she leaped through that window not because she became consumed with her own delusions, which is after all an occupational hazard of all university employees, but rather because she had asked a question that really was genuinely important?

Reflecting that I had just spent the night in the same chair that Sandra Hidecock had warmed moments before her heroic plunge, a frisson of empathy pulsed through me. I felt a stirring, anti-authoritarian inclination. I discovered a new spring in my step, a sense of injustice tightening at the back of my knees. I thought again about Sandra's papers and wondered whether I might have misjudged her.

Leaving the Law School yard, I bypassed the Jefferson Laboratory and the Music Building, skirting the McKay

Laboratory to reach Oxford Street. Then I turned north. Although it was early in the morning, it was already hot and I was thirsty. The streets of Cambridge have never appealed to me. I knew I had to get away from the river and well away from the university. I needed to think things through and there is no university in the world that is conducive to that occupation.

So I walked and I thought, and at some point – I don't know where – I wandered past a black mongrel sniffing at a garbage can, a weak and pathetic creature but perfectly content, and it turned my thoughts to John Stuart Mill's pig. It was Mill who, in 1863 in his sublime *Utilitarianism*, wrote those portentous words:

> It is better to be a human being dissatisfied than a
> pig satisfied; better to be Socrates dissatisfied than
> a fool satisfied. And if the fool, or the pig, is of a
> different opinion, it is because they only know their
> side of the question.

What if we all were like Mill's pig? I wondered. What if we were all vaguely content, just as hapless animals are, but oblivious to the powers we might wield if we only knew where to seek them? What if there is a world beyond the physical laws after all, only we don't see it – because we don't know how to look?

At some point I turned eastwards. The sunlight seemed unusually bright. I wished I had sunglasses or a hat. I looked back on my life and mused about the choices I'd made. I pondered that I had expended so many years learning so rigorously about the rules of nature and admiring their beautiful coherence – in physics, mathematics, geology, botany, zoology, physiology, chemistry, pharmacology, and so many other rigid and uncompromising disciplines. Had I been taken in? Was I Mill's foolish pig? I had studied on four continents and in twice as many specialties. From a young age I'd aspired to become a professor. I had worked with and then led some of the most inspired scientific minds of my generation.

Yet now, a vision of Sandra Hidecock's office still fresh before my eyes, the sobs of her colleagues still ringing in my ears, and with the recollection also of Amelia's plaintive gaze, I found that a new emotion had begun to exert pressure on me. I was still young, and I'd always had a heterodox streak. Was I not the perfect man to test this unorthodox and confronting hypothesis?

I crisscrossed the streets of Somerville, walking in a rectangular figure eight. I felt my mind stretch this way and that as I tried by turns to shake off or swallow Sandra Hidecock's strange ideas. Then something unexpected happened once again that engendered a whole new line of thinking. I passed a young girl, perhaps eight or nine years old. She was getting out of a car, squinting into the light. She had brown curly hair and in some strange and intangible way, she reminded me of Sandra Hidecock. What if this girl should grow up, I mused, into a woman of boundless intellectual integrity like Hidecock? And what if she was schooled in an even zanier branch of the humanities? What if she too should feel compelled to leap from a fourth-story window?

A shudder ran through me, like a breeze on a leaf in late fall. In a future world where every school child has access to powerful concepts like post-modernism, post-structuralism, deconstructionism, and philosophical relativism, the likelihood that others would someday discover the work of Sandra Hidecock and follow in her footsteps seemed nearly certain. I watched the girl follow her long-legged mother through the drab wooden door of a house. Was there no way, I wondered, to save people like these?

In the 1930s, the Germans developed a concept known as *vorsogeprinzip*, or the precautionary principle. It's since become a very fashionable concept, especially when thinking about environmental problems. Conservationists frequently maintain that where the potential consequences of inaction are severe or irreversible, one should always be ready to act. Staring at this young girl who might one day jump to her death, was I not obligated, I pondered, to apply the precautionary principle? As a man of knowledge and a citizen, was it not my duty to try to protect her from any potentially fatal future impact caused by gravity? On the other hand, what could I, a mere scientist, a mere describer and interpreter of reality, not its creator, do about these all-powerful laws?

I stumbled on, and the quaint streets and family houses of suburban Cambridge drifted past, shimmying and shifting like desert mirages with steep atmospheric gradients. I thought about Sandra Hidecock's dying act. I thought about what Marcia Ortez had said and also about Emmanuel Porphyrin's perceptive remark. Why hadn't any of us been able to save her? And what did it really mean to be a scientist in the midst of all this? Was I complicit, I wondered, in these devastating and inhumane injunctions of nature?

All young scientists are taught that the process of discovery is inherently benign. The pain only comes, we are told, with the human application of our discoveries. The laws themselves are fixed and eternal, without moral dimension; they are simply there. "They are nothing to do with us, we merely uncover them!" we all disclaim. As one well-known philosopher once wrote, "A scientist is a priest whose job is no more creative than the reading of Nature's catechism." Yet, what if this is false? What if we don't just discover the laws but inadvertently write them as well? What if a scientist is no mere constable on the beat of natural justice, simply following orders? What if, unbeknownst to ourselves, we are in fact the legislators? Or, worse yet, what if we are the bruising, insensate thugs whose entire existence perpetuates the laws and the repression that comes with them?

These are some of the questions that inflamed my imagination and set my intellect into a state of turmoil, and so lost was I in my thinking about these serious matters that I collided with a trash receptacle and came to an abrupt halt with a cut on my thigh. At once I was seized with a passionate indignation at the injustice of the world, and at the infuriating devastation wreaked upon us all by the laws of nature. Why shouldn't I be able to walk through matter? And why shouldn't an able-bodied woman with beautiful handwriting be able to fly out the fourth story of her faculty building? I suddenly felt only the greatest compassion for Sandra Hidecock. It seemed so unjust that her meager, innocuous attempt to circumvent those laws should have been so brutally denied. To insist on the absolute impossibility of such an act seemed repressive in the extreme, even a little absurd.

Of course, I knew it was madness to think this way. There had been no successful precedent for an attempt to change or avoid the laws of nature. Throughout the whole of human history, every known effort to subvert them had met with failure and hardship. I knew this fundamental truth as well as Sandra Hidecock must have known it when she stepped out from her office window. But as I thought about her dying leap and her beyond-the-grave epistolary appeal for assistance, I began to ask myself whether there might be another option; another way to rescue humanity, at least in part, from the limitations of the natural world, and from the perverse constraints of our unyielding universe.

The problem with Sandra Hidecock had never been the question she'd asked; rather, it was her methodological approach. Clearly she was not equipped to transcend the laws, but another might succeed where she had failed. As soon as I accepted this proposition, I knew that I had to act upon it. What counts in life is not what is possible, but what is right. I recognized in that instant that I had to discover a way, if there was one, and perhaps even if there wasn't, to prove Sandra Hidecock right. It was up to me to take up the baton and repudiate her work.

This awareness came like the booming voice of an ancient god speaking to his prophet, alone in the dirt and dust of a raw desert – only I was just a simple scientist in a crumpled suit, with a grazed thigh, standing on a city sidewalk. I heard no voice. I answered to no gods. I possessed nothing but my own conscience, my own curiosity, and my own mind to guide me. I was but a man, just an assemblage of atoms, perched atop a slab of suburban asphalt with the finite sky above and eight thousand miles of rock below. Yet I understood with a deep and solemn clarity that I would be compelled from that moment on to try to discover some way to stand up to nature and to renounce and defy what was clearly a universal, inhuman, and inherently detestable scientific interpretation of reality. I walked home in an electrified agony of expectation.

CHAPTER V

THE MILLION-DOLLAR IDEA

Throughout the history of mankind, there has been no shortage of people ready to try their hands against the laws of nature. Engineers in twelfth-century India tried to develop a wheel that would turn itself indefinitely, without human intervention and without recourse to any external source of energy. They failed. In the Renaissance, a handful of Italian pioneers attempted to construct their own subversive water-pumping technologies, the so-called "recirculation mills", self-pumping miracle-machines that were supposed to circumvent the laws of gravity, hydraulics, and thermodynamics all at once. They failed. Then there were the Alchemists, who from the Middle Ages to Victorian times tried every conceivable form of subterfuge to elude the laws of chemistry and thus to convert lead into gold. Of course, they failed too.

They all failed utterly and unequivocally. Terrifying as it was, through all the many centuries that mankind has struggled systematically to define and characterize the natural world, there had been no known precedent for moving beyond the laws. The harsh lesson, so often repeated and so widely accepted, was that the laws of nature permit no exceptions.

Yet later that day (the day after Sandra Hidecock's funeral), I rang Emmanuel Porphyrin's office and booked an appointment. A week later I found myself perched in a sumptuous reception area, wearing my best suit, with my shoes lacquered and my chin shaved, waiting to see the President of Harvard.

I knew I had to be extremely careful. After all, I had everything to lose. I held a prestigious, tenured position at the greatest university in the world. My students had just begun to admire me. When they looked at me, there was a pleasing new dimension to their gaze. It was almost as if they regarded me as a superior being. The week before, I had caught one of them stroking his nose while he thought, a mannerism I have had since childhood. Imitation is a form of admiration, and I enjoyed adulation as much as the next man. Among my colleagues I also had a level of respect. Just the year before, I'd proved an important theorem in the analysis of detergent bubbles, and Emmanuel Porphyrin had made special comment about my talents in academic administration. My reputation seemed assured.

Yet here I was with a mad idea, and worse still, a big idea – the sort of idea that university administrators usually claim they are looking for, but which they sedulously avoid in practice. I have never liked begging for money, as it implies dependency and ultimately places one in thrall to another. But what choice did I have? The door opened and a well-preened woman, with thoroughly impractical fingernails and a dress even more Lilliputian than her frame, informed me that Professor Porphyrin was ready.

His bulging eyes gleamed as I approached. "Nice suit, Karlof. So, how much do you want from the President of Harvard?" he said with just the faintest smirk.

His own suit was beautifully tailored in a quiet aquamarine, with a crimson silk tie and a putty-colored shirt. He gestured at a leather sofa, intimating that I should be seated, and placed himself in an armchair opposite. The portraits on the wall behind him distracted me momentarily. There was Edward Holyoke, Urian Oakes, Benjamin Wadsworth, Leonard Hoar, Charles Chauncy, and Cornelius Felton, among others. I realized that Emmanuel Porphyrin had created a small pantheon of all the previous presidents of Harvard who had died in office.

My pitch was a simple one. I told him that I was going after the laws of nature, but that I was determined to do it in a way that would maximize the benefits and minimize the risks to the Harvard name. My approach would be rigorous, scientific, and empirical rather than slap-dash, artsy, or purely intellectual. I reminded him of what he'd said about Sandra Hidecock at her memorial service and I suggested that no other organization in the world could pull off a venture of this kind.

Emmanuel Porphyrin closed his eyes and then began tenderly massaging his nut-brown forehead with the first three fingers of his right hand. "I was rather worried somebody might propose something like this," he said, gazing at the floor. "That foolhardy woman ..."

His words petered out and we sat in silence for a second or two.

"Have you ever heard of Bessler?" he said, fixing me suddenly with those watchful, bulging eyes. I nodded, but my assent was ignored. "Johann Bessler was an eighteenth-century German scientist who dedicated his life to making 'inert material' move of its own accord, spontaneously and without the application of any external force," he said, still watching me closely.

"Yes."

"Nature's solemn and unquestionable verdict was that he was trying to act in direct defiance of Newton's first law of motion, and he failed."

"Yes."

"But equally hurtful was the way in which his peers, and history itself, chose to judge him. He is widely remembered as a madman."

"Yes, I know."

My repetitious agreement seemed to irk Emmanuel Porphyrin. He leaned forward, planting his hands on the little table between us, and lowered his voice the way men of power often do in the belief that it increases the weight of their words.

"Perhaps you are ready for this personally, for the ridicule and derision," he murmured, "but it won't do for the world to hear that Harvard has embarked upon a serious scientific program to circumvent the laws of nature, the very laws that we, perhaps more successfully than any other organization in history, are continuously discovering."

"But Sandra Hidecock –"

"Sandra Hidecock was a lawyer. The world expects this sort of lunacy from her kind. But you are a scientist and in science, the standards are higher."

He stood up as if to embody those higher standards. In his mind the interview was over. I'd been told I would get twenty minutes, yet it seemed I would gain less than five. I clambered to my feet.

"In some respects, I do like your idea," he said, injecting a conciliatory note. "It is thoroughly unorthodox. It has that whiff of Harvard audacity ..." He smiled. I think he wanted me to understand that he was not entirely disapproving – that he didn't wish to dissuade me from developing other grand or daring schemes in the future. "Yes, I do admire your nerve," he went on. "But boldness is not enough. If you were to fail, as you almost certainly would, how could you possibly protect me, and the rest of us here, from the public relations disaster that would follow?"

He gestured at the portraits behind him, at those serious forefathers decorating his walls: men of conservative instincts, whose destiny and determination had been to avoid risks and thereby expand the influence of their beloved institution. He sighed gently and his great, globular eyes roamed the room as if restless, yet seeking something to rest upon – anything but me.

"We are a community of wise men and women, not a home for crackpots and charlatans. I simply don't see how any proposal along these lines could possibly work within an organization such as ours," he concluded.

I handed him a piece of paper. "This is how," I replied.

Slowly he read the page and when he'd finished, he looked across at me with raised eyebrows and a smile of contained delight. "Ah," he said. "Now there's an idea. So how much do you want?"

"A million dollars."

"So little – but where's the ambition these days?" he replied with a shrug.

He turned his head, and again raised his hand to his brow as if kneading out a thought. I felt suddenly that the entire world would someday owe him a tremendous debt for this moment of decision. "Okay," he said, ushering me to the door. "But you've got twelve months to match it with ten million from outside."

What was written on that humble piece of paper? Nothing more than elementary strategy; the outline of a plan that could not fail. On that momentous day when I decided to follow in Sandra Hidecock's footsteps and to make a scientific assault on the laws of nature, I knew that my situation was precarious. Nature itself would be a most challenging opponent.

But I must admit I was also afraid – like Porphyrin – of what my colleagues, my countrymen and my friends would think of me. I had no desire to be thought of as eccentric, no desire to discover how many true friends a man has when he steps off the common path. Probably I feared contempt even more keenly than Emmanuel Porphyrin dreaded tarnishing the Harvard name. I understood as well as anyone that idiosyncrasy generally exacts its price ... unless it is successful. My only hope was to project success before I'd even begun.

Yet how to do this? I'm a simple man. I have always striven for simplicity and the simplest idea is often the biggest one. I based my strategy on the almost infallible premise that if you go big enough you cannot founder, and I knew that the only way to think really big in science is to think deeply and seriously about money. If I could only attract money, and a lot of it, I knew all those reputational risks would fade.

My plan was based on Yuri Govnovych's dictum: that the necessity of success in science shrinks in inverse proportion to one's funding – or, to put it another way, only the worst funded scientists need worry about their results. Although not well known in Western countries,

Yuri Govnovych was an inspirational Soviet astrophysicist who convinced Stalin to invest millions of rubles into extraterrestrial research during the famine of 1932–33, and still managed somehow to survive the purges afterwards. Today, he is considered the grandfather of the contemporary field of astropaleontology. In his *Pocket Manual for Socialist Scientists* (published posthumously in 1955) he wrote:

> When people have committed serious funding to
> anything, no matter how foolish or pointless, they
> acquire a vested interest in seeing it succeed. They
> will pretend it has succeeded for years afterwards,
> even for decades after it has failed – and this usually
> requires not too much self-delusion, for if you
> spend enough on anything, you will usually have
> something to show for your investment, something
> to justify your existence, even if you never achieve
> your original objectives.

The plan I showed Emmanuel Porphyrin was a pure Govnovychian arrangement. My aim was to use Harvard's million to leverage not ten million, but a billion. My goal was not to fund one paltry new research project, but to create a whole new branch of science. In implementing these ambitious ideas, however, I included another essential and entirely original element.

In the week before my meeting with Porphyrin, I'd gone down by train to New York to see my friend Bobby Merlin at Columbia University. It had cost me a day to get there and back, but it was worth it. Bobby was a convivial and beady-eyed sociologist of the old-fashioned stamp. He took me to a little Hungarian pastry shop in Morningside

Heights. It was a well-known place with postcards on the walls, uncomfortable plastic chairs, and a purple laminate floor. We sat down inside and drank black, soupy coffee and devoured pastries with poppy seeds in them.

"Ah, Duronimus," he said, chuckling at my plan, "you really are going out on a limb with this."

"I know, but I believe I can pull it off. The question is how do I raise funds on such a vast scale?"

"You need just the same thing that everyone else needs in science."

"What's that?"

"Credentialed men and women willing to stand up and say 'yes, this is very important' and 'yes, this needs to be funded as a matter of urgency'. You need a visible community of support." He slurped his coffee. I took a bite of seed cake. "You know the Gospel of Saint Matthew?" he continued.

"It's a Broadway musical, right?"

Bobby grinned. "Not quite – to those who have, more will be given," he explained. "Very unfair but it's true. The only way to get others to endorse your plans is to ensure that there are scientists out there who are already funded to do something similar, and include them in your proposal."

"But if these people already exist, why would they want to help me?" I asked.

"Money, Duronimus. Scientists will do nearly anything for extra money," he observed dryly.

"And what if these people don't exist? What if there's no field yet; can I start from scratch?"

"Nothing ever starts from scratch in science."

"So, how do new things get off the ground?"

"Very gradually."

"Yet surely there's a way to galvanize a group of peers to throw their weight behind someone or something new."

"Not for a harebrained scheme like yours," he replied with a smile.

I gazed at him for a moment, wondering why a pessimist should have such a big, soft, friendly face. I was not especially surprised by his assessment. One can usually trust a social scientist to be despondent. In the world of knowledge, the social science professors have traditionally played the role of "human barbiturates", which is to say if you talk to them for a short period, you become relaxed by the confidence they have in their own understanding; if you talk for them for a little longer, you become depressed by their gloomy prognostications; and if you spend a really elongated stretch of time with them, you fall asleep.

"Okay then, Bobby, is there some other way to get funding?" I pleaded.

"I doubt that very much," he murmured, licking the sticky poppy seeds off his fingers. "Besides, you wouldn't want to adopt another approach. Whatever happens you'll need a large community of supporters to share some responsibility when your experiments fail."

He was right. I knew he was right. But the thought of taking the train back to Boston with nothing to show for my journey but a sociologist's grim realism left me rather despondent. The room was suddenly very noisy. A group of workmen had entered and the proprietor was talking very loudly to them.

"But surely there must be something else I can do," I persisted. "Can't you think of anything?"

Bobby drained the last of his coffee and shook his head. "Not really," he replied.

Yet this wasn't his final word on the subject. Afterwards, as we strolled back through the Columbia campus, he stopped suddenly as if struck by an important thought, and a quizzical frown stretched over his face. "Did you know this campus was originally the site of the Bloomingdale Lunatic Asylum?" he mused.

"I hadn't realized that."

"Yes, it was – and sometimes I wonder whether much has changed."

"What do you mean?"

"Well, look at all these people."

He gestured to the academic crowd sauntering past: men with their threadbare jackets, unkempt hair and scuffed shoes; women with their air of elegant poverty; students in their jeans and ironic T-shirts; everywhere a curious mismatch of dreary attire and a preponderance of spectacles.

"You know," he said, "there aren't so many great books or scholarly articles being written here as people might assume. Most of us teach only a few hours each week."

"Yes, but isn't that true everywhere?"

"Absolutely," he went on, "but what happens the rest of the time? Sometimes it seems to me this university is not so different from that strange and rather frightening institution that preceded it. Both are places where people on the fringe of society go to do work that ultimately amounts to very little."

We shook hands warmly. Bobby returned to his office and I went to catch the subway to Penn Station for the train back to Boston. I thought he hadn't helped me, but he had. Bobby Merlin was a man with a handy intuition and a useful imagination. Whether or not he intended it, he had reminded me of the great slack that exists in our academic system, for he'd recalled to my mind the talentless majority.

In those days, there was a growing number of scientists at Harvard and Columbia and elsewhere who were clearly not top class researchers. These people represented a community of disaffected scholars, whose work (if published at all) was rarely published in the top journals, and whose careers had never lived up to their self-imagined promise. Just like the rest of us, in their student days they had weighed up whether to dedicate their lives to knowledge and fame, or to money and happiness. They'd chosen badly, for now they had neither knowledge or fame, nor money or happiness. Indeed, they had not much of anything, except bitter cynicism, a detestation of a world that never properly recognized their abilities, and an abhorrence of their institutions for failing to give them the resources they believed they'd needed and deserved in order to do the great things of which they were sure they'd been capable.

The plan I put to Emmanuel Porphyrin was to capitalize on the unmet aspirations of these people, the overlooked and unheralded ones. My strategy was to give this group a goal so distant and so grand as to make them feel important once again, and thus win their loyalty. These people represented a community of vast numbers. There were multitudes of them. They couldn't be fired and weren't old enough to retire. They were simply moldering away. I wanted their support, for as Bobby Merlin had observed, without deep community endorsement, I couldn't hope to raise even a fraction of the funds I required. But I also realized that their backing would be easy to obtain. In exchange for their favor, I could offer them a role in something much greater than themselves. I could create something that gave them kudos in the eyes of their deans and departmental chairs, and reignite in their hearts a sense of mission and destiny. I could give them something to brag about at dinner parties, something to make them feel fresh and clever again in a way that none of them had really felt since leaving high school.

It was a stroke of genius, if I do say so myself, to galvanize this group, and to turn a failed majority into an unstoppable new movement within the scientific community. Emmanuel Porphyrin had understood this instantly. Of course, he grasped the symbolic value of big money too, but I like to think that he most appreciated the prospects I would provide for Harvard's weaker staff, and indeed for the weaker scientists and academics operating all around the world. Perhaps I am wrong, but I truly believe that he saw with the clearest precision what I'd only at first glimpsed: that my plan would use these people not just as a means to an end, but that it could bring a wider benefit to mankind along the way, for it would revitalize all the wilted, under-nourished, over-shadowed shrubs that were struggling in those dark days to thrive in the garden of knowledge.

CHAPTER VI

ASSEMBLING THE B TEAM

Having received Emmanuel's seed funding, dispensed so generously by him on behalf of the Fellows of Harvard and the Board of Overseers of the university, I set about finding five of our leading second-rate scientists. Any more would have been unmanageable, but five seemed enough to galvanize the rest of the community. I already had one candidate in mind, a colleague in my own department:

RUBIN

Rubin Weisensteiner was a professor of theoretical astrophysics, a man whose full title gave him a status and gravitas far grander than his actual achievements. For twenty years, Rubin's notional research interests had lain with the fine structure constant and the chain theory of the universe – the notion "that everything is linked, that everything is interconnected, and that everything happens one thing after another". He was a highly knowledgeable theoretician, but hadn't published a serious scientific article in years. He was also a minor participant in Hawaii's famous Infrared Nebulous Astronomical Nuclei

Experiment, but as far as anyone knew, he'd never visited the facility nor analyzed a single byte of data from its telescopes.

The week after Hidecock's funeral, I was walking down the corridor in the Jefferson Laboratory and there he was, just five paces ahead of me: bow-legged and wiry, with a wild head of hair. He'd cultivated an intellectual's disregard for personal appearance that begins as a badge of honor, and then settles into a careless habit. That day, he was casual to the point of despondency in an orange T-shirt and blotchy brown shorts.

"Hey Rubin!" I called, catching up and falling in with him at a common speed.

"Duronimus," he replied flatly.

We walked on in silence and I began to feel uneasy. Rubin was normally a gregarious fellow, eager to impress with news of the latest esoteric theorem described in the scientific literature.

"I hear there's a new theory of dark matter," I offered, by way of making conversation.

"*Physical Review Letters*. Yeah, yeah."

His dismissive tone surprised me. On many subjects, Rubin could be maddening. He'd forget what he was saying halfway through saying it, or (even worse) not remember what you'd told him just moments before. If he didn't care for a topic, a conversational amnesia could suddenly engulf him – but if one kept to his favorite themes (neutron stars, black holes, nuclear astrophysics, dark energy, dark matter, and gamma ray bursts), he was usually a most affable and loquacious companion.

I shot him an inquisitive glance. "What's wrong, Rubin?" I asked.

"You haven't heard?" He stopped walking suddenly and faced me. I shook my head. "They've thrown me out," he said.

"Who have?" I asked.

"Hawaii!" he exclaimed bitterly.

I was not surprised. His involvement in that program had more than outlasted expectations. But now he was probably at risk of losing his position at Harvard. Outside the university, he was known for his popular physics books, and for a theorem about the cosmological constant that he had originally developed as a graduate student. Within the institution, however, it was widely accepted that he hadn't done anything original since he was a child, when his Czechoslovakian-born mother had banned him from playing in the family garden, forcing him to pass his time solving mathematics puzzles instead.

I glanced at him gently, with sympathy. "I am sorry to hear that," I said.

We walked on till we reached his office door. Inside, the walls were decorated with posters of galaxies, supernovae, distant moons, neutron stars, the Magellanic Clouds and so forth.

"See there – the Whirlpool?" he said, uncharacteristically mournful, pointing to a brightly colored image of a vast, churning, spiral galaxy.

"Yes, I do – remarkable!" I replied.

"That galaxy is twenty-three thousand light years away and there are times I really wish I was somewhere in the middle of it," he observed wistfully.

Poor Rubin with his fractured personality: marvelously intelligent, but also profoundly stupid; passionate and knowledgeable about his field, but unable to focus creatively and successfully upon it.

"Rubin, there's always a bright side," I said, trying to be positive.

"And what's that?" he asked bitterly.

"Well, you could say it frees up time for other things."

He made a small sound of resignation and it suddenly occurred to me that if he'd never actually spent any time in Hawaii, then losing this association would not, in fact, free up time for anything. Time was not his problem.

"Sorry!" I said. "Just trying to be helpful."

He nodded, and I think he understood. I decided not to share my idea yet. Rubin's disappointment seemed too raw. I didn't want him to think I was offering something out of charity. However, I did make a mental note that he would suit my plans. Rubin Weisensteiner was a man with enormous intelligence who had never achieved his potential.

"I guess I'll see you round," I added.

He nodded again and stood forlornly by his desk, eyes light years away, inside the Whirlpool.

COLIN

I found my next candidate in the *Harvard Magazine*, that monthly piece of dross then distributed to all staff, students and alumni, as well as to their first and second-degree relations. This publication sought to instill institutional loyalty and pride, and to perpetuate the long-standing association of the Harvard name with unparalleled academic excellence. Every edition contained glowing profiles of Harvard researchers. Yet there were only so many staff, and only a small subsection were doing anything noteworthy. Inevitably, as the appetite for research profiles expanded, the quality of people left to be profiled diminished, making this the perfect resource for discovering the people I was looking for.

Of course, there was no point approaching anyone who'd been recently profiled: they'd still be feeling a temporary sense of elation and self-confidence. I needed those with a stable history of mediocrity, those for whom recognition had been a distant, temporary aberration. I decided to visit the Harry Elkins Widener Memorial Library to browse the magazine's back issues.

The Widener is one of the more memorable buildings at Harvard. A flight of steps leads up to its imposing entrance – a grand portico in the Greek style with twelve Corinthian columns. Perfectly devoid of any practical function, these columns have proved invaluable to Harvard in a purely psychological, photogenic capacity. Even today, few students or tourists would leave before having their picture taken in front of the Widener. However, what seems graceful and contained from without is convoluted and tortuous within. I had to penetrate deep into the building's dark interior to locate the back issues of *Harvard Magazine*, their colors now faded and their narrow spines powdered with dust.

I flicked through several volumes at random. To my surprise, identifying mediocrity was not nearly as straightforward as I'd anticipated. For one thing, there was a heavy emphasis on the social sciences, achievements within the business school, the humanities, medicine – I was looking for proper scientific minds. Furthermore, the magazine's editors were adept at disguising their subjects' inadequacies. In a statistical sense, I knew that the majority of those profiled were conducting research of very little significance yet, when contemplating their individual stories, I found it almost impossible to distinguish between the genuine stars and the genuine washouts. Everyone was made to seem so dreadfully high-powered and distinguished, so utterly unique.

Then I stumbled across someone who seemed to hit the mark. In an older edition there was a picture of a large man with an impressive beard, standing in front of a huge gray apparatus with a pine forest backdrop. He was a rough-looking fellow in well-worn jeans, with sandals on his big feet. He wore a massive Texan-style belt buckle and a bright red and white checked shirt, with a rim of yellow undergarment peeping out at the collar. The caption in the article described him as Colin Capstone, Professor of Geophysics. But really it was his apologetic eyes that held my attention.

Apparently, he had invented a novel geophysical exploration technique known as an Oblique Oscillating Polarizing Sensor. This was a new technology for discovering molybdenite, niobate, and tantalite deposits, which had been piloted ten years previously in conjunction with the Colorado School of Mines. Capstone was asked about the pilot program and whether this technology had a practical future, to which he was quoted as saying: "It was a great experiment and we learned a lot, but we discovered that the apparatus would have to be as big as the Empire State Building to work properly. It never has been, nor ever will be, used in the field."

I admired his honesty, but what also caught my eye was an annotation that some other reader had scrawled in the margin: "White elephant ... biggest waste of research money in Harvard's history!" I knew for a fact this wasn't true. It did strike me, however, that Capstone's best years were behind him. If he was still around, I thought to myself, I would add him to the top of my B-list.

LEWIS

My third candidate was a biologist I'd been inadvertently studying for some time. In those days Harvard had a steady flow of investment for new buildings, one of the more prominent of which was the Straubenzee Center for Multidisciplinary Research Involving Animals. The Straubenzee was not a colossus, but it was notorious around campus because an acclaimed architect had designed it with the idea that people work better if the world is watching. Adjacent to my own building, its exterior was constructed almost entirely of transparent glass. It was like working next to a gleaming ant farm: across its entire façade, you could watch people in lab coats perched at their benches, chatting in corridors, performing assays, watering plants, tidying up pipettes, and scurrying to and fro. From the minute it opened, the building was a talking piece, a monument to scientific industriousness crying out to be the subject of an anthropologist's PhD thesis.

More interesting to me than the Straubenzee's incessantly moving inhabitants, however, was the occupant of a large corner office on the second floor. While all around him was a flurry of activity, this man stood out by staying still. I was acutely aware of him because his office was directly across from mine. I would see him hunched at his desk, reading, sorting through paperwork or gazing blandly at his computer screen. He never seemed to have visitors. Sometimes he would twirl in his swivel chair. Often, he would simply stare out the window as if unendurably bored.

He usually arrived at ten and left at three-thirty, and his work pattern seemed a dreary monotony. Assuming he must be dissatisfied, two weeks after my meeting with Emmanuel Porphyrin, I decided to make an approach. I watched him arrive, gave him time to settle, then left my department and briskly crossed the yard. Entering the Straubenzee, I took the glass elevator to the second floor, followed the corridor along to the far corner, and then knocked at his door, which was marked ADMIN.

"Yes?" said a surprised voice.

I thought I detected a British accent. "Sorry to bother you," I said.

"Yes?" he repeated.

It was interesting to gain a closer look at this person, whom most of Harvard must have observed at some point as he went about his daily life. He had watery blue eyes, pinkish cheeks, and a sharp, beak-like nose.

"My name is Duronimus Karlof," I said. "We're virtual neighbors."

"Oh?" he exclaimed. "In the Straubenzee?"

"No, I'm over there," I said, pointing through his window to my office across the way.

"Oh!" He stood and peered at the brick building with small windows that dominated his view. I observed that he had a slight stoop. He was tall and remarkably thin. He gestured to a chair. "Well sit down, please."

We sat together, looking out across the yard. He was not a natural conversationalist, but eventually I conquered his reticence. His name was Lewis Winterbottom. A British graduate of Cambridge University, he had dedicated his life to studying the lifecycle of the blood fluke, rising over the years to become Deputy Director of the Straubenzee Center for Multidisciplinary Research Involving Animals. Lean and florid, it occurred to me that – like pets and their owners – he evoked something of the organisms he studied. I also surmised that his stoop was permanent, brought on no doubt by long periods spent bending over microscopes. Such activities, however, were no longer his main preoccupation for, as he explained, he was now a full-time administrator.

"But don't you ever miss the lab work?" I asked casually.

"Oh, I do. I miss it terribly. Tremadotes – you know, flat worms and flukes – I loved the little buggers," he observed enthusiastically.

"Then why not go back to it?" I asked.

"Well, you know how it is ... You reach a certain level. All your best ideas explored, all controversies settled. Productivity falls. You're not publishing as much ... It's hard to climb back." He gave a tired smile.

I sat forward in my chair and gestured at the forms on his desk. "But you're not really satisfied just doing this, are you?" I asked.

He looked at me, defensively. "Oh, I wouldn't say that," he said. "I like it well enough. It's just ... well, you know ... you don't exactly need a PhD to run a puppet show." He laughed, and I was pleased to discover that he had a sense of humor.

"You're right, I suppose. I do an awful lot of paper shuffling," he added. "It's important stuff, of course, and someone's got to do it, but sometimes I have my regrets. I do wonder now and again how I've ended up here ..." He glanced at me as if gauging my reaction, uncertain whether he'd said too much.

I decided to take a chance on him. "Lewis, I've enjoyed our conversation," I began.

He nodded. "Me too ... I don't have many visitors. Most forms these days are emailed," he said.

"I'm currently looking for participants for a new, special kind of research center here at Harvard. Any chance you'd be interested?" I asked.

"I might be," he said, eyes wide and fingers twitching on the arm of his chair.

·I didn't tell him much, just that I was getting a team of "genuinely outstanding" people together to work on something big and exciting, and that I hoped he might attend a meeting with a few others in my office. He nodded with guarded interest. He didn't ask for any more information – just the time and place.

I stood to go and shook his hand. It was limp. Lewis Winterbottom's dissatisfaction was clear: he would jump at any opportunity of a role with less administration and more real science. I left the Straubenzee and headed back to my office. Adding his name to my list, I felt a growing sense of excitement.

JACK

I chose my fourth candidate from within my pool of existing acquaintances. In those days, I was teaching a joint course with colleagues from different departments, including Chemistry. This course sought to convey the interrelationship of knowledge across disparate fields, and to demonstrate the essential unifying character of scientific discovery. To this end, I had been asked to deliver an occasional lecture in the main Chemistry building and, as it happened, I was scheduled to present another such lecture on the same day as my meeting with Lewis Winterbottom.

The Chemistry lecture theater was just awful – all their money went into laboratories. The seats were uncomfortable and the ceilings always felt oppressively low, but my subject matter more than compensated for these deficiencies. My topic was the Ornstein-Zernike equation in statistical mechanics. I began with the equilibrium theory of classical fluids, explaining the radial distribution function, the direct correlation function, and the importance of Fourier transforms. I worked through the various closure relations, including the Percus-Yevick approximation, the hypernetted-chain equation, and of course, the Karlof solution.

It was one of the best lectures I had ever given. The audience of about a hundred undergraduates sat pinned to their chairs in a kind of electrified silence. But afterward, one kid with a torn sweater came up to me rather boldly with the complaint that the mathematics had been too difficult for him. He asked whether I could pitch my next lecture at the same level as Professor Jack Gasket, a well-known organic chemist.

"You like Jack's lectures?" I asked.

"Oh yes! They are very simple. We always understand them," the boy said.

This was no surprise. Jack could always appeal to the lowest common denominator. It was said that he'd been a fine chemist in his youth, but he published sporadically and almost entirely by reproducing other people's experiments. He was better at affirming knowledge than advancing it. Consequently, he'd never won any prizes for his work and he was known to be very bitter about this. On the other hand, his salary was considerably larger than that of most other Harvard professors. The Gogol-Squibb Corporation, a Fortune 500 firm, paid it – and seemed to expect little in return, except for his occasional appearance as an expert witness when Gogol-Squibb was suing or being sued by its competitors for patent infringements.

"I'm glad Professor Gasket gives good lectures," I said to the boy.

"Yeah. He's the reason I chose Chemistry as my major," he added.

"Are you being sarcastic?" I asked, studying him closely.

"No," he said, and seemed sincere.

This astonished me. Jack Gasket the inspirational figure! Gasket the guru! After I'd gone over the Percus-Yevick approximation with my mathematically challenged young interlocutor, I wandered on up to Jack's office to pass on this unexpected compliment.

He was situated at the end of a long research laboratory that reeked of bananas. The students must have been synthesizing amyl acetate. I walked past the stained benches and sinks, the beakers, the burets, the Bunsen burners and the Büchner funnels, the malodorous fume cupboards, and the blue rows of magnetic mixers. Jack's door was open and he was seated in a plastic chair on the wrong side of his desk, legs splayed, reading what looked like the latest catalog of chemical reagents.

He was a squat man with a clean-shaven head and the character of a drill sergeant. His perfect hairlessness, said in part to be the consequence of an experiment gone wrong, gave his cranium an embryonic quality. You could often observe the veins at his temples pulsing beneath his semi-translucent skin, and when he got angry, his eyes would bulge like someone with a thyroid condition. I poked my head through his doorway and stared at him. "Hello, Jack," I said.

He turned and looked up. "What do you want, Duronimus?" he demanded gruffly. He always was an aggressive fellow.

"Actually, I have some good news for you," I remarked.

He looked at me suspiciously. "Who've you been talking to?" he asked.

"One of your undergraduates," I replied. I passed on the boy's kind remarks.

"Well, that's not much use to me, is it?" he said. He shoved the catalog across his desk.

"What do you mean?" I asked. Jack was a perplexing animal. I'd expected him to be pleased.

"What I mean," he said, "is that it doesn't matter what you do around here. Do a good job or do a bad job – you'll be overlooked either way. Harvard doesn't care."

He leant back in his chair and kicked the side of his desk. "See!" he said. Then he kicked the desk again, even harder. "See! It doesn't care," he said, raising his voice. "It's an inhuman institution. Harvard doesn't care! Doesn't need to care. I can give the best lectures in the world, but is anyone in this place going to pay any attention? I don't think so."

"Well, the students ..." I began, then remembered something that I perhaps ought to have recalled before visiting. He would never admit it, but I knew what was on his mind. For some people, being a Harvard professor just isn't enough. Jack was desperate for an honorary title – a second named professorship, a Distinguished Service Professorship, or a Distinguished Research Professorship. Status mattered to him. I remembered that the Faculty had just announced its next series of promotions. Jack must have applied for something and been knocked back.

Of course, I wasn't surprised. He didn't deserve an honorary title, but I felt sorry for him anyway, and I wondered in that moment whether he might be a good candidate for my project. He was a man of some moral ambiguity, as organic chemists often are, but there were plenty of Harvard chemists whose research performance was weaker than his. I reminded myself that nobody is more easily attracted to a radical cause than a man who thinks he has been overlooked; a man with a chip on his shoulder. Without saying anything, I added Jack Gasket to my list, alongside Rubin Weisensteiner, Colin Capstone, and Lewis Winterbottom.

MILLICENT

I now had four people in mind to help me launch my idea, all Harvard professors in different fields. If I could convince them to join me, then I felt we might have a team capable of creating a groundswell of support for almost any scientific initiative. However, they were all men, and I couldn't do without a woman. Any significant undertaking in academic life needs the affiliation of at least one woman. The larger one's aspirations, the more important this is – and it's as true at Harvard as it would be at the Alabama Central College in Tuscaloosa. There's no point fighting it.

Yet implementing this principle was not simple. I didn't know any second-rate women. So I telephoned the chairs of several academic units to see whether somebody could recommend one. I spoke to the heads of the Rowland Institute, the Sham Institute, the Wyss Institute, and the Kavli Institute. I chatted discreetly with the department chairs of Astronomy, Chemistry, Physics, Earth and Planetary Sciences, Mathematics, and Molecular and Cellular Biology. I contacted the directors of the Center for Advanced Brain Science, the Center for Advanced Computational Science, and the Center for Advanced Research in Materials Science. None were willing to put anyone forward.

Eventually, I had some luck with Harold Neville, Dean of Engineering and Applied Sciences. I liked Harold. He had a bizarre interest in the history of bowties, a subject best avoided, but he was a genuine fellow with a sincere concern for the future of Harvard. To keep things brief, I called him on the phone.

"Hello, Harold," I said, "it's Duronimus here."

"What's up?" he replied.

I explained that I was working on a new research initiative funded directly by Emmanuel Porphyrin, and that I was looking to assemble a group of people with diverse expertise.

"Yup," he said. "So what can I do for you?"

"I am looking for a woman," I explained, cradling the phone hopefully.

"I see," he replied. "Aren't we all?"

He thought for a moment. Then he mentioned a young woman called Millicent Parker, an assistant professor in nuclear engineering.

"She sounds great," I said.

"There's just one thing," he replied.

"What's that?"

"Well, she's very good – very competent," he hesitated, "but to be truthful, I'd say she's not likely to progress to great heights."

"Really? Why ever not?" I asked, my curiosity stirred.

There was a pause.

"Is this off the record?" His voice sounded slightly suspicious.

"Sure," I said.

"Look, it's very simple," he explained. "Millicent is good, but she's too generous with her time. She takes on too many responsibilities."

"So she works hard?" I asked.

This sounded like a sign of competence to me. At the other end of the line, Harold coughed uncomfortably.

"Well, yes, she does work hard, but I should clarify," he said. "Millicent works very hard – but at all the wrong things. She writes half my papers for me, she has twice the teaching load of the male assistant professors, and if any student runs into trouble, she's always the one they go to. She doesn't leave any time for herself."

I understood. She was apparently one of those modern people who believe that universities should be genuine communal organizations, where everyone chips in, and for whom the journey, the experience of working together toward a common goal, is actually more important than reaching that goal. For my purposes, she sounded perfect.

"One more thing, Harold ..." I began.

"Yes?"

"Is she easy to get along with?"

"What do you mean?" he asked.

"I mean, she's not a trouble-maker, is she?"

I had to ask. Community-minded people can be real nuisances if they want to be. I wasn't after someone who'd want their photo in the *Harvard Magazine* every time someone in our group achieved anything of note or, even worse, a person who would run directly to the union if things didn't go the way she liked.

"Oh, no!" Harold laughed. "She's not like that at all – quite the opposite. She's a perfectly sensible person: conscientious, considerate. Let me tell you, Duronimus, I'm not putting her up in order to offload her; I'm suggesting her because I think working with you will do her some good. It might make her a bit more selfish. She's not one of our very top people but if you have straightforward expectations, I think you'll find that she can contribute."

This sounded good enough to me. I thanked Harold and put down the phone. A woman whose main failing was excessive helpfulness sounded ideal. Millicent Parker was on the list. I finally had my five.

CHAPTER VII

THE PROPOSAL

The next challenge was to bring them all together and sell the concept. I invited them to my office at eleven o'clock one Monday morning, just a couple of weeks after Sandra Hidecock's death.

The first to arrive was Colin Capstone, the geophysicist. It turned out that he was still with us, looking very much the same as his *Harvard Magazine* photograph, only wider in girth and grayer in beard. He knocked genially on the door then stomped in, hauling a large briefcase almost overflowing with undergraduate examination papers. He was out of breath and sweating profusely. I offered him my seat – the only one without the constriction of armrests. He smiled and sank into it like a Zeppelin deflating.

Second to arrive was Millicent Parker, the nuclear engineer. She proved to be a plain and well-meaning young woman. She had none of the usual reticence one expects among junior faculty. Dressed in a simple blue denim skirt with a plain, white shirt, she seemed straightforward and enthusiastic. When introduced, she gave Colin a friendly grin and offered us cold bottled water. Then she sat down comfortably in one of the smaller chairs I'd placed in front of my desk, smiling earnestly at nothing in particular.

The next two arrived almost simultaneously. Lanky Lewis (blood fluke) Winterbottom didn't seem certain he wanted to be there. I introduced him to the others, but he said very little and seemed wary. I had a small bookshelf in my office, just beneath the windowsill, and he leaned on it tentatively and looked across at his office.

Coming in just behind him was Jack Gasket, the pugnacious organic chemist.

"Very good to meet you," he growled, jowls like a bulldog, clasping everybody's hand in an emphatic, almost intimidating way. He sat on the edge of my desk, as though he owned it, although his feet barely touched the floor. "Okay, Duronimus, we're ready for you!" he stated, impatiently.

"We're waiting for one more," was my terse reply.

Jack folded his arms across his chest and frowned. I sensed now that he wouldn't be easy to deal with. I couldn't very well eject him from the first meeting, but I did wonder right then whether I would later regret my decision to involve him.

The last to show up was Rubin Weisensteiner, our theoretical astrophysicist. As usual for this time of year, he was sporting a pair of shorts. He apologized for being late, waved to Colin and Lewis, whom he seemed to know, shook Jack's hand rather formally, calling him "Professor Gasket", and then pulled up a chair alongside Millicent.

"And who are you my dear?" he asked in a manner clearly intended to be amicable and perhaps even flattering, but coming across as syrupy.

"This is Millicent Parker – one of our up-and-coming engineers," I said.

"Oh!" he replied, with great interest. "What sort of engineer?"

"Nuclear," she said proudly.

"Oh, really?" he said, with apparent delight. "We should have a chat sometime about thorium tetrafluoride and neutron moderators."

It was good to see Rubin Weisensteiner back to his normal gregarious self, and it was funny to watch him trying to impress Millicent. He was so much older and more intellectual than Millicent Parker; yet at that moment, I perceived that Millicent might be his complement, a small salty cracker to his big cheese, the woman who could get him to comb his hair and eat a proper breakfast. But I didn't wish to get ahead of myself with this line of thinking.

The key thing is they all seemed perfect: not great scientists, not the crème de la crème, but just pretty okay scientists, slightly out of their depth. They were five solid exemplars of the average. I looked keenly at them so that they might appreciate the gravity of what I was about to say. Then I addressed them as follows:

"You're not the most famous people in Harvard. You are not the most successful. You are not even the best loved by your colleagues. Yet I have explicitly selected you because I believe you are honest people – scientists of real integrity; genuine knowledge seekers; good, old-fashioned researchers; people who value truth more than earthly rewards."

Lewis Winterbottom nodded vigorously, and I sensed a glimmer in Colin Capstone's eye and a smile brewing behind Millicent's thin lips.

"I realize, of course, that you've not always received the accolades that you probably deserve, but I don't believe external recognition is what really matters. You are all people who have dedicated your careers to pushing back the frontiers of knowledge rather than playing those underhand political games one has to take part in to get on in the world today."

They were all nodding now, demeanors relaxed, except for Jack Gasket who still frowned, arms crossed at his chest.

"I admire your integrity as members of the Harvard faculty, as people, and as scientists, but I also believe, if you don't mind my saying so, that you all have the potential to achieve so much more."

There was a slight bristling as I said this.

"Please don't take offense," I added hastily. "You all know it's true. But have you ever wondered why? I'd like you to think carefully about the people here at Harvard who have been really successful – overtly successful, that is – in recent years. What defines them?"

"They're mostly assholes," said Colin Capstone, giving Millicent a droll wink.

"No ... I mean, yes, there is some truth in that, but there's something else too."

Actually, there were many things: hard work, good luck, and the imagination to operate in a visionary rather than an incremental way. Successful scientists have the ability to work with others, to attract and nurture students, and to write as well as think. But I didn't mention these things – they didn't serve my purpose.

"Our world is changing," I said. "Science is changing. The expectations of our institutions and of our funding bodies here in America are shifting. Science is no longer an individual pursuit. Our funding councils are seeking out big teams with big ideas. They want people who can work across disciplines, traverse boundaries and bring together disparate expertise to answer really big questions." I paused for a moment. "And I have an idea exactly along these lines; an idea for the six of us."

Gazing at them, I sensed their rising attention, their academic hunger growing.

"So what are you proposing?" asked Jack Gasket. It was the first time he'd shown even a begrudging interest.

"Something I cannot do on my own. Something I need a strong multidisciplinary team for – and people I can trust. Something very big," I said.

They were certainly curious now. Without fail, modern scientists adore big concepts. They yearn for them and fantasize about them. And why should it be otherwise? It's the big ideas that enable researchers – especially the second-rate ones – to live in a blissful, imagined future rather than the humdrum reality of the present. I took a deep breath.

"For centuries, scientists have operated in the belief that the laws of nature are fixed and eternal and universal in application," I began.

"It's a fundamental tenet of physics," said Rubin Weisensteiner.

"And chemistry," said Jack Gasket.

"And biology," said Lewis Winterbottom.

"And geology," said Colin Capstone.

"Yes, indeed – it's what we've all been taught. It's what we all accept. It is the one assumption that unifies all sciences ... But what if it's not true?"

I let the idea hang for a moment.

"You mean ... what if the laws of nature are not universal?" Rubin Weisensteiner asked tentatively, sitting up as if his chair was suddenly uncomfortable.

"Yes. What if the laws of nature are not fixed and eternal?" I continued. "What if the laws are neither universal nor consistent? What if there's a way to get around them?"

They looked at me with undisguised bafflement.

"Sorry, but you'll have to be a little bit more explicit – at least for me. I am not exactly sure what you mean," Rubin said.

"It's simple really," I explained. "I want to test the universality of scientific discovery. I want to find a way to circumvent, let's say, the law of gravity or the laws of refraction or the laws of electromagnetism."

"But that's impossible ... isn't it?" said Millicent.

"It seems extremely doubtful to me," muttered Lewis.

"It's completely unscientific!" gasped Jack.

"No ... well ... it depends what you mean," said Rubin, surprising us all.

"What do you mean, Rubin?" asked Millicent.

As mentioned, she was rather plain and matter-of-fact and she asked her question in the same way she might have asked what time it was. But let me say this and underline it for emphasis: <u>There is nothing in the world a theoretical physicist loves more than to be asked what they mean</u>. To put it another way, "What do you mean?" is not only the most common question theoretical physicists are asked, but it's also the most gratifying. It is a question that swings the gates wide open for them to expatiate freely, and to exhibit their knowledge and genius until the quarks come home. Furthermore, Rubin Weisensteiner was a quintessential man of his discipline. He responded to Millicent's question like a bellboy who'd just been asked to draw Sophia Loren a bath. He adjusted his hairy knees and waited slowly, almost indulgently, until he was sure he had everyone's complete attention.

"Well ..." he began, and then paused. I sensed he had a rare gift for exploiting his moments in the spotlight. "What is a law?" he said, waving his hands in the air. "It is merely refined experience. The laws as we describe them are constantly being modified and changed and adjusted as we learn more about nature. We change our formulae; we improve our models. This is how physics advances."

"Yes. Einstein showed that Newton's law of gravity was only a special case of the law of general relativity," Millicent chipped in.

"Absolutely," Rubin said. "Einstein showed how to circumvent the law of gravity, as we previously understood it, by taking it to its limit. Anyone can give the appearance of getting around a law, simply by operating in an environment where different laws apply."

"But he doesn't want –" Jack started to say.

Rubin held up a hand. The floor was his. "No, Duronimus doesn't want to do things so simply. Actually, if you ask me, he doesn't really want to contradict the laws of nature at all. Our laws are merely descriptions; they are all imperfect and they all have their limits. But that is not your point, is it, Duronimus? If I've understood you correctly, what you really want to do is to repudiate nature itself."

"Yes," I said, steadying my tone, "that's exactly it. I want to test our deepest, most fundamental assumptions about nature. I don't want to find a standard way to break a law, simply by taking some system to its limits. I want to break a law in that very regime where it has been proven to operate. I'm not talking about extending or refining the laws, I'm talking about transcending them altogether."

"But that's impossible, surely," said Millicent.

"Some would say it is impossible by definition," said Rubin. "After all, everything we know suggests that nature is unequivocal in its consistency."

They looked at me, and I looked at them. It was clearly something they hadn't thought about before and this made them curious. On the other hand, they were not enthusiastic. Still, I had not yet revealed my trump card. I let them run for a while.

"Sounds more like philosophy than science to me," said Lewis Winterbottom.

"Yes it does, doesn't it? The sort of thing we might expect from our colleagues in the humanities," agreed Colin.

"Actually, it is mysticism," said Rubin, making me wince.

"Do you have any evidence to suggest this might be a worthwhile endeavor?" asked Millicent.

"None whatsoever," I replied.

"Any ideas about approach?" asked Lewis.

"None yet. We start from scratch. It's a question that has never really been asked – at least not in a scientifically rigorous manner," I said.

"So how would you propose to do such a thing?" asked Colin.

"Honestly, I don't know – that's why I need your help. To me, it's a profound and interesting question, but I cannot attack this on my own. I am sure it can only be resolved by a team approach, and for this very reason I am seeking your help. I am proposing a major new interdisciplinary research program starting here at Harvard, but extending nationally and internationally. We will study in a rigorous and experimental way the fundamental basis of humanity's persistent belief in the laws, and I want all of you to help me lead it."

This was too much for Jack. He was standing now, arms down, shoulders rounded, gruff and truculent. It was obvious the group was not really buying my proposal. Certainly it was a big idea, but it was too risky. I could see Jack's veins pulsing on his forehead. He had read the mood of the room and now he was going to step up to the plate and close the conversation down.

"Hang on a minute. Let me just get this straight," he said, taking a step forward, looking around at the others while he ran a hand across the roof of his hairless braincase. "You want us to help you lead something that is notionally *impossible*?"

"Correct," I said.

Jack took a step back, shaking his head. "Then you are totally nuts," he opined. "Just who precisely is going to fund a harebrained operation like this?"

Studying them closely, I said, "I've already raised a million dollars."

In a millisecond, everything changed. It was as though I'd struck a large match. I saw the light change in Jack Gasket's eyes. Colin Capstone sat up in my chair. Millicent shifted her body angle away from Rubin, toward me.

"I am going to match this by raising some additional funds. You know my own record in research. I don't foresee any special difficulties. The first thing I can promise you is that this is not going to be a tin-pot enterprise."

"Okay ... Okay, we're listening," said Jack.

And so they were. I told them they were the "luminaries", evoking a term used years ago by Robert Oppenheimer during the Manhattan Project. But privately, I called them the "gloominaries", for there was a sense of wretchedness about them. They knew and I knew, and they knew that I knew, that they were only really going along with this because of the money. However, this was our turning point. One by one they agreed to come on board. We all shook hands, and our remarkable project was up and running.

CHAPTER VIII

BUILDING THE CASE

Our first objective was to initiate groundswell support across the community. We took a multi-pronged approach to this, dividing the tasks among the group according to ability.

Rubin Weisensteiner agreed to write a monograph asking why physicists from Nicolaus Copernicus to Stephen Hawking had concluded that nature implements its rules with unfailing consistency across all times and places. He was also going to suggest surreptitiously, toward the end of this piece, that there could be ways of bypassing the laws of physics, and that if only we could discover them, any number of amazing new technologies could become possible: teleportation, intergalactic travel, immortality, invisibility, telepathy, telekinesis, and so on. Rubin planned to call this tract *A New Philosophy of Nature*, or perhaps *The Origins of Scientific Ideology*, but Millicent persuaded him to consider alternatives likelier to engage a more general, younger audience, and for a while the book was slated to be called *Is Physics Forever?* In the end, however, this was deemed rather too trite – "too light-weight for Harvard" is how Lewis Winterbottom phrased it – so at my instigation, Rubin also contemplated *Anarchy in the Cosmos* and *Making God Play Dice*, before finally settling upon *The Freedom Manifesto*.

It was an ambitious, big-picture title. It projected the science of our venture into the socio-political sphere, which would suit us in the short term. Sadly, the document itself was not as invigorating as its name, but that's not uncommon in the modern world where anyone who can write a three-word slogan will eventually find a publisher. *The Freedom Manifesto* was not long in print, but Rubin tried very hard with the project. He took on the subject with a gusto that made us momentarily recast him as a scientific Che Guevara, and whatever one thinks of it, the book served its purpose. It raised awareness and contained one memorable passage that is quoted to this day:

The scientific process is the greatest invention of human history, but does it liberate us – or does it merely open our eyes to our chains? Science has rejected the arbitrary rituals of culture. Science shows us that culture is the enemy of truth. Science has placed culture on trial and found it wanting. We say then that we are liberated because we no longer have to live with false representations of reality. Yet by showing us reality as it really is – inflexible, dominating, uncompromising, infinite – science reveals that it is not God, or ritual, or superstition, or culture, but nature itself that ultimately constrains human aspiration and liberty.

An ethical scientist has a duty to ask what we can do about this. Science has revealed the world not as our forefathers imagined it but as it really is. But does this mean that we must accept things precisely as they are? Throughout history, it has been those thinkers who tremble with indignation at injustice who have proved the greatest friends of mankind. Yet what of nature's injustice? It is the tyranny of reality that has caused nearly all the misfortunes of the world. Naturally, there will always be people who say it is unrealistic to transcend the boundaries imposed by reality, but we must demand the impossible.

Today, the most ambitious scientists think as freedom fighters. Like Emiliano Zapata, they would rather die standing up than live life on their knees. As a scientific civilization, once we comprehend the sheer force of the reality that surrounds us, surely we must recoil instinctively from its total control over us.

In its better parts, Rubin Weisensteiner's monograph was a call to arms. Over time, it proved an important inspiration for the younger generation and was critical in ensuring a healthy flow of graduate students. Its immediate significance, however, should not be overstated. It took Rubin some time to complete this document and even longer to find an appropriate publisher. In truth, *The Freedom Manifesto* played only a small part as we sought to build momentum for our ambitious project.

Far more important, in the first instance, was the parallel work undertaken by Lewis and Colin. Both had some weight in their disciplines by virtue of age and experience. They began writing provocative viewpoints in the major scientific journals. As a biologist, Lewis Winterbottom took on the life sciences, writing stimulating and thought-provoking commentaries in the medical and biological journals. Consistent with his background in geophysics, Colin Capstone began to cast aspersions within the earth sciences and multidisciplinary journals. Together, these two became dedicated renegades, assiduously raising fundamental doubt about the laws of nature.

What's more, unlike Rubin, they never exaggerated the importance of the matters they raised. As far as they were able, they wrote in a detached and objective way. With insouciance, not swagger, they were careful never to "climb out on a limb". They said nothing that could be seen as angling for money or pushing a barrow. Their style, indeed their craft, was one of nonchalance. They drafted every line many times, finessing each word and element of punctuation so as not to seem excessively dogmatic or self-interested. They excelled in presenting our issue almost as if it were just a fascinating but largely philosophical matter. Sure, it was unfinished business for the scientific community, but not something that should be seen as a serious threat to the scientific endeavor. Their presentation was cautious, yet off-the-cuff. This was simply an interesting problem that would ultimately make science stronger – if it could only be resolved quickly and efficiently.

Fortunately for us, they were published in the most prestigious journals, such as *Science*, *Nature*, and the *Proceedings of the National Academy of Science*. Such is the advantage of publishing viewpoint pieces; they don't receive the same rigorous peer review that research articles require, so they can gain quick and easy exposure in even the very highest profile outlets. Looking back through the literature, it is interesting to summarize their approach. Typically, they wrote things like this, excerpted from an article published by Lewis in the *American Journal of Oligochaetology* under the title "More Unfinished Business":

Few ideas are so relevant to so many fields of enquiry as the concept that the laws of nature should be fixed and eternal across space and time. Yet the universality of the laws of nature has never been thoroughly and rigorously tested. We believe it is high time to remind ourselves of this important philosophical question, and though we agree this is not the most important issue in contemporary science, it certainly remains one of the most fundamental – at least from a theoretical perspective.

Naturally, following the publication of words like these with the Harvard name attached, the scientific literature erupted with responses from all over the world. On one particularly memorable occasion, twenty-seven senior German physicists, including three Nobel Laureates, submitted a joint letter to the editor of *Nature*, criticizing the journal for allowing one of Colin's more speculative pieces into print. The German argument was that the universality of the laws of nature was not untested at all, but had in fact been confirmed over and over again, on occasions too various to be calculable. They wrote:

Every time a person drops a tennis ball and observes it fall, they are testing the law of gravity. Any time someone presses the accelerator on an automobile, they are testing the laws of mechanics. Every time anyone hits a light switch and sees a light turn on in their home, they are testing the laws of electromagnetism. What more confirmation of universality do we need from nature?

Colin and Lewis responded to this particular piece of criticism with a confident but conciliatory note, which the journal also published. The journal's editors took the approach of agreeing wholeheartedly with each of the German physicists' observations, but rejecting their conclusions. They liked the back and forth nature of the exchange and noted that experience of *what is* should never be taken as proof about *what is possible*, concluding with the line: "We do not question what it is that nature does routinely, but whether it might be conceivable to make it do things in another way."

Fortunately, the German response was not the most common. To our delight and astonishment, we discovered that there was a great deal of support in the scientific community for the idea of challenging the laws of nature. An eminent astronomer from the University of Nottingham published a fervent letter in the *Proceedings of the Royal Astronomical Society*, advocating an international program to test whether the constants of nature were the same on earth as in the furthest galaxies. A distinguished quantum physicist from Lund University in Sweden wrote a fascinating theoretical account in the *Transactions of the Berzelius Society*, suggesting that nothing in the universe is real unless it is first observed and that the laws of nature, while fixed, have only become so since humans have been conscious of them. With an avidity and enthusiasm that belied his dour Northern European heritage, he exhorted experimental scientists all over the world to turn their attention to "this most fascinating and impenetrable mystery".

Perhaps the most interesting and unexpected reaction came from a group of epidemiologists from Universiteit Utrecht, who wrote a very supportive article in the *New*

England Medical Journal drawing attention to the fact that there was already a lack of universality in the area of clinical trials. "What applies to the Northern European does not always apply to the Latino, and what applies to the Latino does not work at all for the African," they wrote, prompting the Chief Scientist of Bolivia and the President of the Nigerian Academy of Science to follow up with a joint article published in the *New York Times* entitled "Is Nature Racist?" This article cited both the *New England Medical Journal* and a review written by Colin Capstone in the *American Journal of Seismology* in order to question whether the only way to abolish racism from the world was to abolish nature itself, and prompted some wunderkind at the *New Yorker* to devote a full feature article to Colin Capstone and the "Harvard Six" as he called us.

This was a particular stroke of good fortune, for it prompted the United Nations Educational, Scientific and Cultural Organization (UNESCO) to respond with an international examination of racism in science, which began to lend some seriousness and prestige to our endeavors. The President of UNESCO himself signed an authorization appointing both Lewis Winterbottom and Colin Capstone to a steering committee looking at new models for the development of African (as opposed to American) science. In his letter of appointment, he wrote: "We are seeking the application of your expertise to create a new African model of science, which might reduce American scientific hegemony and emphasize the importance of plurality in ethnic approach when interpreting nature." It was an utterly pointless initiative, but one that benefited us just the same, as it lent us an exceptional and more international imprimatur.

In this intellectual climate, it should surprise no one that a good number of new research initiatives with relevance to our mission began to spring up in many parts of the world. In a move that illustrated a national gift for not being outdone, the Chinese government founded a new *International Center for the Re-Interpretation of Science in the Chinese Context*, based at the Ningbo Institute of Virtue, Truth, and Honesty in eastern Zhejiang province. The Russian Academy of Science announced that it would embark upon a new wheat-breeding program to try to create new "gene-free" foods specifically tailored for the "unique Russian digestive tract". A Californian philanthropist opened a new research center at the La Jolla Institute for Paranormal Research in affiliation with the University of California, San Diego. And in an interview for *Scientific American*, the Chair of Chemistry at the University of Utah announced that two of his most talented employees were designing a novel apparatus to test the laws of nuclear fusion in a glass beaker at room temperature.

Soon enough, the idea of questioning the universality of scientific law was being treated very seriously and over time, we succeeded in making our problem fashionable and created a strong impression of global competition. Yet there was more to this achievement than merely writing books and papers. Just six months after our initial meeting, in the midst of our efforts to stir up the academic community, I took four of the gloominaries with me to Washington D.C. (Jack Gasket was unable to attend due to an expert-witness obligation.) It's one thing to talk about ideas, but the fastest route to enhancing one's credibility in research is to engage financially with the Department of Defense.

CHAPTER IX

DARPMA

I t certainly was a gloomy day as we flew into Washington. The clouds were low in the sky and our distant view of the Capitol afforded only a muted pleasure. We landed at Ronald Reagan National Airport, where we took a black and orange cab a short way to a small office building in Arlington, not far from the Pentagon. It was an unremarkable, anonymous structure; no nameplate at the entrance, only a street number. Next door there was a hair and nail salon, across the road a Taco Bell. It was all very unassuming, the sort of building in which one expects to find the offices of tax attorneys or podiatrists. Yet these were the headquarters of the Department of Arbitrary Research Pretending a Military Application (DARPMA), an important subsidiary of the Department of Defense.

Over the years, I'd been involved in a range of important military research projects. I'd received funding from the Office of Naval Research, from the Army Research Office, and from the Office of Air Force Research. DARPMA was where the slightly more unorthodox and imaginative projects were funded. It had enjoyed something of a renaissance during the previous administration and, given the growing interest in our topic within the scientific literature, it seemed a natural funding partner. DARPMA bureaucrats tended to be conspiratorial and instinctively jealous, and they abhorred the thought of missing a chance to associate with a hot new area of discovery. I felt we had a good pitch and there was now more than enough competitive momentum in the wider research community for us to point to.

We entered the building and gave our details to the straight-faced concierge. He made a call, then took us through a basic security gate and up an elevator to the sixth level. When the elevator opened, a small woman with eyes that seemed to be looking in different directions stood waiting for us. She shook my hand brusquely and led us along a dreary corridor. Eventually, we came to a door with a faded walnut veneer and a large aluminum handle. Our guide knocked on it and without waiting for a response she ushered us in.

The man I'd arranged to see was program director, Walt Martin. He was in charge of codified classified research: work so secret that not even he was allowed to understand it. A bespectacled bureaucrat of medium height, we wore a navy double-breasted suit with remarkably large lapels. He had a square, slightly stupid face that would have looked right at home in military intelligence. Upon our arrival, he briefly pretended to reorganize some paperwork. He then leaned back amiably in his swivel chair and asked how he could help. I handed him a folder of journal clippings (actively stimulated by Colin and Lewis's steady stream of reviews, opinion pieces, and articles), and began to explain our project.

"Don't say any more," he quickly interjected. "It could all be classified."

"But don't you want to know what it is we're proposing?"

"No," he said. "This isn't the National Science Foundation. We don't like too much information around here. If we know it, then at some point in the future we could be compelled to release it. We worry about overly zealous journalists and whistleblowers. Our policy is that of the Defense Department as a whole: Don't know, can't tell."

"So what can we tell you?" I asked.

"Well, let's think about that – are you working on a new weapon system?"

"Ahh … I suppose it could be a weapon," I said. I didn't know that this was really the case, but I figured it would be difficult to convince DARPMA to fund us if our proposal didn't have some relevance to the military.

"Can it be used to terminate enemy combatants?"

"Well … yes, why not?" I thought this was fair enough too. Even a pencil sharpener or a paperclip can kill someone if used in the right way.

"Will it have any deleterious consequences for Americans?"

"No – certainly not!"

"But it can be used against the enemies of the American people?"

"Yes … I suppose it could."

"How much are you asking for?"

"A million dollars."

"How much do you already have?"

"Harvard has given us a million dollars."

"Oh!"

Clearly this impressed him. I knew it would. As a general rule it excites someone when they hear that Harvard has backed something with its own money. Not that Harvard has ever been short of money, mind you, but it's the principle of the thing. Outsiders always imagine that the people running Harvard are the smartest. If Harvard is doing it, so the thinking goes, then we should too. This has always been a part of the secret to the institution's success.

"So what do you call this thing?" Walt asked, apparently wanting to skirt around the subject of money.

"Which thing?" I replied.

"This thing that you are doing. What is it?"

"I thought you didn't want us to explain ..."

"No – you mustn't! Don't describe it. Just give me the name of it."

"But we don't have a name yet," said Colin.

"Oh," said Walt, his eyes narrowing into a disappointed frown.

This was a sticking point. We hadn't thought of a name. Why should we? Truth be known, we still hadn't the least idea what we were actually going to do. Until now, our focus had been on promoting the question we wanted to answer. I saw Millicent and Rubin exchange looks. It's very difficult to give something a name before you've decided what it entails, but I understood where Walt was coming from. He was worried that he might not be able to brag about the high-tech nature of our project unless he had a high-tech name to go with it; without a name, he would have nothing to write on his budget papers and, above all, he was worried because he couldn't be seen to fund something called "Top Secret" because that's when people start asking questions.

"Could we give it a code name?" Rubin suggested tentatively.

"It's an Ooala Reactor!" I blurted out the first thing that came into my head.

"An Olala Reactor?"

"No. It's Oo-a-la. The Ooala Reactor," I corrected.

"That sounds pretty serious." Walt was visibly impressed.

"It is. We were thinking of calling the project the National Ooala Reactor."

"You mean this is going to be a national venture?"

"Yes, absolutely – a national team venture."

"But not a nuclear reactor?" Walt had gone slightly pale.

"No, no," I said, "it's all above board. Strictly sub-atomic."

I explained to Walt that there would be nothing nuclear going on. Our goal was to raise a national team of leading experts across a broad range of fields. We'd realized, I said, that by working together we could do something infinitely greater and more exciting than we could ever manage by working on our own. I hastened to suggest enthusiastically but imprecisely that ours was one of those vast and rare challenges: a problem of such magnitude that it could be properly resolved only with substantial investment and a nationally coordinated multidisciplinary approach. This kind of argument excites most bureaucrats. They are nearly always seduced by the idea of national teams and big ventures.

"You know, I've never had five Harvard professors in my office before, all at the same time," Walt said.

"Oh, I'm only an assistant professor," said Millicent.

"Yes, but I've never even had two Harvard professors in my office before, at the same time. It's amazing ... Everything okay over at Harvard?" he asked.

"Yes, it's wonderful," I replied, and the others nodded enthusiastically.

In the end he gave us two million dollars. I think he wanted to go one up on Harvard. In only half a year, we had tripled our money. We had enough now to talk about a multi-million-dollar prototype. There was also palpable interest across the scientific community. We had real traction. Yet our success was still not assured. We now faced a new set of problems. What was the Ooala Reactor and what was it actually going to do?

I knew from previous experience that our project's momentum was very strong but likely to be temporary if we didn't act quickly. We needed to grip our opportunities with both hands and promote them as widely and loudly as possible. I knew this as implicitly as any other intellectual visionary who is dependent upon the charity of others to realize his dreams. But now there was something else for us to worry about. It was only a question of time before the Harvard donation and the DARPMA support would lose their currency. From now on, we needed more than the beguiling allure of the Harvard name. We had reached the stage where we had to define, at least in broad terms, our actual plan of work. It was time to demonstrate that we actually knew what we were doing.

CHAPTER X

BRAINSTORMING AT THE OLD ARLINGTON

Following our DARPMA visit, I called an urgent meeting of the Harvard Six with the intention of discussing the experimental ideas by which we might practically – if not realistically – attempt to circumvent the laws of nature. I arranged for us to meet at the Old Arlington Hotel down in Boston's Back Bay area. I wanted to meet off campus to stimulate fresh thought, but also to remind the group that we were already successful, or perhaps more explicitly that we weren't short of cash.

The Old Arlington Hotel was ideal. A converted Victorian apartment building, with large sash windows and a grand staircase, its formal meeting room had an old world ambiance that captured the imagination. The drawing-room elegance, the antique printed map of Boston above the fireplace, the sketches of politicians and other rogues hanging upon the walls: all these furnished the room with a conspiratorial flavor. It was exactly the right place to concoct a majestic scheme, to dream up a scintillating new mechanism or, more exactly, a bold and ambitious experiment with the real potential to confound the laws of nature and to expose the vulnerability of our scientific perceptions of the world.

We began the day, as is customary on such occasions, with a cup of strong coffee – except for Lewis, who always brought his own teabags. Then I sat the crew down in an eclectic assortment of overstuffed armchairs and sofas, arranged in a huddle.

I asked Lewis, our biologist, to speak first, largely because I expected the least from him, and he didn't disappoint. Not a natural public speaker, his hands shook as he meandered through his elaborate and convoluted proposal. Sometimes as he spoke, he gazed solemnly into his cup. Sometimes he lifted his eyes to the chandelier. Occasionally staring in astonishment at his vibrating fingers, he seemed to be holding a symposium not with us but with his own pink knuckles. It was an exemplary performance of academic elocution in the finest British tradition, and in this way he described, if somewhat erratically, how we might revisit one of the great dead ends in the history of science: Lamarckian evolutionary theory.

Lewis's idea was that evolution might be forced away from the Darwinian ideal. According to established understanding, an organism is born with a particular genetic blueprint and passes on to its progeny a random subset of this blueprint, with modest mutations. Under this arrangement, evolution depends upon the laws of chance. There is no capacity for individuals to determine which of their genes will be inherited, or to direct the evolution of their descendants. Evolution thus occurs randomly and relatively slowly over a timescale measured in generations. Lewis felt our mission should be to compel nature to proceed along different lines. He cited a discredited theory proposed in the eighteenth century by the heroic French botanist and taxonomic enthusiast, Jean-Baptiste Pierre Antoine de Monet Lamarck.

"In the Lamarckian theory of evolution, an individual's reproductive blueprint could actually be improved over the course of their life and their descendants could inherit acquired characteristics. By this arrangement, evolution within a species would not occur over generations but within individual lifetimes," Lewis mumbled.

This was the theory. In practical terms, he wanted us to breed mangroves in the desert, to train polar bears to eat bamboo and lima beans, to rear saltwater fish in freshwater tanks, and to shine bright lights into the eyes of little moles. "By subjecting these organisms to environmental extremes, perhaps we can create the circumstances for the passing on of an acquired trait," Lewis said.

He also proposed a longitudinal study on the progeny of short men, comparing the children of those who have lived normal lives "with the children of those whose bodies have been extended prior to reproduction by the application of a human stretching apparatus". The idea vaguely outraged us from an ethics and public relations standpoint, though this was flagged only in passing.

Lewis's main suggestion was that we embark upon a major experimental project using the blood fluke as our model. "Blood flukes are the ideal template for any major initiative in the biological sciences. They are neither so simple as to be already well understood, nor so complex as to be beyond comprehension," he said. He recommended that we should build a massive facility holding more than a trillion flukes. "This is my idea for the Ooala Reactor – that we construct a massive-scale breeding reactor. Only by working on an enormous scale can we expect to see Lamarckian patterns," he concluded.

"Lewis, I don't like it," Jack said abruptly, his voice ricocheting around us. "Your idea is brazenly biological and you sound like that Russian fellow, Trofim Lysenko."

Trofim Lysenko was one of the very few twentieth-century Lamarckian biologists, a famous fraud, another favorite of Joseph Stalin, and a man widely held to be responsible for the degradation of biological sciences in the Soviet Union and for the arrest and death of many Russian biologists who happened to disagree with his views.

"As a matter of fact, Lewis, I don't like it either," chipped in Colin, though in a gentler tone. "Dealing with all those blood flukes sounds revolting."

"And what if they escaped? Surely there are huge environmental and public health implications!" said Millicent.

I asked Rubin what he thought.

"Actually, I'm attracted to the general philosophical approach," he replied, scratching his forehead. "But why Lamarckian evolution? Why pick this particular dead end? Why not do N-Rays or the ether or phlogiston?" He went on to cite several failed theories from the history of physics, and to explain why nobody could ever hope to be successful in reinstating them.

Lewis's concept had no support. It was a legitimate approach with a certain beguiling logic, but we couldn't feel any enthusiasm. It was not remotely original and given Lewis's personal interest in trematodes, it looked awfully self-serving. It also seemed guaranteed to fail. Demonstrating Lamarckian evolution in a complex biological system would be the equivalent of an alchemical miracle and blood flukes were not experimentally compelling from anyone's perspective except Lewis's.

Millicent, our nuclear engineer, spoke next. In stark contrast to Lewis's tortuous monologue, she had rehearsed a short statement, which she delivered with the earnestness of a girl scout. She also chose to stand, which irritated me. I knew I shouldn't hold it against her, it simply reflected the conscientiousness she brought to everything, but I felt she misjudged the situation and with each word, she slowly diminished in my estimation. Despite her quaint enthusiasm, her arguments were about as advanced as one might expect from a high school debater. Her essential thesis was that it was difficult to contravene the laws of nature because we ourselves are a part of nature.

"This is the Heisenberg paradox," she explained soberly, referring to the perplexing German physicist, Werner Heisenberg. "How can we be confident about what we observe when we are a part of what we are observing?"

It was a valid and well-worn philosophical point, as well as being a fundamental aspect of quantum mechanics – a concept with incontrovertible, empirical underpinnings. Yet it was also an idea that the rest of us were very familiar with, and hence contemptuous of. Apparently, Millicent didn't appreciate that her audience had all once been sixteen-year-old boys with scientific predilections and no girlfriends, routinely given to a form of transcendental rapture over precisely this kind of pseudo-philosophical moonshine. But by the time young men of this disposition attain the intellectual maturity of their twenties, they are usually completely over and done with the subject. Indeed, as they move into adulthood, the idea that there might be an interesting interplay between science and philosophy pales until it becomes a painful topic to remember, a subject that reeks of immaturity and broken dreams, a slum city of the mind they'd prefer not to revisit.

So, as Millicent spoke primly of Heisenberg's uncertainty principle, the collapse of the wave function and the paradox of objectivity, I noticed Jack Gasket yawning, Lewis Winterbottom studying the map of Boston above the fireplace, Colin Capstone rubbing his eyes, and Rubin Weisensteiner frowning with a decidedly forced expression of concentration. Like most scientists we all wanted to believe we'd improved with age. None of us wanted to reignite the passions of our teenage years. The only exception perhaps was Rubin, who may have relished Millicent's dissertation simply out of intellectual vanity. After all, there is a certain sort of scientist who will sit through a dull presentation quite happily if it enables him to gloat privately at the notion that he is thirty or forty years ahead of a colleague.

I have no idea how much of this Millicent picked up. If she did notice she gave nothing away, and in any event she soon progressed to other themes. She spoke of a precedent set in 1882, when the Cambridge philosopher Henry Sidgwick founded the Society for Psychical Research with a mission to prove the existence of the human soul. She mentioned the origins of psychology and the contemporary breakthroughs in cognitive science. She tried to excite us about advances in brain scanning that were emerging from the new technique of magnetic resonance imaging. Then she delivered her conclusion. It turned out she wanted us to circumvent the problem of human participation in the world, including our dual role as observers of and participants in nature, by studying both the "untapped power of human consciousness" and the "potentiality for mind to exert control over matter".

With one palm lifted as if taking an oath, she gravely stated, "At this stage I don't come with a definitive proposal, but surely it is only by unlocking the mystery of consciousness that we can discover whether it is really possible to liberate humanity from the constraints of nature."

"It may surprise you, coming from a nuclear physicist," she added, "but my concept for the Ooala Reactor is that we try to develop a device to channel psychic power. Mankind has invented the lens to focus light. We have harnessed the magnet to channel electricity. So why not something similar for brainwaves?"

I think the five of us wondered for a brief moment if she was proposing a scientific experiment or the creation of a new spiritual ashram. For my own part, I wasn't sure if we hadn't been momentarily teleported to a meeting of the World Theosophical Society. I looked across at the others, nervously.

"I don't like this mind-over-matter angle. What do you all think?" I asked, fearing a deluge of criticism. Scientists can be extremely antagonistic about this sort of thing.

"We'd have every neuroscientist and psychiatrist in America breathing down our necks," observed Jack ominously.

"As a biologist, the brain has always terrified me. Best to stay away from the brain," said Lewis.

"I don't like it either. There is something a bit weird about parapsychology," said Colin.

"I know," said Millicent, meekly. "I realize that psychic research has a bad reputation. But I'm not suggesting we team up with some psychic spoon-benders.

All those people are frauds for sure. But I do believe this: the one thing that separates us from the rest of nature is human consciousness. If we embarked upon a massive, serious program of research into the human brain, we just might find something."

Leaving aside the painful Heisenberg reference, it wasn't actually such a stupid suggestion, and in contrast to Lewis's proposal, there was something refreshingly generous about her approach. For one thing, she hadn't pushed her own field of nuclear engineering. But now we had the opposite problem. She was proposing that we persuade the world to invest in a major project, with vast amounts of international funding and thousands of researchers, and all this to be led by the six of us who had simply no history or track record whatsoever in the field. It was utter naivety!

I asked if anyone had experience in cognitive research, and they all pursed their lips and shook their heads. I asked if any of them knew someone with the capability to lead a project like this, and again they said no, though they recognized that such people must exist. I asked if any of them thought this was an avenue we should pursue, and their answer again was no.

"It was just an idea. Thanks for hearing me out," said Millicent.

"That's quite alright, Millicent," I replied. "That's what we're here for – to listen, to brainstorm. But we do need to frame our ideas with some measure of practicality. Our aims are very unusual."

"Essentially, they are preposterous," said Rubin, rubbing his hands together.

"Yes, which means we have to be courageous, absolutely – but also extremely cautious," I said. "Our challenge is a bold one. Therefore, our ideas must be imaginative, creative, and revolutionary. But this alone will not be enough. We must show ourselves to be both imaginative *and* rigorous, creative *but also* practical, revolutionary *and at the same time* conservative. And this means, above all, that we must do what we know."

"Absolutely," said Lewis. "That's why I suggested the blood fluke facility."

"Yes," I said. "But the rest of us know absolutely nothing about them."

"And we're quite happy to keep it that way," quipped Rubin.

Before we could descend into a disparaging cycle, I reiterated my strong preference for doing something that could be seen as an extension of our existing expertise, and also suggested that we look for something highly controlled and systematic with a watertight methodology, affording us not only the greatest chance of success, but also the greatest protection from failure.

"But how can you possibly achieve this when you are trying to undermine the very fabric of reality?" asked Millicent.

It was at this point that Jack injected himself more forcefully into proceedings. "Can I describe my idea?" he barked. "I won't get up," he noted with a surly glance at Millicent. Then he cleared his chest with a self-important, deep-throated cough.

"I don't agree with you," he began, turning to face me with a sneer, "I don't agree with you at all."

Jack Gasket had a reputation for inducing a high level of mental fragility among his graduate students. It was said that his PhD students would arrive perfectly normal and well balanced, only to leave five or six years later with elements of their personality shattered or completely dissolved. I wondered how working with him would affect me. He was a provocative individual, with the air of a cocksure monkey.

Contrary to my suggestion that we focus on what we know, Jack's staunch opinion was that the Ooala Reactor should be some sort of facility for tackling the "soft sciences", by which he meant those areas of research where the laws are still not so well developed.

"Look, in my career I've spent a lot of time dealing with the legal implications of science. My expert testimony has helped a bucket load of lawyers interpret science in the context of human law as opposed to natural law. And one thing I've learned is that it's much easier to break the law in Haiti than it is in Washington D.C.," he said.

Colin and Rubin enjoyed a good chuckle at this and Jack smiled and puffed himself up in his armchair.

"Anyway, we all know it'll be a darn sight easier to contradict the laws of psychology or economics or geography, say, than the laws of chemistry or physics or mathematics," he said. "So why not go for nature's soft underbelly? I say we hit one or two of these weaker disciplines and just start ripping them to shreds."

My heart sank. I had hoped that Jack Gasket, of all people, would be more hard-nosed, and a little more precise. I asked him to give us some specific examples.

"Well, obviously we have to finesse the details," he said.

"Yes."

"But I have a range of ideas. For instance, we could make it snow at the equator. Anything to do with the environment or climate is going to be pretty soft. Or we could focus on behavior. We could train cats to chase dogs and mice to chase cats, or we could get a goat to mate with an oyster." (He looked up, hoping for a rise from the audience, but didn't get one.) "Or we could pick an area like sociology, or economics. We could seek to reduce the homicide rate in Honduras to zero. We could convince a Frenchman that capitalism works. We could ..."

"And the Ooala Reactor?"

"The Ooala Reactor would just be a facility for achieving any of these objectives – or something different again. My point is really the principle: not only that we try to make things happen that shouldn't happen, but that we do it in those weaker, softer fields, where the laws are less well defined," he said.

I could tell from people's faces that nobody thought much of this idea. Jack's perception that nature is easier to controvert in some areas than in others was wrongheaded. Of course, nature may appear vulnerable in those fields where the laws are still imprecisely known or largely statistical in character, but in these same fields, it is also hard to know when you have genuinely succeeded in circumventing a law. After all, how can you be sure you've really broken a law if the law is not clearly defined to begin with?

Colin made these arguments – with Jack all the while glaring back at him furiously. Colin tried to do it tactfully, but Jack was not one to take criticism as lightly as he dished it out. I watched his eyeballs expanding with every word, and I found myself wondering if he had received some of his education in Russia or Eastern Europe. His tetchiness reminded me of a Hungarian mathematician I'd worked with earlier in my career, and I could see that his temperament would not have been out of place on the faculty of the Moscow Institute of Physics and Technology, where they have installed lead-lined walls to contain the intensity of interpersonal interactions to prevent them from detonating into the psychological equivalent of nuclear explosions. It seemed to me he'd also be at home in at the famous Budker Institute of Nuclear Physics in Siberia, where the winters are long but the fires of envy, pride, and intellectual rage provide warmth all the year round, even when the central heating fails.

To defuse the situation, I told Jack in as conciliatory a tone as I could muster that although his suggestions were highly impractical, they were still extremely interesting. Lewis Winterbottom asked him a detailed technical question about goats and oysters "from a biological perspective".

Rubin Weisensteiner reminded him of the great New Zealand physicist Ernest Rutherford's words: "The only possible conclusion the social sciences can draw is: some do, some don't."

Even Millicent Parker, who'd endured Jack's negativity only moments before, went so far as to confess very sweetly that she admired his ideas and his imagination, although she couldn't resist making one provocative observation. "Just for the record, Jack," she murmured. "In the interests of intellectual inclusiveness and fairness, a number of our colleagues in other disciplines would be insulted by your use of the word 'soft' in this context. You shouldn't think of them as the soft sciences but as the non-physical sciences."

"Is that so?" said Jack, irritably.

"Yes," said Millicent.

I stood up to open a window, but it had been nailed shut. The air in the Old Arlington Hotel was getting stuffy. We had reached an impasse and I could see it was time to refocus. I directed everyone to stand and wriggle their shoulders a little. Then I got them to embrace one another. I'd picked up this technique some years previously at an intense planning session in Zurich for a world congress on non-Euclidean geometry. I have always remembered how, following a heated discussion about the parallel postulate, a young woman from Berkeley had suggested that everybody stand for a moment in order to hug one another. It had been a surprisingly touching experience to see the Lobachevskian geometricians, the Minkowskian geometricians, and the Riemannian geometricians briefly clasped together, hypotenuse to hypotenuse. I realized then that even the most abstract science is a distinctly human endeavor and also therefore an emotional one, and I saw the benefits in emotional release and collective physical contact, especially for individuals who'd been trained from a young age to channel their feelings and physical impulses into intellectual activity and disputation.

Whatever the general merit of the hug, that day in the Old Arlington it seemed to work. Lewis tittered about being British. Colin chortled about the scale of his waistline. Millicent joked that she was feeling rather hot all of a sudden. Rubin quipped that we'd just broken a law of nature: the "academic aversion to interpersonal contact". Everybody laughed and relaxed, and I was able to suggest a new focus for our discussion. I told them, if we wanted to be serious in our endeavor, we had no option but to contend with reality head on, which meant concentrating on the hardest of all laws: the laws of physics.

CHAPTER XI

IMPOSSIBLE BY DEFINITION

There has always been a hierarchy of truth in the scientific academy. Everybody knows that the laws of physics are the laws in their clearest and most general forms. They are the exemplars, serving as models for the laws at large. Many of them are universal too. The force of gravity, Sandra Hidecock's nemesis, operates at the level of the cosmos, the elephant, and the electron. As far as I was concerned, our plans had to match this level of universality.

I sat up in my leather wingback armchair. I pointed out that it was no accident that I'd selected a majority of physicists to join our group. Whereas any young ignoramus may aspire to be a scientist, only an elite minority has what it takes to become a physicist. Physicists are the guardians of reason, the standard bearers for natural order, the ultimate legislators of truth. They control the Upper House in the Parliament of Knowledge. I argued that if we could succeed against the laws of physics we would really achieve something meaningful, while to claim success in any other area would be to leave ourselves open to reproof.

"It is only by working at the frontiers of physics that we can hope to accomplish anything truly significant," I said.

As I brought my comments to their conclusion, I stared squarely at Rubin, who wriggled in his seat, becoming almost tongue-tied in his eagerness to support my position.

"Absolutely, Duronimus! I couldn't agree more," he said. However, he went a step further. He believed that although the laws of physics were the most clear-cut, well defined, and powerful of all the laws, they were also in one respect the most vulnerable.

"Whatever do you mean?" Millicent asked, her eyes glimmering with fascination.

"How do I explain this?" he asked himself aloud, and scratched his chin, as if pondering the remotest reaches of the universe, far beyond the Whirlpool galaxy. "Well ..." he began, and then paused. "Let's put it like this," he said, and paused again, this time to inspect his bitten fingernails. "Okay, it's like this," he said finally, chuckling for a moment as if what he was about to say was a really profound joke. "In an eternal and infinite universe, almost anything will eventually happen if you are prepared to go far enough and wait long enough. Yes?"

"Yes," Colin agreed.

"At the atomic and sub-atomic level, the laws of nature involve irreducible randomness, and in any equilibrium, all kinds of fluctuations can occur. Yes?"

"Yes," said Millicent, shifting her body to the edge of her chair.

"So why don't we just wait? Something strange – something lying in direct opposition to the laws – is bound to happen eventually. In fact, we know this happens in the quantum regime. Particles can form from nothing in a vacuum and then disappear again. My suggestion is that we tap into this sort of effect. It is just a matter of knowing where to look, and then waiting long enough to see it happen."

He looked around, his eyes glowing with self-satisfaction. I had a sense that he was expecting to be nominated for the Nobel Prize, or that he wanted someone (probably Millicent) to throw off her clothes and rush through the streets of Boston shouting "Eureka!"

Instead, Colin asked flatly, "So you're saying we just measure stuff and wait? For how long?"

By way of explanation, Rubin launched into a history of the Homestake Experiment, run in those days from the Homestake Gold Mine in South Dakota – a massive facility five thousand feet underground, involving a giant tank filled with 100,000 gallons of dry-cleaning fluid. Every few weeks they'd test it to see whether they'd captured any neutrinos.

"It's a fascinating project," he said. "They simply set up the apparatus and wait. It's the same with other similar initiatives for detecting, say, dark matter. When looking for statistically unlikely events, the secret is often just to set it up and then wait."

"Yes, but for how long?" asked Colin again. "A year? A century? You're potentially talking geological timescales here. Won't DARPMA want to see some results before then? Besides, Rubin, I'm not even sure if what you've described meets our objectives. I could argue that these fluctuations occur within constraints imposed by other laws. More precisely, if fluctuations in the laws as we know them are a part of nature, then observing them is not to disobey a natural law but simply to notice the impact of some other underlying law. Isn't that so?"

"No, no, no," said Rubin, his leg jiggling up and down with suppressed defensive energy, "not necessarily."

It seemed an obvious point to the rest of us, but Rubin was determined to argue the case. He was adamant that rare fluctuations in the fabric of reality, apparently contrary to the laws of nature as we know them, need not be evidence of some pre-existing, underlying natural condition, and he went to great lengths to explain why.

He asked a series of rhetorical questions and quibbled over every response. He drew complex equations on the back of a lunch menu. He raved about Niels Bohr and Albert Einstein. He pretended that a stack of paper cups were sub-atomic particles, and began arranging them on the carpet like an elaborate MIT shell game – then fell into a fury when Lewis accidentally trod on one. He waved his arms about and knocked over a lamp. He reprimanded Millicent and Jack for not listening properly. He rubbed his forehead with great vigor. He went red in the face and taunted Colin for being an "ignorant geologist, not a real geophysicist". One second he would agree, then he would disagree. His brow crumpled under the strain of his thinking. His hair seemed to rise off his scalp, as though he was sitting on a Van der Graaf generator. His voice grew hoarse. I began to think we might need another group hug. Finally, he cocked his head to one side and with a degree of wistfulness and a surprising amount of decent, apologetic good humor, he openly recognized that Colin was quite right and that his idea was not a good one after all.

Unfortunately, Colin wasn't much help either. Sparing us the public cogitations we'd had from Rubin, he confessed that actually he'd had a very similar idea: building "the biggest goddamn laser in the world" – but in the end he couldn't see the point. "As far as I can tell," he admitted, "the best we can ever hope to do is to take a law to its limit.

But if we do that, won't we just discover more laws? Other laws? Different laws?"

"Seems like a dead end to me," said Jack.

"Yes – that's absolutely true," I agreed.

Colin looked down forlornly. They sat in silence and a somber mood descended upon the room.

"So what's your idea, Duronimus?" asked Millicent.

"Well, it's evident that our old thinking won't be enough. You've all established that," I declared. "I think we need to be much more ambitious. We must do more than simply observe nature, or probe nature. That's what science has always done and we know where it leads. As Colin says: at best to the discovery of new laws, and at worst to the entrenchment of old ones."

"So what are you proposing? What else is there?" asked Colin.

I paused. I remember the moment well. I remember their eyes upon me, expectant and alert. For a few seconds, I studied those second-rate Harvard professors and wondered why I had invited any of them to join me on such a mad and perplexing journey into the unknown.

"It seems to me," I continued, with unflinching resolve, "that we must disprove nature completely. To disprove a single law is not enough for our purposes. After all, what is a law of nature? It is merely a generalization based upon precedent. If we find a way to transcend some specific precedent, what does that prove? Nothing definitive, for there is always the possibility of exceptions, of other laws that lie behind the laws we already know."

This was Colin's point, but I was happy to elucidate. It was only too likely that if we transcended merely one law, then people would respond by saying "But haven't you just unearthed a different law?" or "Doesn't that point to some as-yet-undiscovered, hidden force controlling nature in a different way?" – and answering them wouldn't be easy. For this reason, I proposed something very different from anything put forward by the others – something exceedingly difficult.

"As I see it, we must disprove nature completely," I reiterated, with added gusto. "But to achieve this we must do more than simply find a way to do something that cannot be done. We must be more courageous than that. We must find a way to do something that cannot even be imagined!"

There was long, puzzled silence. Colin, Lewis, Millicent, and Jack all looked at me with a modicum of fear. Their alarm bells were ringing; they were thinking they'd been brought here under false pretenses and that they'd need to make a quick exit, first out of the Old Arlington, then out of the group. Why, they were asking themselves, had they signed up with this lunatic masquerading as a professor? Why, for a mere million dollars, had they gone along with such a ludicrous, impossible dream?

Rubin was the exception. I sensed something useful crystallizing behind his dilated pupils. I waited. I let the idea mull. I felt my heartbeat quicken. As the silence grew, so did the uneasy terror in the eyes of the others but, just as I'd hoped, I discovered that Rubin was with me. He straightened his back.

"Yes," he said, and everyone turned to face him expectantly. "Yes," he said again in a tone of calm amazement. "If we are to succeed, we must look to the impossible – not at what's impossible by law, but at the *absolutely* impossible – in other words, at what is impossible even by definition!"

It was as though a window had been flung open. We all sat up in our chairs and Rubin leaped to his feet.

"Don't you see?" he said, turning eagerl,
Millicent to Colin. "We must do the impossibl
by transcending the laws, but by transcending
itself. Duronimus is absolutely right. We mustn't worry
specifically about this law or that law. We must go deeper.
We must subvert the very logic of reality."

"Oh, really!" scoffed Jack. "So how do we do that?
Or maybe that's too logical a question?"

"Well," said Rubin, rubbing his chin. "It shouldn't be
that difficult. Nothing ever is, really. The only important
thing in science is to ask the right questions. If you can do
that, the answers usually fall into place."

Jack stared at him blankly. "And what's an example of
the 'right' question in this context?" he asked.

"No idea," replied Rubin. "Let's think about it ..."

Everyone became remarkably still – I suppose they
were thinking, or pretending to think – and an eerie hush
descended upon the room. For a moment, I almost wished
we had a philosopher, or a psychologist, or a comparative
literature person present. They can't keep quiet for long,
whereas scientists tend to think in silence. I had my own
proposition of course, but I held back just in case someone
else dreamed up something better. Also, I wanted to
give the impression that we were all arriving at this idea
together; people are always more willing to get behind a
concept if they feel it is theirs to begin with. Finally, Rubin
spoke up.

"I am probably going out on a limb here," he said.

"Go for it," I replied.

"Time goes backward and forward. Um ... how do I
put this?" He laughed awkwardly. "Can we make it move
sideways?"

"Sideways?" said Millicent.

"Yes," said Rubin.

"What does that mean?" asked Millicent.

"I have no idea. It just seems a suitably subversive concept," said Rubin.

"You can't be serious!" gasped Jack.

"If we could decide what it means, there might be something in it," I said. "But maybe Jack's right. Maybe this one's too difficult."

"What about space then?" asked Colin, tugging on his beard, getting into the swing of things. "Can we do something unusual with space?"

"Perhaps we could fill it up ... over-fill it, I mean. You know, put more into it than can possibly fit," mused Rubin.

"Or take more out of it than is comprehensible," responded Millicent. "Has anyone ever tried to take a vacuum below zero pressure?"

"You mean like an anti-vacuum; a space with less than nothing in it?" asked Colin.

"Interesting ... very interesting," mused Rubin. "But surely ... no ..."

"What?" said Millicent.

"Well," said Rubin, "if you have a space with less than nothing in it, you could still end up with something."

"What?" said Millicent again.

"Anti-matter ... well, possibly anti-matter ... I'll need to think about this."

Jack Gasket stared at Rubin in disbelief. Lewis Winterbottom ran a hand through his lank hair as if the discussion was all too intangible. The others, though, were just warming up.

"Okay, so we can't do space – then what about motion?" asked Colin.

"Time and space together, you mean?" said Rubin.

This was precisely the entrée I'd been waiting for.

"My idea," I noted gravely, "is that we make a particle decelerator."

"A what?" said Millicent, obviously still flustered.

"A particle decelerator," I repeated.

"You mean a particle *acc*elerator," said Rubin.

"No, I mean a particle *dec*elerator," I replied.

"You mean a brake then?" asked Colin, scratching his beard.

"Yeah, doesn't Ford do that?" Jack remarked dryly.

"Yes, I suppose so. But what I'm talking about would be no ordinary brake."

"So what would it be?" asked Colin.

"A giant brake, for small objects," I replied. "I'm saying that we make our Ooala Reactor a massive, internationally sponsored facility – a landmark scientific facility – for slowing things down. Everything in the universe is moving. But what if we could create an environment that slows things down, and slows them to the point where they are stationary in relation to all other points in the universe?"

"Yes, that could be possible, but I don't see the revolutionary angle here," said Rubin. "How exactly does this subvert the laws of nature?"

"Well, my idea is that we don't stop when it's stationary. We keep slowing it down, even after it's completely still."

"You mean ... we start to move it in the other direction?"

"No. That wouldn't be slowing it. That would be speeding it up again, just in another direction. That would be moving it, wouldn't it?"

"So it stops. Then what? What else is there?"

"Well, that is precisely my point. I propose that we slow it down so much that we go beyond stationary …"

"Beyond stationary?"

"Yes, sub-stationary."

"Sub-stationary?" Rubin looked at me quizzically. "You mean super-stationary?"

"No, sub-stationary. No one has ever done that before."

"Hang on!" Jack interjected. "I don't understand. Why isn't that just motion in the other direction?"

"What I'm talking about is not going forward or backward. On the contrary, it's the opposite of movement. It's anti-movement."

"But that's impossible," said Jack.

"Precisely," I said. "That is precisely my point."

"But it doesn't make sense. It's just … meaningless."

"Yes, I suppose it is," I replied. "But it is still potentially possible. And unless we try it out, we'll never know. And didn't we just decide that the only way to transcend the laws is to transcend meaning itself?"

There was another long silence as this concept sunk in. I gave them time to reflect, and then asked them one by one whether I'd have their support to pitch for funds along these lines. I explicitly sought an opinion from each of them. I wanted to be sure that we all agreed: the Ooala Reactor should be the world's first particle decelerator.

"I like it. You've got my vote," said Rubin. "It will give the high-energy physics community a run for their money anyway. They'll all be thinking *Why didn't we think of that?*"

"I like it too," said Colin. "It's got a sense of profundity about it, and that's going to be crucial."

"It is big science, isn't it? And it's clearly multidisciplinary. This could be a truly global initiative. I'm all for it," said Millicent.

"I'm not sure that I really understand it," said Lewis. "But if you're all keen, I'll go along with you."

"Oh, Lewis," said Millicent coyly, "you mustn't worry about that. If people understood modern physics, nobody would ever fund it. Our greatest advantage will be that nobody understands what we're doing – not even us."

Then I turned, finally, to Jack.

"I think I need more time to think about it," he responded uncomfortably.

CHAPTER XII

A NATIONAL ACADEMY

Jack Gasket's hesitation about our agreed direction did not trouble me. When it comes to making communal decisions about a course of action, unanimity is usually a fantasy. The meeting at the Old Arlington had been a great success as far as I was concerned. We now had a genuinely grand idea. We knew precisely what we were raising funds for. Ooala would be the kind of capital-intensive project that politicians love to support. Most of our group had departed believing that they had personally contributed to the formulation of our goals. Jack was undecided but we could hook him as the money flowed in.

For a while after that, everything was plain sailing. We contacted those who had followed Lewis and Colin's lead by writing in the literature about the problem of the laws, and we founded a new scientific society: the National Academy of Unlawful Science. I was the inaugural president, Millicent Parker was the secretary, and Rubin Weisensteiner was vice-president. To defend ourselves from criticism, we also instigated a new, peer-reviewed journal in which to report our findings: the *International Journal for the Refutation of Nature*. I was the editor, Colin was the deputy editor, and Millicent, Rubin and Jack were the first three members of its editorial board.

We agreed that Colin, Lewis, Rubin, and now Millicent too, would continue, in the wider scientific literature, to suggest that humanity should determine if it was possible to challenge the hegemony of the laws of nature.

Sadly, Jack remained intransigent. For the time being, he was happy to be associated with the project, but he did not want a public role. This didn't matter, however. We drummed up support from colleagues around America, and our National Academy of Unlawful Science membership expanded steadily.

I also arranged to visit key colleagues and dignitaries in Europe: notably the President of the Royal Society of London, the Secretary of the Swedish Academy of Science, and the President of the European Science Directorate in Brussels. I was able to convince the Europeans that our work was fundamentally important, and that the US would go it alone on this project unless they too became involved at an early stage. It was not long before the bureaucrats in Brussels agreed to stump up $4 million to initiate an international consortium with the brief of drawing a design plan and undertaking a preliminary costing for the Ooala Reactor. Then I managed to finalize $2 million in out-of-round funding from the National Science Foundation back in Washington. I subsequently secured participation agreements from the Mexicans and the Brazilians, both involving a small amount of funding. Then we signed the Argentinians, the Chileans, and the Costa Ricans. Less than a year after Emmanuel Porphyrin's initial grant, I had raised $10 million.

All of a sudden, we were on a trajectory that could not fail. Even if we struggled scientifically, I knew we would receive ongoing support from those who had chosen to invest. For political reasons, they would now need to justify these initial investments, and the surest way of doing that is always to invest more. So we prepared a preliminary design and costing for the Ooala Reactor, and contacted a group of Nobel Laureates. Rubin and I flew to see many of them personally in order to explain our proposal. In the end, we convinced six Laureate physicists to write an open letter to the President of the United States. They wrote in support of our venture, requesting direct US government support to build our reactor, and the letter was published in many of the mainstream newspapers. It read as follows:

Dear Mr President,
Recent work by Professor Karlof and others at Harvard University, which has been communicated to us by manuscript and in person, leads us to expect that there is potential to devise a scientific system that can undo certain aspects of reality.

The significance of this work clearly calls for quick action on the part of your Administration. Any power capable of circumventing reality would possess a military and economic advantage unprecedented in human history, affording it a strategic edge in global affairs. Furthermore, we understand that scientists in the Chinese National Academy of Science have already commenced work on a similar project in the Jia Qizha Gorge near the Shandong Institute of Piaoqie.

In light of these developments, we hope you will establish permanent contact between the Administration and our scientists. One way of achieving this might be to entrust the task to a person who has your confidence and who could serve in an unofficial capacity. You may also see

merit in special budgetary arrangements being made
for the National Academy of Unlawful Science,
which is currently serving as the umbrella group for
American researchers working in this area.

Yours sincerely –

The success of this letter was remarkable. Denis
Doberman, a senior adviser in the White House, was
appointed as our direct contact and he orchestrated the
federal funding arrangements for us over the next three
years. The value of this relationship was enormous, as the
US government quickly evolved into our major investor.

But I should stress that this was always an international
initiative. We contacted the United Nations and sought an
international working party to look into this issue of the
laws of nature, proposing this as an important mechanism
for improving international relations through science.
After only a handful of meetings in Paris, this group
(which I chaired) proved hugely effective in stimulating
British, Canadian, and Japanese backing for the Ooala
initiative. It galvanized a global community interested in
addressing "the problem of the laws" (a phrase that was
fast becoming a watchword), and it was critical in exciting
foreign policymakers about our project.

Soon we had collected over one billion dollars in
funding commitments from the governments of all the
major Western economies. None of our funders ever really
grasped what an Ooala Reactor was. How could they,
when none of those involved in the project were quite sure
yet, either? Nobody on the planet understood the potential
benefits of supporting our project, but we all agreed that
this was the nature of the beast. Scientific research isn't
really discovery work if you know what you're going to

find in advance, and if you know exactly what the benefits will be. For a new venture, focused on such deep and fundamental questions as ours was, it's always impossible to predict the outcomes.

When I look back on that tumultuous year, I sometimes wonder what Sandra Hidecock would have thought. Her solitary effort to counteract nature's laws suddenly seemed so amateur and so inconsequential, compared with our major scientific undertaking. Our Ooala Project was an initiative of massive scale and profundity, backed by the economic power of the entire Western world.

CHAPTER XIII

CHIEF OPERATIONS OFFICER

esigning the reactor took another year. Building it took three. None of this was easy, especially given the tensions and behavioral quirks that began to emerge within my group. On almost every front, as our project gathered steam, our personal relations deteriorated. Luckily I was assisted through this, at least initially, by my re-acquaintance with Amelia Middleshot.

I recall it was a quiet Harvard day in late fall. Most students were away for the holidays and many of the faculty members were hibernating. Occasionally one saw a body or two hurrying across campus. Always they moved in straight lines, their scarves wrapped close and their jacket collars turned up against the chill air. Their thoughts seemed to be turned inwards, closed to the world about them, presumably preoccupied by mathematical proofs, far-flung galaxies, points of philosophy and logic, the interactions of sub-atomic particles, or distant civilizations and languages.

I had just stepped out of a very positive meeting, reporting to Emmanuel Porphyrin on our considerable progress, and I was feeling in a communicative mood.

Yet tasting the crisp Massachusetts air and looking up at that glorious collage of fall foliage, I was shocked by an unexpected rush of memory. Thoughts of Sandra Hidecock surfaced, and I was suddenly possessed by a desire to communicate with her memory. I am not usually retrospective but I wished she could have known about our progress and known, too, that her death had prompted the creation of something extraordinary.

It was unscientific and illogical, but there was one obvious place to go. A huge statue had been erected in Sandra's memory outside the Law School. It was an ugly abstract work with green cylinders, yellow squares, and black inverted pyramids, interconnected with reinforced chicken wire and all seemingly balanced so as to defy gravity – to jump but not to fall. At the base was a polished brass plaque, inscribed:

In loving memory of
Professor Sandra Hidecock:
Strive for the impossible!

As I approached, I saw a woman standing in front, gazing up at this monstrous work. Catching the sound of my footsteps, she turned and gasped, and I was transported at once back to St Crispin's Crematorium. I saw again that excessively long fringe falling carelessly across those pale green eyes. I saw the demure expression of innocence and hope. It was Amelia, Sandra Hidecock's graduate student.

"Oh, Professor Karlof!" she said, her mouth held open with astonishment.

"Hello, Amelia," I replied, and hugged her.

It was a short, enjoyable embrace. The laws of physical attraction between humans are not well understood scientifically, but it is generally accepted that an excellent bosom clasped impetuously to one's chest, even in the most casual or indifferent manner, can inadvertently stimulate a rudimentary form of animal magnetism. Although we hardly knew each other, I experienced an intriguing emotional charge at her touch.

Things were different for Amelia. Our embrace evidently reminded her of the wretchedness of those days after Sandra's death. As we broke apart, I noticed that she was slightly short of breath. She blinked her emerald eyes at me apologetically, her expression deeply regretful.

"Come with me," I said, impulsively. "Let me get you something warm to drink."

We stopped at the first spot we came to. It was neither comfortable nor private. Amelia perched herself on a stool then looked nervously over at me. Her coat was open at the front. Beneath it, she wore a formal black skirt and matching jacket, and I noticed that her smart, muscatel-colored shoes had formidable heels. She looked nothing at all like the student I'd left behind in Sandra's office. She seemed to have grown in some way, and it suited her.

After we'd ordered, she told me her story haltingly: how she'd never finished her thesis but tried writing a novel instead; how she'd returned to Wyoming to be with family but despaired of their provincialism and departed after just two weeks; how she'd been on antidepressants, and how she'd finally found employment in the Harvard legal unit. She finished with a flick of her hair.

"And do you know what?" she said. "I've discovered that I'm really good at legal work. I suppose it was all those years interpreting and reinterpreting texts, constructing and deconstructing documents, encoding and decoding narratives. My parents were always proud of me for pursuing a PhD, but they did worry whether I'd ever be useful for anything. Now I've been able to set everyone's mind at ease. Even mine."

Amelia sipped her hot chocolate and our eyes met briefly over the rim of her paper cup. There was something matter-of-fact about her now. Her voice was still warm, but she had evidently matured. The fledgling scholar, bedazzled by dreams of intellectual achievement, had grown up. Still, she retained an aura of vulnerability or, more precisely, the grace of disappointment.

"It sounds as though you are doing well," I said.

"I do have one regret ..." she began, but her voice failed her.

"Yes?"

"Well, in the first place, I'm disillusioned about Sandra."

"Of course."

She looked at me, and frowned cautiously. "She is not remembered in any meaningful way. Yes, there was the memorial service, and of course the monument. But that's not what she'd have wanted. To have her work continued, to leave an intellectual legacy – that's the only thing she hoped for and that's the one thing she's been denied. Everyone has forgotten her."

"Not everyone."

"No – you haven't." She looked up at me suddenly. Her glance was warm and thankful, and I acknowledged this with a gracious nod. "But mostly, it's as if her life and death were utterly irrelevant. They held a conference in her honor in Stockholm. She was lauded in every lecture. But now all that is forgotten. In the arts and humanities, everyone has moved on. Her old colleagues hardly talk about her. They've pushed her from their minds."

"But this is natural. This is what happens. Not everyone can be celebrated after death."

"Yes, I suppose so. But it makes me sad."

We sipped our drinks in silence. My mind returned to the former patron of the Harvard Squash Club. I remembered her passionate way of talking, and her witty turn of phrase. I reflected on the astonishingly courageous – and remarkably stupid – nature of her death. Amelia seemed to be thinking something similar, and I was struck again by the greenness of her eyes.

"So how about this current job of yours?" I said, returning to my original question. "Do you like the work?"

And I was genuinely curious. In academic life, one doesn't often get to see what happens to people after they throw in the towel. Amelia struck me as an interesting case since she was out of academic life but still operating in the academic milieu. Her answer surprised me.

"To tell you the truth ... I don't really know," she said. "I originally took the job hoping to be able to support equity measures within the university. I thought I could introduce anti-discrimination practices into all Harvard's legal agreements."

This sounded like the old Amelia. "It didn't turn out that way?"

"No. Within a month, I was moved into intellectual property law and the management of grant contracts. I work within a team that processes nearly six million pages of legal documentation every year."

"And how do you feel about this?"

"I don't mind it ... most of the time. As I said, I'm extremely good at it." She looked at me dolefully then glanced away. "The truth is," she concluded, "I do like

119

what I do but I feel somehow I've betrayed myself; that I've sold out. I used to believe I could change the world with an idea. Now I support other people's ideas."

"There's nothing wrong with that."

"I know, but sometimes I feel like a failure. A bureaucrat."

"But isn't that a common destiny for those with a higher degree in the humanities?" I asked.

"Yes!" She laughed awkwardly. "That's how it seems sometimes, but I don't have to like it. If I look at it objectively, I have become a part of the ongoing corporatization of this university, and I'm not comfortable at all about that." She took a long, deep breath and looked at me wistfully. "Still," she continued, "I can tell myself that at least it's Harvard. At least there are others here working on important research, teaching the next generation, carrying the torch ..."

"Oh yes? Who?"

She seemed thrown for a moment. Then she lifted her chin so that her hair fell off her face and her eyes were turned fully and confidently toward me. "Well, people like you. Everybody knows about the Ooala Reactor. They say that if you succeed, you'll win the Nobel Prize."

I don't know what possessed me in that moment. The gravity of the decision I made next would not become clear until much later. Perhaps it was a sense of guilt or obligation, an irresistible surge of vanity, or maybe something less definable – an essentially ungovernable component of the biological relations between the sexes. Whatever its cause, in an act of spontaneity I offered Amelia a position with the Ooala Reactor, working as my legal adviser and chief operations officer.

"I am flying down to check out a potential construction site in California next week," I said. "Come with me, if you like."

Her mouth broke into a big smile, she clutched my arm and her eyes glistened, those long, innocent lashes a dam for her tears.

CHAPTER XIV

THE BIG SLOW

In academic life, friendships are born of misery and success is a high-octane fuel for animosity. Anyone who has ever worked in a university department or government agency learns this lesson early, and rarely has cause to forget it. This was certainly the case with us. In the initial phase of our project, while the reactor was designed, scoped and then built, one by one I found myself falling out with the others. Those bonds of trust built so readily as we raised our first billion dollars steadily deteriorated as we began to spend it.

Our disagreements were mostly trivial but this did not diminish their ardor. For instance, our technical scoping team decided that in order to create a stationary environment we should build our decelerator deep below ground, preferably situating it in a desert, remote from other human activity or any other sources of external vibration. This was largely based upon Colin Capstone's advice, and was his first recommendation after I had appointed him Director of Geophysical Positioning and Vibrational Control. His preferred location for our experiment was Death Valley in California. His second choice was a plain in the northern part of Western Siberia, the world's largest frozen peat bog. His third choice was the Black Rock Desert in Northern Nevada.

Once word got out, however, that there could be benefits to building our experiment underground, Rubin Weisensteiner, whom I had appointed Director of Theoretical Analysis and Contingency Planning, pleaded instead that we do everything under New York City. He came to see me in my Harvard office.

"There are sixty thousand miles of unutilized subway tunnels under New York City. Why can't we use them?" he said.

"New York is out. We need a desolate place – a place free from vibration."

"But the best theoretical scientists in the world all want to live in New York," he mewled.

"So?"

"You instructed me to think of contingencies. I am concerned about the caliber of our workforce. The best physicists don't just work anywhere, you know. We need stimulation. We have active minds. We need synagogues."

"My main consideration is the quality of the site."

"So what are you proposing? Millicent tells me you are going to choose one of these deserts Colin is so keen on."

"Yes, Death Valley is our favored site."

Beads of sweat formed under his frizzy hair and rolled onto his forehead and I noticed that his yellow American Physical Society T-shirt looked unusually damp.

"Surely you can't be serious. The heat –"

"Death Valley is 282 feet below sea level. It is completely barren, geologically inactive and far from human industry. In short, it's ideal."

"But it's a horrible place. How do you think it got its name? For months on end, the temperature scarcely drops below 100 degrees."

"Yes, it will be a hot house in every sense."

I said nothing more to him but I confess that I saw considerable psychological as well as physical advantages in Death Valley. I liked the idea of working with people who had nothing else to do in the evening but tend to our experiment. I liked it that our staff would be forced to live in close quarters, where they could not help but share ideas and discuss work after hours. I was delighted by the concept of an environment that blurred the distinction between work and social life, where the young people would inevitably start to worry about who was sleeping with whom, and where the achievements of Harry working on Project X might spur on Joe who was working on Project Y. In my opinion, the whole spartan barracks arrangement seemed ideal.

Rubin stormed out and refused to speak to me for three weeks. He took every opportunity to complain to the others, saying that I'd failed to understand the peculiarities of physical scientists and was deliberately compromising the intelligence of our workforce. Unbeknownst to me at the time, Rubin's antipathy was not really related to optimizing our workforce. The real problem, as would later emerge, was that he suffered terribly from heat allergy.

This incident triggered a permanent rift in our relationship. This was not unusual; I had similar altercations with all the others, the ferocity of our interactions usually escalating and diminishing in inverse proportion to the seriousness of our points of contention.

I suppose conflict of some kind was unavoidable, given the magnitude and complexity of our project. Our plan with the Ooala Reactor was to build an infrastructure capable of holding an object perfectly motionless, and then to render it more motionless still. Our work demanded not just a low-vibration environment, but also an environment completely free from motion of any kind. We needed to be able to control the motion of our object relative to our apparatus, the motion of our apparatus with respect to the earth, and the motion of the earth with respect to the rest of the universe – no mean feat. The level of precision and the extent to which we had to call upon different disciplines of knowledge were unprecedented, and the technical demands of our project inevitably pushed us into disagreements. But this was only part of the story.

Our disputes were also a function of personality: ego, envy and pride. Most of those involved in the Ooala Project had remained deeply offended since childhood by a spirited sense of their own under-recognized importance. Consequently, there were occasions when it rankled with the other members of the Harvard Six that it was I, not they, who was the director.

At times, too, they bitterly objected to our division of labor. In constructing the reactor site each of us played a critical role according to our expertise, but the design of the core of the reactor fell to me, which meant (as everybody realized) that I would gain most of the credit if our experiment worked. Their resentment at this led to strange acts of insubordination. "Overly helpful" Millicent abruptly stopped making me coffee. Colin developed a curious resistance to answering anything I asked him directly; he wanted everything in writing. Lewis would disappear into the nearest doorway whenever he saw me coming. But my relationship with Jack Gasket became the most fraught.

As predicted, Jack's reluctance about our venture had waned as the amount of money we raised increased.

I didn't object to his venality, since his work ethic rose in line with his interest and, unlike the others, he was surprisingly keen to assist with administrative matters. Indeed, I made him Director of Administration, in which role he proved assiduous and energetic, although he was also the quintessential scholar, critical of any decision I ever made.

Issues of contention could be small or big. It didn't seem to matter. One day, he would rail about my method of disbursing funds to our partner institutions on the basis that "it gave the director too much discretion"; the next day, he would storm into my office and shout about the color I'd chosen for our logo or criticize my intellectual property and profit-sharing arrangements. Everything provoked the same passionate intensity. He had absolutely no sense of proportion. He was as much a hothead over the layout of our corporate letterhead as he was on the hiring of Indian or Chinese nationals (or as he called them, liars and spies).

He was also singularly jealous of my interactions with our funders and associated administrators. If ever I organized a meeting with Denis Doberman, the senior White House adviser, without also inviting Jack, he would charge into my office (even if I was in another meeting), and snarl that I was unreasonably secretive, and threaten to resign if I was not more "inclusive" in the future.

Worst of all was his attitude to the publicity the rest of us attracted as the project took off. When the National Geographic Channel ran a profile on the Ooala Project for their *American Scientists* series, they broadcast an extensive interview with Lewis Winterbottom. Unfortunately, Lewis gave the most boring interview conceivable. Indeed, I believe the footage is still used in various journalism schools as a glaring example of What Not To Do. The day after it screened, Jack marched in, determined to know why I hadn't given him the interview.

"How could you?" he demanded.

"How could I what?"

"Have you not seen it?"

"Seen what?"

"The National Geographic documentary! The *American Scientists* episode!"

"Oh yes ... what about it?"

"It's appalling!"

"Yes ... it's a little dull, I suppose."

"Dull!" His eyes bulged. "The man's a blithering idiot."

"Oh come on, Jack," I said. "He may not be a natural public speaker, but Lewis made some good points."

"What? Tell me one!"

Unfortunately, I couldn't think of any off-hand.

"I really don't understand you," concluded Jack. "Lewis is a bumbling amateur. Why do you let him do this? I mean, why didn't you do the interview?"

"I was busy." By way of elaboration, I waved at the paperwork piled on my desk.

"Then why not ask Rubin, or Colin ... or me? The program is called *American Scientists*, and Lewis is not even an American for God's sake – he's British. What I really don't understand is why you didn't ask me. I was available and at least I'd have had some goddamn thing to say!"

Why not Jack? This was the most persistent theme of our disagreements. He seethed incessantly about his lack of public profile. Every time there was a report about the Ooala Reactor in a newspaper or on the radio or television that didn't mention him personally, he would charge into my office and hurl his complaint. He would extol the simplicity of his time in the army where he'd learned the "true value of teamwork". He would rage against the "divisive individualism of Harvard's research culture". He would contrast the "frank" and "supportive" processes that he'd observed within the American pharmaceutical industry with the "underhanded" and "undermining" traditions of academic life – and my spirits would sink. It got so bad that I even considered locking my office, or working from home.

For a while, I managed to keep him at bay by suggesting that he publish more: gratuitous advice that answers many complaints in academic life. He would respond by grumbling about all the administration on his plate: the gratuitous response that nearly always answers the gratuitous advice. We danced like that for a while, following the customary ritual for interactions between the successful and unsuccessful, a formula that tends toward equilibrium but never quite gets there, yet which ensures that no argument among academic peers ever really gets out of hand.

I wished he would resign or learn to suffer in silence. But try as I might, Jack had committed his soul to a lifetime of complaint. Eventually I didn't even bother to argue. I just stopped answering his protestations and, as Amelia suggested, started imagining him as some kind of mechanical instrument. Gradually, I learned to ignore his smoldering attitude of grievance.

My capacities for both cajoling and disregarding the others were strongly extended over this time. Amelia was a calming influence, but in some respects it was a miracle that we got anything done. Like Sisyphus, I was constantly laboring to push them all up the hill, driving them continuously to transcend their more negative instincts. In time I realized that Rubin might be right: working and living together in the desert was not going to be an easy prospect for any of us – though at least it would be flat.

This brings me to a key point. I must explain that while we did end up operating near Death Valley National Park, we didn't end up in Death Valley proper, owing to a range of impediments created by the Californian government. When broaching prospective locations in California, we had to satisfy requirements for an extraordinary number of government entities. The Californian Office of Historic Preservation drew exclusion zones around many culturally sensitive sites in the desert and surrounding areas. The California Biodiversity Council and the California Department of Pesticide Regulation sought assurances that our experiment would not operate to the detriment of the flora and fauna of Death Valley National Park. The California Energy Commission wanted a ten-year forecast of our proposed energy use. But these were only the first of the prerequisites presented by Sacramento's tentacular bureaucracy, and I recollect only a tiny subset of their other stipulations.

The California Architects Board wrote seeking input into the exterior design of our facility "to ensure its compatibility with the native aesthetic of Death Valley". The Californian Department of Alcoholic Beverage Control asked for legal assurances that research students would not use our site "as an unlicensed drinking venue". The California Department of Community Services and Development insisted that we partner with a variety of private non-profit organizations to ensure that any low-income workers operating on our site (such as cleaners and construction workers) would be accommodated in appropriate housing, "free from lead and asbestos". California's Earthquake Authority wanted a study to address concerns about the implications of our work for the San Andreas Fault. The Californian Board of Barbering and Cosmetology asked for assurances that an influx of out-of-state scientists would not diminish "Southern California's well deserved and highly prized reputation as a mecca for attractive people". And the Commission on the Status of Women advised that we would need to include a certain quota of women on our governing boards and in all managerial positions – much to the disgust of Rubin, who said that this "final straw" would make his work "absolutely impossible".

Amelia helped me enormously in dealing with these matters. Her efficiency and persistence pleased us all – even Jack, who rarely praised anyone. She had an office at Harvard adjoining mine and I found her working there at all times of the day and night, sitting with her back erect, dressed in sober, professional attire, churning out reports of the most perfect banality, all of them written in flawless bureaucratic English. I discovered that she was a gifted user of the passive voice and that she had a flair for vapid phraseology. With her artistry and stamina, I thought we could eventually fulfill all the tortuous requirements of the Californian regulators. At a critical juncture, however, her lack of experience showed.

Our coup de grâce came at the hands of Dr Barbara Fissure in the Californian Environmental Protection Agency. She wrote to us once our bid to construct the Ooala Reactor in California began to look serious and I went to see her at the agency's headquarters in downtown Sacramento, bringing Amelia to take notes and Colin and Lewis too in case I needed their technical bluster.

Dr Fissure was a middle-aged woman with lank brown hair and dull eyes. She dressed all in brown, with wooden beads the size of chestnuts around her neck, and her thin smile drew lines upon her face that seemed quietly resistant. She had a very efficient manner though. Her office door opened at exactly the designated time, revealing a spacious room with natural lighting and a large red-brown carpet hanging on the wall. She whisked us in and surprised us with super-quick handshakes, gestured us into armchairs then sat on the edge of her own chair, picking up and opening a surprisingly thick file marked "Ooala?".

"I am sorry to have to call you down here," she said, flicking deftly through the pages.

"Not at all," I replied.

"You know, we are very pro-science here in California."

"Yes."

"We really love to challenge the boundaries too; that's one of the defining attributes of this state."

"Yes. We love the Californian spirit as well," I said. "This is one of the main reasons we're keen to bring our experiment here."

"And of course we're attracted by the scale of your investment," she responded. I smiled at that and she smiled right back at me. "On a personal note too, I really love what you guys are up to. But it's my job to see that things are done properly," she added. Her smile didn't change, and we all nodded as sincerely as we could. "So please tell me," she said, "what will be the environmental consequences should the Ooala Reactor succeed in going sub-stationary?"

I looked at Lewis. Lewis looked at Colin. Colin looked at Amelia. Amelia looked at me. Lewis looked at me too. Then we all looked at Dr Fissure.

"There won't be any environmental consequences," I said.

"Oh!" she responded, unsmiling now. "Can you be so sure?"

"Of course," I replied, with Lewis, Colin and Amelia nodding perhaps slightly too vigorously beside me.

"In that case," Dr Fissure continued, "can you clarify something for me? What will happen when you go substationary? I mean, what does it actually mean?"

"Well, we don't know. That's what we're hoping to discover," I replied.

"So it could produce something unexpected."

"Undoubtedly, but –"

She raised one thin finger to stop me right there. "Then how can you be so certain that there'll be no environmental consequences?" she asked triumphantly.

This worried me but I knew better than to voice concern. I kept my outward demeanor as calm and expressionless as I could.

"I know you've met the requirements of the California Biodiversity Council," she went on. "But the matters raised in that report only concern your construction. What I'm talking about are the consequences of your actual experiment."

I explained that whatever happened within our experiment would surely be contained within our experimental structure, which was designed to withstand an earthquake of level 10.0 on the Richter scale. Colin chipped in to add that our apparatus would even withstand a direct thermonuclear explosion.

"Not that anyone is expecting one," he hastened to add.

"Yes, but all this is beside the point," said Dr Fissure matter-of-factly. "What concerns me are not the precautions you've taken but your total inability to predict the outcome. We simply need to understand the consequences of your experiment. This is a highly sensitive region. If you go sub-stationary, we need to know it will not be to the detriment of any ecosystems in Death Valley –"

"You mean the desert?" Colin interjected before she had finished.

"Yes, if you like. The delicate ecosystem of our desert," said Dr Fissure, primly.

"But isn't this already the worst desert on earth?" said Amelia suddenly. "I mean, how much worse could we make it?"

· There was a long, shocked pause. Amelia told us later that she'd asked the question in all innocence but also maybe as a joke. Either way it didn't matter. It was game over.

"This is what you will need to find out," said Dr Fissure, bristling. "I don't mean to be a nuisance, but given the risks, I have to inform you that we will need proper technical and scientific assurances. In a case of deep uncertainty like this, it is compulsory under Section 514 of the *State Environmental Risk Assessment Act* to conduct a full impact study."

We never provided it. The cost for such a study as quoted by three different environmental engineering consultants was between ten and twenty million dollars. No matter how great the appeal of Death Valley, I didn't feel we could justify it. Even after the impact study, we may still have been denied access. I drew a line under the project and promptly informed Colin and the rest of the Harvard Six that California was out of the question. We were going to Nevada instead.

CHAPTER XV

NEVADA DREAMING

Things were much simpler in Nevada. Although our favored site, Black Rock Desert, was being used by the military for unspecified purposes, the state government paid us a cool $200 million to situate our facility at the edge of Nevada's little corner of the Death Valley National Park, in a region known as the Sarcobatus Flat. People like Barbara Fissure did not exist in Nevada back then. We had to deal with only one level of government: the governor's office. It was there that I had a fifteen-minute meeting with an affable young man called Joe Cave, the governor's adviser on development.

His Carson City office was a miniature gallery of Nevada state icons: the Las Vegas Strip of course but also Wheeler Peak, painted snow-capped and desolate; posters of bighorn sheep, mesquite trees, and the Hoover Dam; pamphlets for ski resorts; a fascinating photograph of an atomic bomb test – glasses and all; a blue and white helmet from the Nevada Wolf Pack college football team, mounted like a headless hunting trophy; sagebrush and Wayne Newton fridge magnets. And unless I was mistaken, an elegant silver statue of a pole dancer rested mid-twirl on the corner of his desk. It was one of the more colorful government offices I had visited.

Yet Joe Cave turned out to be a practical man with a business-like approach. He was clean-shaven, neatly combed, and had an honest gaze. He wore a crisp white shirt and a dark blue tie. He was very focused and kept our meeting to the point. He listened to my outline, added a few brief, constructive comments and then he closed in on the important details.

"How much are the Californians contributing?" he asked.

"I am not at liberty to discuss that," I responded.

"Then how much would it take for us to site this thing in Nevada?"

"$300 million would guarantee it."

"Would you take $200 million?"

"Yes, that should do the trick," I said.

We shook hands and that was that. A bill was passed in the Nevada Legislature the following week. A month later, I sent Colin and his team down to the Sarcobatus Flat with their seismic equipment to determine the facility's optimal location.

At first Colin was rather despondent not to have the Black Rock Desert, which he said had "unusually positive geotechnical properties" and "interesting inclusions and intrusions". He also expressed real concern about "abrupt seismic discontinuities", about the number of "batholiths" and "laccoliths", and about the possibility of confusing "anticlines" and "synclines" in the Sarcobatus region. However, when I told him he could take $100 million out of the Nevada matching funds in order to support his program's equipment budget, his complaining ceased. Not that we ever really had a choice. The site we wanted was technically desirable but politically impossible. The site we were offered was politically possible but far less desirable technically. In such a context, we had to be realistic. There is no power on earth that can prevail over political impossibility. Our science was strong, but not omnipotent.

In the end, Colin chose a site roughly 120 miles from Las Vegas, some way off the Veteran's Highway, midway between Death Valley and Area 20 in the old Nevada Nuclear Test Site. The closest place was a ghost town called Rhyolite. Not that we had much use for towns or ghosts. Once up and running, we planned to operate entirely within an enclosed perimeter. In order to minimize vibrations, we would need to impose severe limits on traffic to and from our location.

Colin's initial task was to measure vibrations rather than control them. To this end, he built a series of fifty concrete monitoring facilities in a vast ring around Sarcobatus Flat. Each of these facilities was built above a shaft extending a mile underground, into which a remarkable range of geological, geochemical, and geophysical sensors were embedded. These provided automated support for advanced magnetic, pleochroic, acoustic, stereographic, and seismic analysis, generating an extraordinary range of data describing the geological environment.

At the center of this ring loomed a single tower, a hundred feet high. It housed a modified version of the Oblique Oscillating Polarizing Sensor – the concept invented by Colin years before but never before realized on such a gargantuan scale. Once all the irritating diggers and trucks and cranes and scaffolding had been and gone, this extraordinary apparatus began operating as a long-range detection system, collating information from the network of facilities and firing deep electromagnetic pulses into the earth for measurement, analysis and interpretation in a range of inter-continental collection stations further afield, typically institutions of higher learning in places like Florida, Mexico, Chile, and Alaska.

Used in combination, these systems proved extremely powerful. Colin claimed that if a single grain of sand on Sarcobatus Flat shifted, then he could identify it. He used to boast that he could hear oranges being picked on the other side of the Sierra Nevada Mountains down in California, that he could detect if someone won a jackpot in Las Vegas, and that he could pick up the vibrations from the tour buses idling in the parking lot of the National Automobile Museum in Reno. He managed to link vibrational anomalies in the Sarcobatus Flat with such remote events as the collapse of an ice shelf in Antarctica, the eruption of a volcano in Indonesia, the underground testing of a nuclear weapon in Israel, and the blasting of an open-cut copper mine in Chile. Every Oscar season, too, he would joke about being able to detect the passed-over Hollywood stars hyperventilating.

"Although that should be factored in as background noise," he would add with a smile, "since there is always someone hyperventilating down there."

The sensitivity of this equipment enabled us to control for underground movement in our immediate environment. Initially, we used Colin's reading of subterranean vibrations to install heavy rocks – mainly lead, bismuth, and protactinium ores – as a vibrational shield at key points across Sarcobatus Flat. This rendered our site arguably the quietest geological location on the planet. But our intention over the longer term was to use Colin's elaborate sensors to pinpoint geologically quiet moments at which to run our experiments.

Colin's work was skillfully executed, and nothing we achieved subsequently would have been possible without him. This is not to suggest, however, that everything proceeded without hiccup. Shortly after Colin first installed and calibrated his Oblique Oscillating Polarizing Sensor, he phoned me at Harvard.

"Something serious is happening," he said, a note of panic in his voice.

"Yes, what?"

"I don't know."

"So why are you ringing me?"

"We think there is going to be an earthquake."

"I see. So you mean the site is no good after all?"

"No. I mean we think we are about to see a major geological disruption. We can sense a new fault line about to emerge, stretching all the way from Reno to Vegas."

"Are you serious?"

"We're talking San Francisco 1906 – only in Las Vegas."

My heart was racing. As I assessed the implications of his prediction, my mind focused with tremendous clarity and acuity. Quickly, loudly, I relayed the information to Amelia, who was working nearby. She gasped and stammered. I instructed her to get the numbers of the State Emergency Service in Nevada and key personnel in the governor's office and at City Hall in Las Vegas.

"How long have we got?" I asked Colin, over the telephone.

"Hang on a minute –" There was paper shuffling and urgent murmuring in the background. "I'm gonna have to call you back," he said. "Standby."

Time passed painfully slowly. I looked through the doorway at Amelia, hunched at her screen. She was white as a sheet. It seemed to me that this was an incredible moment, a moment we'd talk about for the rest of our lives. Every researcher relishes the instant when their ideas impact upon the world.

I tried to think ahead. We'd need to evacuate Las Vegas, Reno, and every town in between. We'd have to work with government agencies to prepare for aftershocks and for unexpected calamities across the region. We'd have to brace ourselves for the public attention afterwards. This was scientific enquiry at its most potent and bewitching. People had been trying to predict earthquakes for years. If Colin was right, we would prevent thousands if not millions of deaths and this would be a historical moment. We'd be heroes. Nobel Prizes and National Medals of Science would follow, and every person in America would know our names. But what if Colin was wrong?

The phone rang and I snatched it up. "Colin, how confident are you?"

There was a long silence at the other end of the line.

"Hello? Are you there?"

The silence continued for a few more seconds, then I heard the sound of someone shuffling something, and then I caught the distant but resonant medley of vocal chords vibrating, an uvula twitching and phlegm shifting as Colin cleared his throat. "Um, false alarm," he said. "Sorry about that."

It turned out that two frisky lizards had crawled into one of their detectors. Thankfully we hadn't called the authorities, but this grim memory hung over us all for weeks. I became ultra-cautious and deeply suspicious of my colleagues' claims, double and triple checking everything they did. All their complaints fell on deaf, stern ears. "Trust is good, but control is better" became my new mantra.

CHAPTER XVI

MOLEFORCE

After establishing our cordon of vibrational sensors, we fenced off a circular inner zone within a six-mile diameter and clear-felled the area to remove all sources of motion, including all forms of life. The fencing was solid steel, reinforced with molybdenum and guaranteed to be animal proof. Its aerodynamic corrugations dampened the acoustics and minimized vibrations from the prevailing winds. To prevent intrusions from burrowing animals, the fence was installed atop a reinforced concrete foundation extending ten feet down into the desert. All these duties fell to Lewis, as Director of Biological Control and Site Management.

He laid traps for the rodents, snakes, sidewinders, lizards, scorpions, jackrabbits, wasps, and spiders in our site zone, and after tagging he released them across the border into California, where most of them were protected species. The only challenge after that was to burn all the greasewood bushes, kill off the salt grass, and tear down the other hardy desert shrubs that speckled the terrain. We were concerned that the transpiration of water or the rustling of a breeze through the indigenous plant life would cause minute vibrations across our landscape. But Lewis attended to this very assiduously, spraying the area with broad-spectrum cyanide-releasing pesticides and multi-target herbicides, systematically killing every weed, shrub, and grub on the surface. He then bulldozed the area so that nothing was visible but the raw, dry dirt. It seemed to us all that he had done a superlative job. To the human eye at least, there was nothing living there with any prospect for movement. Yet Colin's seismic instrumentation continued to detect miniscule, sporadic motion beneath the ground.

I asked Lewis about this during a site visit. The two of us were sitting in his Land Rover, with the air-conditioning working at full capacity. Outside, it was so hot we'd had to let some of the air out of the tires.

"What is going on, Lewis?" I asked.

"I am afraid we have moles," he replied, not quite looking at me.

"Moles?" I said incredulously.

Stretching out his neck and lowering his lean face to peer eagerly between his knees, he reached into the glove compartment and extracted a small plastic container.

"Do you see this?" he said.

I gazed at the little plastic box. Inside, there was something gray and roughly half an inch long. "It looks like a piece of putty," I said.

"It's a new species," Lewis noted, proudly puffing himself up like a mantis about to engage in the courtship ritual.

He handed me the box and a small lens, through which I peered carefully at the creature. As far as I could tell, it looked no different under the lens than it looked to the naked eye. I was struck once again by its drab, gray formlessness. More than anything in the world, it evoked analogies with a little piece of painter's putty.

"It looks like putty," I said again.

"Yes, doesn't it?" he responded cheerfully. "Have you ever seen anything like it?"

"Well, yes ... putty ..."

Lewis reached out with a small penknife. "And look at this," he said. He cut the specimen open. "Incredible, don't you think?"

I hardly knew what to say. Inside, once again, it looked just like putty, albeit slightly pinker. Lewis's hands were shaking slightly with excitement. He was clearly experiencing a life-defining moment. I was aware that this was the sort of thing many younger biologists would dream about before they fell asleep at night.

"So, what do you think?" he asked again. "Isn't it extraordinary?"

"Yes, Lewis," I replied forlornly. "I am deeply impressed. It is truly remarkable."

"It's the greatest discovery of my career."

"Yes," I said, and I could well understand it, "but how do we get rid of them?"

"Get rid of them!" Lewis looked at me, mildly horrified, then gulped and stumbled through an argument he'd clearly been rehearsing: that the discovery of any new species is a stupendously important matter for the whole of mankind; that we were redefining the limits of human knowledge; and that we were introducing an entirely new form of life into the taxonomic textbooks.

When none of that moved me, he added that these creatures were uniquely adapted to live for long periods without water and might someday help humanity to survive in a water-constrained world. He also noted that they had an "extraordinary" attraction to rubber, and would often "emerge upon the surface around the tires of a parked vehicle", a trait that might reveal a unique set of biochemical pathways, which could be utilized in petroleum exploration and more broadly exploited in generating artificial sensors – possibly even in the creation of an artificial nose. In short, he avowed that this was a major discovery of long-term significance for humanity.

"But, Lewis," I said, cutting him short, "we need to get rid of them. We need our site free from vibrations and that means free from these creatures."

"But you can't."

"We only need to eliminate them from our enclosed area. Surely they exist in other parts of the desert."

He shook his head solemnly. "I've searched the whole of the Sarcobatus Flat and not found a single one."

"Are you telling me they only exist in this one particular location?"

He nodded, almost gleefully I thought. "It would seem so."

We discovered later that they needed a low-vibration environment to breed or, more specifically, to communicate. They'd evolved on our site for the same reason that we'd been attracted to it – its geological stability. At the time, though, it seemed to me that there must be more of these pests in other parts of the Flat. Shaking my head with resignation, I asked Lewis if he had a name for his putty mole.

"*Neurotrichus porphyrin*," he said with a note of satisfaction.

"After Emmanuel Porphyrin!"

We shared a sly smile. No university president would be anything but delighted at having a mole named after him. It would have been better, of course, had Lewis discovered a new species of lion or eagle or owl. Given the size of Emmanuel's eyes, perhaps a new species of goldfish would have been most appropriate. But then, you take what you can get in this life.

Lewis accompanied me to my next meeting with the Harvard president back in Boston, and I shall never forget the glee on Porphyrin's gnome-like face when we told him about the discovery.

"A mole?" he gasped, his fountain pen quivering with pleasure.

"Yes, that's right," Lewis beamed like a schoolboy on prize day.

"You named a mole ... after me?"

"Yes."

"I don't know whether to be honored or insulted."

We took one out and showed him.

"This is it?"

"Yes." Lewis nodded solemnly.

"It looks like a piece of putty."

"It's a very unique piece of putty."

"Well," Emmanuel observed gravely, rolling the mole carefully in his hand, "I don't know about you two, but I'd like to see this precious species preserved."

Lewis was nodding now with increased vigor.

"Who knows," Emmanuel went on, "it might be useful someday. Perhaps we should delay construction to sort this out, Duronimus. Don't you think?"

My hands were tied. We had to figure out how to save this species before we began our more local systematic eradication. Fortunately, Lewis found a way. He created a new mole breeding ground ten miles north of our enclave. Colin installed a ten-mile long subterranean barrage filled with scrap lead metal to serve as a vibrational shield between the moles and us. Lewis then attracted the moles to the surface of our enclave with rubber oil, and relocated them within truckloads of dirt to the other side of the barrage. It was all very Pied Piper.

The whole process took six months, during which Lewis published numerous papers in the *American Journal of Terrestrial Vertebrate Ecology*, the *International Journal of Advanced Soil Science*, and in *Anatomica Facta*. Sensing my frustration, he regularly assured me that his work was invaluable to the global community of invertebrate zoologists. This brought me little joy but was of great advantage to Lewis: for his discovery he was eventually made a Fellow of the European Linnaean Society and appointed a member of the International Taxonomy Committee.

I should also point out another unexpected consequence. As part of his plan to ensure the future of *Neurotrichus porphyrin*, Lewis started a business called Moleforce, exporting his putty moles to California, where they proved beneficial to orchard farmers trying to rejuvenate marginal dry lands. Ultimately, there was far greater commercial return from Moleforce than was ever derived from intellectual property developed in the Ooala Reactor itself. Indeed, putty moles eventually made Lewis a multi-millionaire, much to his bemusement and the chagrin of the rest of us.

CHAPTER XVII

SARCOBATUS SPRINGS

Although Lewis's success with the putty moles affected our timeline, there were still other matters needing attention. For one thing, we had to build accommodation for our researchers on location. Mostly we used demountable buildings, prefabricated in Texas and trucked in. The buildings were not salubrious, but they were air-conditioned and the layout ought to have been adequate for people who professed a greater interest in the universal and eternal than in the here and now.

Originally I asked Millicent to oversee the design of this little community, thinking she might bring a practical woman's touch, and she seemed happy enough with this at the time. I appointed her Director of Energy Generation and Site Management, but a few days later Rubin objected, catching me after a departmental seminar to explain his reasons.

"You can't get Millicent to do the housing," he said.

"But why not?" I murmured, genuinely baffled.

"Well, she's a woman."

"Yes, I know. That's why I asked her," I replied.

"But you're stereotyping her," he hissed through clenched teeth.

"I'm not stereotyping her. I thought she'd do a better job than we would."

Rubin's elevated eyebrows seemed to say *quod erat demonstrandum*.

"Okay then, Rubin. Why don't you do it?" I said.

"I couldn't possibly," he opined, "unless you want a statistical mechanical analysis of ceiling fans."

I broached the issue with Amelia later, hoping that her experience with Harvard's legal matters would give her some insight.

"Was I really wrong to ask Millicent to do this? I mean it's housing design, not washing up," I said.

"It makes no difference. Full professors have been forced to resign over much less than that," she replied. "Indeed, if Millicent were a lawyer instead of a nuclear engineer, she'd probably be suing you for sexual discrimination by now."

"But there are plenty of male architects and urban planners," I protested.

"That's not the point, Duronimus," she said. "If you'd asked her because there are so many male architects out there, you wouldn't be in this situation; the fact is you asked her because she's a woman."

"But I never told her that. How could she know?"

"Women always know."

In the end, I asked Amelia to do it – not because she was a woman, mind you, I was sure to make that explicit – but because someone had to. Thankfully, she agreed. Days later, I overheard Millicent quizzing her about this decision.

"Aren't you worried about the gender implications of doing this?" she asked.

"Not really. It's one thing to be alert to the symbolic implications of my actions, quite another to be ruled by them," Amelia purred.

She was an excellent choice. Amelia's preternatural administrative efficiency and cost-cutting prowess were stunning. From the outset, I directed her to measure every budgetary decision in terms of its implication for our scientific projects.

"If they want a television in every cabin, calculate how many PhD students or interferometers this will cost us," I said. "If they want double beds and hot showers, price this in terms of deuterium-fluoride lasers or technical support staff."

She took me at my word, instructing our architects to cut costs down past the bone, to the shoestring. The others could hardly believe what they saw when our scientific village opened. We took the Harvard Six down to inspect the accommodation a week before we moved in. From the exterior, it looked like military barracks: a cluster of colorless, fiberglass huts atop a concrete slab. But on the inside, it was even worse; the fixtures and furnishings were cheap and dreary.

"The carpet is a little thin," said Lewis.

"And where's the coffee machine?" asked Rubin, his face knotted with concern.

"The furniture looks a bit flimsy," murmured Colin, lifting a plastic chair with his oversized hands.

"It is extremely austere. Not my taste at all," said Jack peevishly.

Apparently they had been expecting something better, something state of the art – or IKEA at least. Behind their clenched jaws and stoic expressions, they were utterly crestfallen. Then Millicent emerged from a bathroom. The bathrooms were especially small – designed, according to Amelia, "in the Japanese style".

"Doesn't this contravene health and safety regulations?" Millicent asked, turning her head to each of us.

"Not in Nevada," replied Amelia. "In Massachusetts it'd be another story."

"But we are employed by an organization based in Massachusetts," said Millicent, wiping her hands on her skirt.

"Yes, but our deployment is in Nevada," reiterated Amelia. "Don't you like it?"

"Oh, it'll do," said Millicent grudgingly. "It'll have to do, I suppose … I just wish it could have been a tad more comfortable."

I didn't say anything but I admired the humble design. Our accommodation was designed for those living a life of the mind. I figured they would learn to like it.

We named the village "Sarcobatus Springs". The expression helped create a sense of affection for what was, objectively, just a hot, monotonous shantytown. By the time the Ooala Reactor was up and running, nearly two thousand people were living and working there. For most of us, Sarcobatus Springs provided the most wretched and uncomfortable conditions we'd ever lived in, but despite a few initial reservations, most were never really troubled by it. Those engaged in the pursuit of knowledge can nearly always be relied upon – eventually – to make a virtue of poverty; and ultimately our wretched circumstances were not just endured, but actively celebrated as proof of our unswerving determination to solve the problem of the laws.

Indeed, the barrenness of our living quarters became an unexpected selling point in attracting talented younger researchers. We offered our graduate students the virtue of science with no distractions. We gave them a pure environment with the bare minimum in material comfort, and like seasoned ascetics they reveled in the opportunity for personal and intellectual development. One student even had T-shirts printed where "Godliness is next to Cleanliness" had been crossed out and overwritten with "Sub-standard is next to Sub-stationary". As Sarcobatus Springs filled with young introverts, nimrods and nerds, I realized that we could have made things even less commodious – and we responded by cutting living costs further and squeezing more and more people in.

After all, there is no shortage of people who will forgo the company of their fellows, live in a cardboard box, or subsist on bread and water for a shot at scientific fame. Many scientists will endure almost anything if they believe they are working for a higher cause, and what cause could be greater than that of circumventing the laws of nature? For a whole generation of researchers, Sarcobatus Springs came to be seen as a dream destination, a great asset to one's curriculum vitae, offering something momentous, something akin to Los Alamos as experienced by those working to create the atomic bomb in the 1940s. And they were right to think that way, for it was just like that. Whichever way you looked at it, we were creating nothing short of a new frontier.

CHAPTER XVIII

POWERING UP

I t was natural perhaps for young, idealistic scientists to interpret our squalid material situation as evidence of our noble preoccupation with higher matters. But there was something extra to justify the poverty of our living conditions – something more than the simple grandiosity of the scientific challenge we had set ourselves.

Before we built the accommodation, we knew that we'd need a secure and reliable energy source, both for onsite staff and for our reactor. Nevada's grid had insufficient capacity and there were questions about the vibrational consequences of connecting with traditional transmission lines. So it was decided that we should generate our electricity locally, and I succeeded in vesting responsibility for this undertaking with Millicent, who was already Director of Energy Generation and Site Management.

We met to discuss this issue very early in the piece at her Harvard office, a cramped, windowless chamber in the School of Engineering. I noticed that there was a large-leafed tropical plant thriving miraculously behind the door, a tribute to Millicent's tenacious, conscientious nature. I also observed what I assumed to be a pile of Rubin's T-shirts neatly ironed and folded on top of a filing cabinet, a fact which troubled me slightly, but which I determined to ignore.

Our conversation was conducted standing up, with Millicent looking uncharacteristically excited and cheerful. Her cheeks were flushed and there was a confidence in her eyes that I'd not observed before. Then I understood: she announced, with great delight, that she'd had an idea!

"An idea?"

I felt anxious. I had assumed that Millicent, the nuclear engineer, would be installing a small, fission-based generator. At that time, modest nuclear systems not much larger than a country cottage were readily available. It was easy enough to acquire such devices from General Electric or one of the big Japanese conglomerates. With such a system, we could fulfill all of our energy needs reliably and cost-effectively. But Millicent wasn't interested in nuclear; she wanted to use Ooala funds to develop a completely novel form of energy technology.

"More cutting edge than nuclear?" I asked incredulously.

"Oh yes!" she said, her smile radiating out at me.

"Okay then, tell me more," I said, feeling uncomfortable.

"If we are going to be in a desert," she began slowly, as if leading up to a concept of tremendous profundity, "why not use the one resource that exists in abundance?"

"You mean moles?"

"No. Don't joke," she chided.

"Sunlight?"

She shook her head. "Solar is old hat. Think of the one thing you can always find in a desert."

I thought for a moment. "You don't mean sand?"

"Exactly!"

Her plan was to generate electricity from the tiny, natural movements of millions of grains of desert sand.

The concept had been prototyped by the Israeli army in the Negev Desert and by a group of government-funded hobbyists in the Nullarbor Desert in Australia, but it had never been used commercially. To me, it sounded whacky.

"What if it rains?" I asked.

"We'll have backup batteries."

"Yes, but what if it rains for a week?"

"I thought Colin wants us in a desert."

"He does. But you never know about the weather – even in a desert. When we're challenging the natural laws, we don't want to be at the mercy of the elements."

"Very well then, so we get two weeks of battery capacity – or a backup generator," she said impatiently.

It was a grotesque idea. I didn't like it and I told her so. Her proposal required commandeering an area six times the size of the main Ooala site and covering it with a vast mechanical superstructure. She called this "technically challenging". I called it lunacy. She insisted that she didn't want to work with old technology. I insisted that I valued nothing so much as reliability. She accused me of being anti-science. I accused her of putting ego ahead of the needs of the project as a whole, and made it clear that I didn't wish to discuss her crazy idea again.

But we did discuss the matter again – a day later – and were still discussing it months down the track, until eventually she wore me down. Yes, she offered some mitigating information: data from the Negev experiment suggesting that inducing electricity from accumulated sand might help us to minimize surface vibrations at our reactor site. She also discovered a man in Poitiers, at the Grande École Nationale Supérieure des Technologies Commerciales, who was working on a similar idea and was willing to collaborate. But information like this played no serious role in my final decision. I must confess that when I gave in to Millicent's scheme, it was not for any rational reason but because I was tired of arguing the other point of view. It was simple attrition: Millicent's persistence triumphed.

The consequences were not entirely bad. The Array for Inducing Electricity from Accumulated Sand (as we came to call it) extended for twenty-four square miles, a massive mechanical apparatus involving approximately sextillion microscopic needles and a similar number of matching miniature solenoids. Each needle was designed to deflect in response to the motion of an individual grain of sand. Technologically it was an extraordinary feat, assembled on a truly American scale. Measured per gigajoule of electricity produced, it was widely considered the most expensive electricity-generation scheme on earth. For many years, it had not one, but two citations in the *Guinness Book of World Records*: first owing to its cost per unit of energy produced; and second because an employee of the Royal Dutch Shell Petroleum Company suggested that it cost more in electricity to build the thing than it could ever generate. This hardly mattered because the main benefit of Millicent's system was not electrical, but psychological.

When we moved into Sarcobatus Springs and looked over at the Array glistening out to the horizon, we were reminded that we were doing something revolutionary and beautiful. Although expensive and unreliable, this energy-generation scheme was our precious jewel, proof that we were operating at the frontiers of technological possibility. It was a testament to the nobility of the scientific psychology, a constant reminder that our ambition mattered more to any of us than our realism. It was a welcome distraction from the harshness of our living conditions and from the tensions that had erupted within the group. It helped us, at least for a while, to endure one another's company and to place our petty disagreements within a wider context. If we were already proud to be involved in a grand initiative to test the fundamental nature of reality, the Array for Inducing Electricity from Accumulated Sand only added zest to our *esprit de corps*.

Thus, when the air-conditioning cut out at midday, we would look out at the spidery crisscross of wires, and glory in the idea that we were hardy pioneers leading humanity to a better future. Likewise, when our electricity sputtered off at seven o'clock in the evening, compelling us to eat cold beans out of cans by candlelight, we would happily speculate about the long-term beneficiaries of our present sacrifices: North African desert nomads and marginal farmers the world over who could extract energy from their dry, disused paddocks. Similarly, when the electric pumps in our sewerage treatment facility stalled and a fetid smell wafted through the area, we would hold our noses in the knowledge of a coming era of energy security for the world and of the cessation of all political and military conflict in the Middle East.

These bright futures were infinitely more important than erratic electric lights or air-conditioning. They helped us not just to endure life at Sarcobatus Springs but to relish it. We knew in our hearts that scientific breakthroughs rarely arise from serenity or sanity; they are won by disparaging the comforts of now in order to change the future for mankind. Every day and night in that place, thanks to Millicent, we never forgot that we were forging that future.

CHAPTER XIX

ACCENTUATE THE NEGATRONIUM

This brings me to the Ooala Reactor itself, and to the picoslumberous decelerometer. In our quest to create a state of matter totally free from motion, we needed to do much more than hold something still. Our dream of moving into the sub-stationary regime required us first to bring an object into a stationary state. But how were we to define stationary? It is one thing to hold an object stationary with respect to the surface of the earth, but the surface of the earth itself is moving, albeit slowly, via continental drift. Nor is it enough to hold an object stationary with respect to the earth as a whole, for the earth is moving with respect to the sun. And, of course, it is obviously insufficient to hold an object stationary with respect to the sun, for the sun is moving too with respect to every other star in the universe. For these reasons, we needed to measure the center of mass of the universe and to determine in which direction and how fast it was traveling. This was a massive problem – a problem of cosmological significance. So I turned to Rubin for help.

His solution was to bring in a team of multidisciplinary experts. At this time, there was a view that creativity in science was a product of communication, not contemplation. According to this view, interaction is always more important than individual thought; a human mind is more likely to receive ideas than generate them; and it is only by sharing our thoughts with others that true genius emerges. Rubin was determined to go down this path.

"It's the only way to solve a complex problem like this," he explained one day as we walked along the Charles River. "We need to assemble a team of complementary specialists. You know, we'll bring the astronomers together with the astrophysicists; the radio astronomers with the optical astronomers; we'll get the quasar guys talking to the pulsar guys; and we'll need to get the dark-matter guys in the same room as the anti-matter guys."

It didn't sound like an easy undertaking. In those days, disciplinary rivalries were notoriously intense across the subfields of physics. I looked out over the speckled water. Young rowers were splashing their oars and there was an occasional whoop from a coxswain. I imagined how different Rubin's team would be to these lithe athletes, gliding down the river so harmoniously. The thought of a quantum physicist and a plasma physicist rowing in unison struck me as somewhat ridiculous but I put my reservations aside.

"Okay. So, how many experts do you think you'll need?" I asked.

"I'm not sure," Rubin said. "Maybe half a dozen, maybe a dozen. It will obviously depend upon the complexity of the problem."

In the end he put together a team of fourteen experts, each from a different physics subfield. They gathered for a week in the seminar room of the Jefferson Laboratory and debated ambiplasma theory, M theory, Tolman's entropy problem, and the continuing importance of orbifold planes. However, deliberations did not proceed as smoothly as Rubin had hoped, so he invited a dozen additional experts to join the group for a follow-up session. At twenty-six, their collective expertise now covered all the main elements of astronomy and astrophysics. This larger group was perfectly equipped to exchange views on an even wider range of themes. They compared notes on the Hertzsprung-Russell diagram, the All-Sky Atlas, and the ten points of the Romanov Escalation; they debated the Lyman-alpha spectrum, superstring theory, the ekpyrotic model, and the Friedman-Robertson-Walker metric. Still their collective efforts were in vain.

In response, Rubin expanded the group once more, including another twenty-four experts with skills in various new and esoteric domains of cosmography. This body of fifty minds now began meeting in earnest – two days per week on an ongoing basis. They contemplated the depth and breadth of the cosmos, the significance of black holes, the role of phantom dark energy fragments, and the meaning of commensurate relativistic mass; they counted the stars and galaxies; they weighed the size, shape, and configuration of the universe. But after a month, it was evident that even this expanded cohort was no closer to a solution. Rubin therefore sought to expand the membership of his group yet again but I got him to hold off. They had still not agreed upon a simple definition for "stationary with respect to the rest of the universe" and their activities were eating up a significant proportion of Ooala's coffee-and-biscuit budget.

Obviously we couldn't wait for all these physicists to concur. The universe itself might not last long enough. So one day I took Rubin aside.

"Is it possible, Rubin," I said, "that this problem is simply too complex to be solved through the coordinated efforts of so many minds?"

I remember his cold indignation and resentful stare. Undeterred, I told him to stop consulting with his ever-expanding brains trust and come down to Nevada with the rest of us, where he would be more likely to solve the problem on his own. He objected, if only on principle. He threatened to quit the project. He mentioned by name one or two Nobel Laureates within his group, whom he said would be offended. He pleaded with me for just a little more time. But I was adamant, and I think he knew I was right. As it turned out, I could not have recommended a better course of action.

Down at Sarcobatus Springs, poor Rubin became a very different man. Previously a gregarious, compulsive communicator, he now withdrew into himself, disappearing almost entirely from view. As he had hinted, he was allergic to the heat or, more precisely, to his own sweat, and a horrible rash broke out all over his body. For the most part he refused to leave his hut, and even there he found little comfort. The unreliable electricity affected Rubin more than the rest of us. For months he sat groaning in front of the sole air vent in the main living space of his cabin, or Millicent fanned him with a scrunched up piece of cardboard. He was said to be furious with me, but it was the perfect environment for stimulating intellectual activity.

Six months after we moved in, Rubin's period of solitary meditation came to an end. I remember the occasion well. Millicent rushed into my office shrieking about a breakthrough. She'd been visiting him a great deal, sometimes staying over, although we'd pretended not to notice. But this time something special had happened. There was an unusual emanation about her. Sweat glistened on the light, downy hairs above her upper lip, and her eyes gleamed. As I rushed up the sandy path to Rubin's cabin, I realized that her excitement had infected me as well.

I found Rubin sitting at the cheap plastic table in his otherwise empty living space. He was dressed only in orange underpants, great blotchy welts all over his curiously hairy body. Nothing was in front of him except a few papers and an empty bottle of loganberry-flavored soda we all liked. He glared at me as I entered the room, his eyes aflame. For a moment, I wasn't sure he had recognized who I was. Then he stood up and grinned.

"I've got it, Duronimus – you scoundrel!" he said, his voice hoarse with exhilaration.

"Oh yes? Well, go on then ..."

He was examining me eagerly, triumphantly. "We've been thinking about the problem the wrong way," he declared.

"How do you mean?"

"We've been trying to determine how to weigh up the universe – you know, how to pinpoint the center of gravity."

"Yes, absolutely," I said. "Isn't this what we need?"

"Not necessarily," he shook his finger at me gleefully. "There's another possibility ..."

He gestured to the table. In front of him was a sheet of paper with hundreds of equations written in a tiny, spidery scrawl. At first I found the workings incomprehensible. I recognized the symbols for pressure, volume, energy, enthalpy, and mass, but the equations were unusual. Some of the formulations reminded me of the von Mangoldt function, others were reminiscent of Category Morphisms, while still others brought to mind the Riemann zeta function. Mainly I was confused by the recurrence of a symbol, "Nm", which didn't correspond to any physical entity I knew.

"But what's this?" I asked, pointing to it.

"It's the negatronium particle," he replied.

Rubin's insight was that we didn't need to measure the universe; we needed to find a force that could do this for us implicitly. This made immediate sense. In research, we often set out with a goal to measure force A, or particle B, or effect C, yet discover nothing at all until we start looking for something else. Indeed, as the history of the pursuit of knowledge demonstrates, it is only when people learn to search for things indirectly – to shine light through a lens, to reflect it with a mirror, or to bounce particle A off particle B and interpret the consequences – that they begin to see things as they really are. We may express the laws of nature in highly explicit statements, but their discovery almost always follows an oblique, roundabout process.

I leaned eagerly over the desk, and in a rapid staccato, Rubin took me through his workings. His argument went way beyond the standard model but I soon grasped that his protracted proof did imply the existence of an invisible and massless entity that would reduce the energy of anything it collided with. I could also see why he'd called it negatronium. I admired the intrinsic elegance of his approach. Remarkably, as sometimes happens in the theoretical sciences, Rubin's new particle seemed to fall in and out of his equations exactly as required.

We cracked open some more cold fizz. As is inevitable with any good scientific idea, I wondered why no one else had thought of it.

"There's just one thing, Rubin," I said.

He nodded and took a sip of his drink.

"Does such a particle exist?" I asked.

"Well, I have theorized its existence right here," he said, pointing at his equations.

"Yes, but does it actually exist – you know, in reality?"

"Oh ... I don't know," he remarked, somewhat unsettled by the question. "To my knowledge, Duronimus, no one has ever seen one, but until now no one would have thought to look."

"I understand that," I said, "but do you think it really could exist?"

He looked up quizzically, his dark, curly hair glistening. He frowned for a moment, and his black eyes took on a solemn, thoughtful expression. Then he extended his fingers, raising both palms outwards, shoulders hunched in a supplicatory shrug. "It certainly exists in theory," he said. "Ball's in your court now!"

It was hardly ideal. I mean, how could we build a giant, multi-billion-dollar facility out of a particle that only existed in theory? I knew not to count on Rubin for implementation. He was a theoretician. By his own admission, he was notoriously inept when it came to practical matters, but when I asked him, insofar as he was able, to try to contemplate the practical side of the problem, he did give us some sense of how this negatronium might be made, if indeed it existed.

On the evening of Rubin's announcement, I gathered the Harvard Six together to explain the concept. I would have invited Amelia too, but she was visiting her sick mother in Wyoming. We assembled for dinner in Rubin's cabin. Following the completion of his theory, Rubin had decided to try the water cure, spending as much time as possible in his bathtub. So while Millicent microwaved a pizza, we sat on the rickety chairs around the small table and Rubin hollered at us from his en suite. It was not ideal, receiving a tutorial from a disembodied voice with the occasional sound of slopping water and gushing of faucets, but it was important that we were all across the physics, insofar as this was possible for the non-physicists among us.

"Like so many other great theories of modern physics," Rubin began with great brio, "my idea starts with the concept of an idealized void." He paused momentarily, as if to let the idea sink in, or maybe to reach for the soap. "Can you hear me?" he asked suddenly.

"Yes, Rubin!" I replied.

"Good," he said, and then he began again, speaking with the crisp diction of a practiced elocutionist. "The idea was inspired by an interesting conjecture first developed in the 1930s by four great Russian theorists. Have you heard of Yakov Frenkel?"

I looked at the others. Naturally, I'd heard of Frenkel but clearly none of the others had. "They probably haven't," I answered, on behalf of the group.

"Vitaly Ginzburg?" came Rubin's voice, wafting through the door.

The others shook their heads.

"No," I said.

"Boris Mamyrin, or Arseny Sokolov?"

"No," I reiterated. "But don't worry about any of that, Rubin. We don't need a history lesson."

"Very well," he continued, amid a little outburst of splashing. "But you should know these men. They were among the first physicists to formalize the idea of the perfectly idealized void – though of course they only proposed it in an abstract, theoretical sense. What I have done," he continued proudly, "is to develop a theory that shows what could happen if we can find a way to make and use an idealized void in practice."

Colin looked up, slightly bewildered. "What's an idealized void, Rubin?" he called out.

"Ah, it's very simple," Rubin called back, using a phrase I'd never heard a theoretician use truthfully. "An idealized void is just an extreme form of vacuum – space that is completely empty. But there's slightly more to it than that …"

We heard the sound of Rubin's body rising in the tub, and the slosh of water flowing around him. Then, with that slightly patronizing patience that is the mark of those who consider themselves the very best lecturers, he explained that true emptiness is not just a function of density (i.e., mass and volume) but also of the specific topological shape that contains it. He pointed out that an idealized void could be thought of as "an expanse that is free, not only of matter but also of space itself", by which he hastened to explain that he didn't really mean space, so much as its "underlying fabric". Then, triumphantly, he pressed home his final arguments: that an idealized void should have no "local trivializations", no "lifting properties", and certainly no "Hartle fluctuations".

It was a very clear definition, I suppose, for someone used to thinking in an encyclopedic format. Yet, for all Rubin's efforts, I doubt that the others were much wiser about any kind of void, let alone an idealized one; although it occurred to me that they may have experienced something similar, firsthand, within the confines of their own minds. Colin was now staring out the window, Lewis was gazing thoughtfully at the table in front of him, while Jack had adopted that feigned look of intense concentration that is the peculiar preserve of learned people who have lost their way in the midst of a difficult intellectual dissertation – a look that is often deployed across university campuses just after three o'clock in the afternoon, part way through the weekly departmental seminar.

I think it was a beep from the microwave oven that roused them. While Rubin was pontificating, Millicent had been busy in the kitchen. We all watched hungrily as she carried a plate of rubbery pizza through to the en suite.

"And if we can make one of these ... um ... bounded ... I mean topologically structured, perfectly empty spaces, what will this achieve ... exactly?" Jack asked, his voice very measured, as if he was making a particular effort to sound knowledgeable.

"Well, an idealized void has never been made before," Rubin replied, cautiously.

"Yes, but what do you expect it to do?" Jack continued.

"What do I expect all this to do if it does what I expect it to do?"

"Yes, that," answered Jack, in slight confusion.

"Well, in itself it won't do anything. It's just a void," said Rubin. "But if we can use such a void to capture part of the fabric of space itself ..."

His voice trailed off. I closed my eyes, trying to contemplate the strange possibility of creating a hole in nothing, but with the aroma of pizza wafting in our direction the only hole I could visualize was the one in my stomach.

"And if we can find a way to concentrate or compress this fragment," Rubin droned on, "then, according to my theory, we will initiate the creation of a new sub-atomic particle ..."

Colin and Lewis exchanged questioning glances, not sure yet whether to be skeptical or visibly impressed.

"My calculations suggest it will be a particle of negative energy: zero-dimensional and infinitely small, but powerful enough, if present in sufficient volume, to take something into the sub-stationary state. I've called it the negatronium particle," Rubin ended with a flourish.

I looked around the table. Scientific personalities do not usually enjoy the revelation that someone else is smarter than they are, but neither do they enjoy admitting ignorance. Their communal expression was one of intrigue, fascination, even excitement. Yet at the same time, it was evident none of them had any idea what Rubin was talking about. For a moment, I even began to doubt whether I'd understood it. Then from the other room we heard him again.

"Mmm, Millie, this pizza is excellent!" he boomed.

Millicent was finally on her way over to us with another platter of piping hot Quattro Stagioni pizza. She tossed her head at Rubin's compliment and blushed faintly. "Thanks!" she called back.

Placing the pizza on the table, she studied me earnestly. "Do you think we can make something of this, Duronimus?" she asked.

"Perhaps ..." I said, not certain yet, but determined to try.

There's often an abyss between mathematical discovery and practical realization, and the theoretician's notion of bridging it is usually to reduce a mathematical construct to a conceptual one, itself still far from implementation. Rubin's discovery was no exception. Like most new theoretical constructs, his proposition was half crazy, and even though I couldn't yet tell which half was the crazy one, I felt confident I'd figure it out in time. Rubin's mathematics seemed sound enough and great discoveries have often been the product of counterintuitive plans. Besides, I could see the potential and obvious utility of the negatronium particle in helping us to go sub-stationary. I didn't want to get the others' hopes up, but the very next day, quietly confident, I set to work.

CHAPTER XX

THESE ARE NOT THE VOIDS YOU ARE LOOKING FOR

We erected a large shed on the outskirts of Sarcobatus Springs. There, I designed a variety of ultra-high vacuum systems for creating environments at extremely low pressure. We found that we could easily adapt existing technology to generate intense vacuums – spaces so sparsely populated that their volume was essentially devoid of matter. However, our techniques for extracting and manipulating that empty space proved to be completely ineffective.

Our most promising invention in this regard was the endodynamic expurgator, a gravimetric tool that when connected to a vacuum was designed to rupture the underlying fabric of the space within, to remove and compress some part of that emptiness, and then detect any sub-atomic particles that might form as a consequence. This apparatus was based upon demonstrated principles of intrinsic energy theory, specifically the well-known Horava quantum gravity phase transition conjecture, but we faced a serious impediment in its application. As anyone who has ever thought about these things knows, it's simply impossible to break open something that one cannot get a hold of in the first place.

Over several months, we explored every imaginable form of empty space. We tried connecting our expurgator to voids organized across a range of diverse magnitudes and dimensions. We made vacuums using imperial units, and then switched and tried the metric system; we formed them in shapes that were cubic, spherical, helical, tetrahedral, toroidal, paraboloid, and icosahedral. We also systematically trialed a vast range of endodynamic nozzles manufactured from a remarkable range of materials, including most of the known elements. None of it worked.

In every scientific project, naturally there are periods of doubt and technical uncertainty, but in my experience such moments are usually temporary. I have always held that perseverance and imagination will prevail. The imaginative capacity of the human mind is infinite, and for a long while I genuinely believed that creative solutions to our technical problems would emerge. Yet, as the weeks and months dragged by without any tangible progress, my quest for the negatronium particle came to seem increasingly laborious, time-consuming, and fruitless. What's more, I received no assistance from the other members of the Harvard Six. I began to doubt what I was doing and to question my own judgment, Rubin's theory, the existence of negatronium, and the entire Ooala project.

Then late one afternoon, I was surprised by an unexpected idea. I'd reached the end of another profitless day and returned to my little plasterboard office in the demountable that was our administration unit. I slumped down at my desk with my head in my hands. I remember the slow, thumping feeling of despair and exhaustion, as if my head was my heart and it was winding down. I remember pressing my eyeballs with the base of my palms, hoping to relieve the tension, cursing Rubin for proposing his ludicrous theory, and cursing myself for listening to him. Then, just as I felt things couldn't get any worse, there was a tentative knock at the door. My heart sank further still. I suppose I expected it to be Jack with another complaint.

"Come in." I sighed, really wishing whoever it was would go away.

But then the door opened and Amelia entered. She was wearing linen pants and an orange blouse. She was always so much perkier, crisp and brightly dressed than all the scientists who worked with us. She placed a pile of mail and some files on my desk, and I saw that a plate rested on top, with a sandwich and a freshly sliced Californian orange.

"I've brought you some lunch," she said.

"But it's five o'clock in the afternoon!" I replied, not feeling hungry.

"You skipped lunch today."

"I skip lunch every day."

She looked at me with the gentlest reproach. "Please, Duronimus," she said. "You haven't been eating properly."

"No – perhaps you're right."

I took the sandwich and bit into it. Amelia sat in a chair opposite my desk and watched while I chewed. I was grateful for the meal. She was right; I had been too distracted to eat.

"Anything I can do?" she asked.

I shook my head sadly. I mumbled about the endodynamic expurgator not working, the difficulties of operating at ultra-high vacuum, the transience of emptiness in a world that was bursting with matter, and the apparent impossibility of manipulating the fabric of empty space. I felt utterly dejected. She listened quietly with that non-judgmental attitude that comes so naturally to the non-expert, and as I spoke and chewed, I realized how grateful I was to have her with me.

"And do you want to hear my gravest fear?" I eventually asked. She nodded. "It's that Rubin's theory is plain wrong, and that we are never going to create these negatronium particles."

She looked at me, the skin around her eyes furrowed with concern.

"Duronimus ..." she said cautiously.

"Yes?"

"Duronimus ..." she repeated, with what I detected as tender concern, "you need to rest. You need to refresh. It's not possible to continue like this ..."

I sighed. I knew she was right, but I felt the heavy weight of responsibility upon my shoulders. For years, we'd all struggled together and triumphed against so many obstacles, and now the success of the entire project hinged on me.

There was a moment of silence.

Amelia gazed at me sympathetically. "What are you thinking?" she asked, suddenly.

"Oh ... nothing," I said.

This wasn't strictly true. I'd been thinking about our calibration process. When we first discovered that our apparatus wouldn't reach into a vacuum, I wanted to check that it could at least grip onto something. To this end we tested the endodynamic expurgator on a range of different materials. Yet contrary to our hopes, we'd discovered that the best connections were typically generated using the densest materials. The strongest contact we'd established was with the densest of all elements – a small piece of pure osmium obtained from the National Institute of Standards and Technology in Boulder, Colorado.

I looked into Amelia's sea green eyes and tried to explain all this: how our contraption had an excellent capacity to connect with the densest forms of matter, but that it had no ability to grip empty space; and how, in other words, it was really good at doing the complete opposite of what we needed.

"I see," she said. "I'm so sorry."

She reached out and took my hand, squeezing my fingers a little. I found myself admiring her lovely mouth and thinking how beautiful she was at that moment, and who knows what might have happened next, but the workings of the human mind defy all rational understanding – for at that precise instant, an idea hit me. There was one thing we hadn't tried. Sure, I had demonstrated that an endodynamic expurgator could effectively engage with osmium. But given everything that Rubin had told us about the importance of creating a perfect void, I had never taken the experiment any further. It had certainly never occurred to me to power the device to full expurgation while it was connected to anything other than a vacuum. This left an intriguing possibility – one I had not yet tested.

I stood up and stared at Amelia, my mouth open and my eyes burning with excitement. What if the endodynamic expurgator could rupture the fabric of space, even when the space involved was itself already full of dense, solid matter? Sometimes, simply describing a problem is enough to trigger a solution. Sometimes, too, a moment of distraction or a sandwich is all that is needed for the subconscious mind to do its mysterious work. I headed straight out the door.

"Thank you, Amelia – you are a genius!" I exclaimed, glancing back at her appreciatively.

I raced to the shed. I called together my experimental team. Some had to be woken from their desks, others roused from their cabins, for now it was after dark. More than forty students and postdocs gathered to watch the event. Two PhD students placed the piece of osmium on the workbench. The endodynamic expurgator was wheeled over, and seven of us lifted it into a cage suspended above the table. Sitting just five feet away at a small computer, I tweaked a few settings on our interface and then we gradually lowered the expurgator's suction valve onto the surface of the metal. As soon as we registered engagement between the outer layer of osmium atoms and the expurgator's nozzle, I initiated surface suction. I also instructed my assistants to activate the sensors so that we could measure the energy profile inside the expurgator. Then I applied full expurgation.

For three minutes there was complete silence. Then we observed an unexpected shift in the resonant frequency being detected by our mobile infrared spectrometer. A hushed whisper of excitement ran through the room. Scarcely a minute later, we recorded two distinct collisions associated with a small energy loss at the very heart of our apparatus. This was met with spontaneous cheering and applause. I turned to my team, one by one, and gave out high fives. It was a monumental breakthrough. We had just recorded the first measured impact of a negatronium particle.

CHAPTER XXI

THE VOID WITHIN

I t is one of the extraordinary attributes of modern theorists that their theories often prove malleable enough to conform to almost any fact. Following our discovery, I sent word for Rubin, Jack and Millicent to come to the shed, their expertise being most relevant to the data at hand. When they arrived I took them to a sample-preparation room, where I had spread the spectroscopic data and the energy trace on top of a large plastic table alongside our clever piece of osmium.

For several minutes they studied the X-ray data, the nuclear magnetic resonance spectra, the Raman spectroscopy, the infrared analysis, and all the other material pertaining to the osmium expurgation. Rubin scratched his nose more than once as he went through the diagrams. Millicent and Jack worked in silence. I said nothing, letting them interpret as they would, for I did not wish to prejudice their analysis.

At last, Rubin turned to the energy trace from the sensors inside our endodynamic expurgator. As he studied this, Rubin's chin slackened and his mouth opened in disbelief. Then he looked up with a curious elation. When he finally spoke, his voice crackled with barely repressed excitement.

"You realize what you've seen?" he said.

"Yes," I answered.

"You've found my negatronium!"

"So it would appear," I replied.

"Amazing!" he said, his top lip quivering. I thought he might cry.

Millicent rushed around from the other end of the table. "Is it really true?" she asked.

"See for yourself ..."

Rubin held up the energy trace, and without really examining it, she gave us both a congratulatory hug. "Oh, that's so wonderful!" she exclaimed.

Jack, however, looked up skeptically from the infrared analysis. "I'm not so sure," he said.

"Why not?" I asked.

"Well, there is just one thing ..." He was looking at me with a strange expression.

"What?"

"Well, it's the manner in which you've derived this result," he replied. "I mean, surely you can see that this is the complete opposite of what Rubin told us to expect?" He reached out and picked up the osmium, holding it out to Rubin in a vaguely accusatory way. "Osmium is the densest of all the elements, Rubin, but you told us that we needed a perfect void to create the negatronium."

Rubin smiled, innocent as a fawn. "Well, the two are not actually incompatible ..." he said.

"Are you serious?" Jack scoffed. "How on earth is there any similarity between a perfect void and a material that's extremely dense?"

With the hint of a smirk, Rubin held out his hand to take the osmium. For a second, he studied it affectionately. "Have you never asked yourself, Jack, what is inside this solid?" He gestured at the dark, murky little osmium chunk in his hand while Jack looked on suspiciously.

"Matter ... atoms ... neutrons, electrons, and protons ..." Jack replied.

"Oh yes, of course there's all that," Rubin said. "But the key things here are not these material constituents, but the spaces between them."

"The spaces between them?" Jack murmured, sarcastically.

"Yes, surely you understand that all matter is full of empty spaces – even dense solids like this one." Rubin held up the osmium, as if to admire it in the light. I thought he might bite into it next. "Inside every atom, there are spaces between the protons and neutrons and electrons, and there are the gaps between the atoms too," he continued. "Surely, as a chemist, you know that even in an extremely dense substance like this, there are points at which there is simply nothing at all ... or an absence of anything, if you prefer."

"Yes but –" Jack began.

"You don't agree?"

"No ... I mean, yes ... it's just that ..." He shrugged helplessly.

"You know it's true, Jack," Millicent said, apparently glad to reassure him. "Surely you must know there are multiple points of nothingness in everything."

Jack picked up the energy trace Rubin had just been studying. He rubbed his eyes, as if bewildered.

"Just think of atoms as little billiard balls," Rubin explained. "If you stack them up to form a neat, three-dimensional array, you will find there are always spaces between the balls, right?"

Jack nodded. "True, but atoms are not billiard balls," he said.

"Yet there are analogies within every material," I chipped in. "All Rubin's saying is that there will always be points of unfilled space inside any piece of matter – even a really solid chunk like that one."

"Yes," said Rubin. "Absolutely – you can think of it as the void within."

"The void within?" Jack gasped.

"Yes – the void within ..."

It was an astonishing idea. Yet scientific explanations often seem counterintuitive to begin with, and Rubin's notion of the void within had one particularly salient attribute. Like any great scientific explanation, it was beautiful in its simplicity.

Jack eventually came round to it. One by one, they all did.

Of course, we never did get our endodynamic expurgator to grip the fabric of space directly inside a vacuum, but ultimately it didn't matter. Rubin was right. Localized voids exist inside all substances, albeit on the sub-atomic scale, and we found that we could routinely extract little fragments of nothingness by expurgating the void within.

CHAPTER XXII

THE PICOSLUMBEROUS DECELEROMETER

t soon became evident that if we could generate enough negatronium, then we could bring any object into an absolutely stationary state. Since the negatronium particles were extremely weak, we needed a great heap of them, but using our new process we found that we could only obtain a few at a time. Over the ensuing weeks, therefore, in a state of enraptured inspiration (with Amelia providing the sandwiches), I made a number of technical improvements and fresh discoveries. First, I dramatically improved the efficiency with which our expurgator identified and extracted points of vacuity. Then, in rapid succession, I invented a series of critical devices.

I created the anacranial canister for storing the fragments of space that we collected, and for combining them into larger homogeneous voids. I invented the introspective valve to transfer these larger voids from the anacranial environment directly into an appropriate compression vehicle. I devised a centrifugal cogitator for compressing different forms of void at high volume, triggering the vital process of radioinactive decay and the production of negatronium particles on a much larger scale. I also invented a novel instrument for channeling the negatronium particles we generated into a single, focused beam.

Integrating all these components, we assembled what is now referred to as the world's first picoslumberous decelerometer – an all-in-one apparatus for storing empty space, and for creating and directing the motion of its associated negatronium.

At the same time, I formed the Ooala Spatial Collection Unit to address the logistics of upscaling our operations. Every member of this team was a PhD with high-level technical expertise in anacranial environments. Together, the members of this group built 185 stationary endodynamic expurgators, and then they went to work collecting fragments of inner space from a variety of sources around Sarcobatus Springs.

There was a concern, however, about the implications of removing too many fragments of empty space from a single location. Since everything is composed mostly of nothing, I was not too worried. It seemed to me that if we removed a little void here and there, it would make no difference to the grand scheme of things. But what would happen if we began to remove a great deal of empty space from within a confined area? This question inspired me to rethink our collection process. As a precaution, I funded a team to shrink the endodynamic expurgators and anacranial canisters so that they were portable. Within a few months, I had members of the Ooala Spatial Collection Unit traveling all over the country and sampling the space between atoms across a remarkable range of substances.

At first they visited federal laboratories and universities, looking for esoteric solids that might yield unusually high volumes of empty space. Then they moved to steelworks, and building product factories, and removed some of the voids from within the structural materials being manufactured there. They plumbed the highways of Los Angeles. They tapped the invisible spaces inside the concrete, steel, and glass of skyscrapers in New York, even venturing into Broadway and Central Park. They went to every mountain range and every significant rock formation in the country, sampling igneous, metamorphic and sedimentary rocks across the length and breadth of the continent. They expurgated the voids inside public monuments and sculptures. They penetrated the spaces in the sequoia trees of Northern California. They even went up to Washington D.C. and collected considerable amounts of empty space from the minds of American public officials. Results were so good that we decided to set up a collection hub there.

In the end, our agents went to every part of the country, and sampled every solid substance they could set their expurgators on. In each case, they channeled just a few fragments of emptiness into a low-pressure anacranial vial, which was then Fedexed back to Nevada. In Sarcobatus Springs, these samples were transplanted into a gigantic anacranial canister at the heart of our reaction chamber, deep underground. I am proud to say that by the time our reactor was built, we'd assembled an impressive volume of empty space corresponding to the voids within millions of objects from all around America.

The invention of the world's first picoslumberous decelerometer, its installation in the heart of the Ooala Reactor, and the work of the Ooala Spatial Collection Unit were not widely remarked upon at the time. They were not photogenic like the haunting concrete tower that housed Colin's Oblique Oscillating Polarizing Probe. Nor were they folksy and profitable like Lewis's Moleforce farm. They did not receive the press coverage of Millicent's Array for Inducing Electricity from Accumulated Sand. But ultimately, nothing was more pivotal to our experiment than this unique device and the dedicated people who supplied it with so many fragments of emptiness.

Following our success with the endodynamic expurgator and the invention of the picoslumberous decelerometer, and once we'd made some real headway relocating Lewis's moles, we began work on the reactor itself. We dug a gigantic pit at the center of our site, six hundred feet wide and seven hundred feet deep. Into this, we installed a thick, energy-sapping conglomerate. It was fabricated using rare, perfidious rocks, which we derived from some of the most stable geological formations on earth. These included heavy, unyielding materials such as deprikite, limitite, desolite, and demoralite, all cemented together with high-density concrete and braced by vanadium girders. This was our structure's outer shell. Within this encasement were seven nested chambers, each one made from an amalgam of dense, dark metals and each layer separated from the next by a thick, insulating pulp of fine-grained hooey dust, viscous hokum sap from Oregon, and a filtered extract of heated air. It was at the very center of all this, three hundred feet below the surface, that we assembled the nucleus of our facility.

Here is where we built the various instrumentation and control compartments, the monitoring quarters, and the storage cavity for our anacranial canister. A warren of reticulated corridors, airlocks, and degassing stages segregated the rooms within this central section. Access to the surface was via a magnetic, levitating platform that moved up and down in a precipitous vertical shaft. It was here, deep within the bowels of the Sarcobatus Flat, that we finally constructed our deceleration chamber: a cavity no larger than a simple coffin, but with walls eight feet thick, fabricated using callous, acid-molded tungsten.

This all-important chamber was intended to support an ultra-high vacuum. A network of channels crisscrossed its ceiling and walls. Filled with liquid helium, their purpose was to cool the entire chamber to −460 °F. Their numerous joins and access points were all fabricated with a crushed thermoplastic composite and meshed with vibration-resistant alloys of compressed polonium and laertium. These enabled access for visualization ports and entry for our instrumentation, the most prominent of which was the protuberant silver nozzle of the picoslumberous decelerometer.

At the heart of this chamber, at the precise point to which that sleek, silver nozzle was directed, stood a small, golden dish, forged in the shape of an earlobe. This golden auricle was enveloped by a superconducting solenoid, capable of creating a field sufficient to levitate and control the absolute position of any magnetic substance placed inside. Our target was a perfect sphere of matter, about the size of a gumball, cut from a slab of pure adamant crystal that the Apollo 11 astronauts had brought back from the moon in 1969. This object was placed within the hollow of the auricle using a robotic lever and thus it sat, in its own little tray, ready for the moment when the solenoid would be powered up and the negatronium particles unleashed upon it.

In the history of science, there had been no experimental apparatus to rival ours in scale, scope, or complexity. Our facility was surely the quietest and most stable structure on earth; we had a reaction chamber that was totally protected from the outside world and a unique mechanism for sucking the motion from our magnetically suspended target; and in our small sphere of adamant crystal, we had a substance that was faultless for our purpose. Yet we still faced one potentially significant hurdle.

Everybody knows there is no place for emotion in modern research. Certainly, all my colleagues should have known this. In those days, we all still believed that hidden truths would reveal themselves only to those who sought them with perfect detachment. We'd been taught this from the earliest stages of our careers: science requires impartiality and open-mindedness; it does not progress through feelings. I'm sure all my colleagues on the Ooala Project aspired to a thoroughly disinterested and unemotional state of mind, even if they found it impossible to achieve in practice. Alas, our needs in this regard were far more stringent than would have been true for any conventional experiment.

Following the Ooala Reactor's construction, we calibrated our onsite instrumentation, and Colin began to detect slight, sporadic vibrations deep within our facility. From the timing of these incidents, we surmised that the problem was somehow related to human operators. Our initial response was the logical one: we banned all mechanical vehicles from the site and constructed a hot air balloon to carry scientists from Sarcobatus Springs to the reactor and back again. We retrofitted much of the instrumentation within the reactor facility, replacing mechanical controls with infrared laser switches and holographic dials. We even installed a series of ergonomic levitating stools, so that staff could conduct their duties without having to perform tremor-inducing activities like walking or drawing up a chair. We sought to minimize human activity of any variety that might cause reverberations, no matter how miniscule, near our deceleration chamber.

Although these measures went some way toward controlling the problem, we continued to find that the presence of any person on site subtly increased the low-level background vibration. When scientists were frustrated or angry, the level of background vibration would trend upwards. Yet when we asked our staff to sit on their levitating stools and do nothing but watch pre-recorded golf on a screen, the background vibration dropped away until it was almost no longer measurable. This gave us our final, important realization – we were picking up the reverberations of human emotion itself.

Such sensitivity in scientific instrumentation has never been equaled. After years of arduous preparation, we were finally on the threshold of unleashing a new human capability – one with the potential, although we didn't yet realize it, to influence the fate of every person on earth.

CHAPTER XXIII

COUNTING THE DAYS

Now that we were ready to run our reactor, we fixed a date for the launch and invited representatives from our funding bodies to attend the event. Life should have been simple at this point. Less than a decade after Sandra Hidecock's death, we were finally on the verge of going sub-stationary. We should have been happy. It was the culmination of everything. But the mood of our group slowly soured as our day of reckoning approached, even beyond what I'd come to expect in the ordinary course of events.

Perhaps it was the tension of getting every detail right as we prepared for the launch. Perhaps it was jealousy, borne of the dawning realization that credit is never evenly distributed. Perhaps it was simply the fulfillment of one of the great truths of experimental work: that the potential for catastrophe never lets up. I don't know why it happened. It was the consequence of no single incident, but rather the effect of a series of unexpected clashes, any of which on their own might have been trivial, yet which collectively proved highly detrimental to morale.

Three days before our launch, for example, there was the crisis when *Newsweek* ran a major feature on our experiment. The article was called "The Incontrovertible Frontier". The subheading was "How American science is revoking the laws of nature and moving us into the sub-stationary regime". It was a useful report – a short, elegant articulation for the mainstream reader. It presented the vast challenges we had faced in building the Ooala Reactor, and it explained in layman's terms how we'd solved every one of them. It was a superb panegyric of American ingenuity, but it failed to mention Jack Gasket. On the day of its publication, he came through my doorway, bristling.

"Why do you deliberately ensure I get no recognition for my contribution to Ooala?" he asked in a shrill, strident tone.

"But I'm not –"

"Then why do I never get media profile like the rest of you?" he said.

"What do you mean?"

"I just read the *Newsweek* piece," he said, waving the magazine at me. "This article mentions every one of you, except me."

"That was not deliberate," I explained. "You know how these journalists operate –"

"They never seem to miss you out."

"But I'm the director," I observed.

"Yes, and the others? These stories rarely overlook them either. With me, though, it seems to be different –"

"It's just a coincidence," I said.

The corners of his mouth hardened. "I don't believe in coincidences," he replied archly, and stormed off.

That was the end of our discussion, but it was not the end of his perception of injustice. From that moment on he was not just angry, but bitter toward the rest of us. This exchange put him in a dark mood from which he had still not emerged when we gathered to launch our experiment.

Next, there was an altercation between Millicent Parker and Lewis Winterbottom. Just two days before the launch, Lewis had discovered that Millicent was harboring a couple of pot plants inside her cabin, and she'd caught him red-handed with herbicide and trowel, in the process of euthanizing them. Attracted by the noise, half the resident population of Sarcobatus Springs arrived on the scene just as Millicent pursued Lewis onto the neutral territory of the dirt road outside her cabin. I had never seen her so enraged. The placid and preternaturally helpful assistant professor had vanished. She seemed to have grown three inches, her eyes were flaming, and she was flourishing a saucepan.

"You've damaged my *Aspidistra lurida*," she yelled.

"But it was ... transpiring," Lewis stammered. "Furthermore, it is an attractant for ... for ..."

"Yes?" Her eyes dared him to go on.

"For ... for mites and mollusks."

"Mites and mollusks! And how are they going to get here? You've killed everything within twenty miles. It's a death zone. You call yourself a biologist? You're a murderer!"

It was obvious Millicent wasn't going to back down.

"But you know the issues as well as anyone," said Lewis, his gaunt cheeks sucked inwards. "It's an inspection. I'm going through every hut. We have no choice but to minimize all life forms in the vicinity –"

"Not mine!" Millicent cut in. "I don't believe that the death of this plant makes the slightest difference."

"But it does –"

"I Don't Care! If you touch my *Aspidistra lurida* again, I will consider it an act of workplace harassment. Do you understand that?"

Lewis shook his head mournfully. "I do. But I think you're acting irrationally," he said.

This is when I interjected. Gesturing to Millicent in a conciliatory manner, I took Lewis aside and gently recommended that he turn a blind eye to Millicent's plants. "For goodness sake, make an exception," I said, and led him away. Thereafter, however, the two of them refused to acknowledge each other, or even be in the same room if they could avoid it.

Rubin was also drawn inexorably into the feud, for he was now very much in Millicent's thrall, driven by a fierce physical infatuation. Colin once noted dryly that he could track Rubin's location across the whole of the Sarcobatus Flat, based upon the exuberant ticking of his heartbeats. Needless to say, in the lead up to the launch, Rubin now became thoroughly contemptuous of Lewis, and Lewis naturally responded in kind by becoming implacably disdainful of Rubin.

Nor was this ridiculous affair the last of our petty conflicts. On the very day before the launch, the Harvard Six had gathered reluctantly in my office for a final planning session, and Jack used this occasion to raise the diabolical idea of a dress code. He began by stressing the seriousness of the event, the eminence of our guests, and the presence of a large media contingent, before insisting that Colin Capstone not show up to the official launch function in his Birkenstock sandals.

"Oh!" Colin said, quite taken aback.

"Yes – great idea – do you mind?" I asked, thinking I should back Jack up for once.

Colin frowned and thought for a moment, gazing down at his feet through his beard. "What if I wear socks with them?" he said.

"No," Jack replied, quite firmly. "We don't want any sandals or open footwear of any kind, with or without socks."

Colin didn't like it, but he acquiesced. However, it was quite another matter with Rubin, whom Jack next asked to wear a collared shirt in place of his usual grubby T-shirt.

"I'd be happy to oblige," Rubin said, "but I don't actually own one."

"So can't you borrow one?" Jack demanded.

"No," Rubin replied firmly, and began describing the symptoms of his cholinergic urticaria.

When Jack told him he sounded like a hypochondriac, Rubin exploded with indignation. He stood up and waved a welt-ridden arm under Jack's nose and pointed out that he could only survive as it was by taking five hundred milligrams of hydroxyzine a day, observing tersely that it wasn't his choice to live "in this subhuman environment".

Rubin then turned to me and asserted that while Jack might be the Director of Administration on the Ooala Project, he had no authority over anybody's "axillary fossae" and insisted that he would not conform to anyone's "superficial social conventions" as a matter of "philosophical principle". He rounded things off with a lecture about his rights under the American Constitution.

A bitter argument ensued in which everything came to the surface: Jack's belief that no one took him seriously and everyone else's annoyance at having to pretend to; Rubin's anger at having to communicate with "uncultured morons who wouldn't know one end of the Schrödinger equation from the other"; Lewis's indignation that nobody listened whenever he spoke at our meetings; Millicent's disgust at what she called my "oppressive management techniques"; and Colin's complete bewilderment at the uncompromising nature of his peers.

In the end, not even the Birkenstock outcome was changed. If anything, it became a competition to look the scruffiest on the day. But more importantly, the attitude of dissatisfaction became so thoroughly cemented that it continued unabated right through to the very moment of the launch.

It was all so perplexing. The source of our disagreements seemed so trivial and yet the consequences had to be taken seriously. I couldn't imagine that my colleagues would do something silly – not at this point. After so many sacrifices and so much hard work, it seemed absurd to presume that any of them might choose to spoil things. Yet the night before our launch, I couldn't sleep. I told myself I mustn't dwell upon my colleagues' jealousies and anxieties, but the thought kept occurring to me that they ought to have been in a better mood. I couldn't shake the feeling that something was bound to go badly wrong.

CHAPTER XXIV

PRETTY IN PINK

The official delegation arrived early in the morning, via limousine cavalcade from Las Vegas, in a cloud of dust. The string of shiny black vehicles made its way slowly up the narrow road across the Sarcobatus Flat. Our security operator, a well-intentioned local man called Frederick Fust, raised the boom gate with unusual alacrity, saluted, then stood stiffly to attention until the last car had passed. It was heartwarming to see that the pride I felt as head research scientist could be shared by one such as he, whose main role in our project had been to watch television in a tiny fiberglass hut and occasionally help our staff break into their cabins when they lost their keys.

For the occasion, we had erected a spectacular marquee in the center of Sarcobatus Springs. The vendor had described its color as "luminescent Hollywood cerise". In practical terms, the marquee was intended to provide an exotic, shady venue for our guests while drawing attention away from the grim landscape and our drab living quarters. We flew the American and Nevadan flags, side by side, from its summit. There was no breeze, so they hung limp, but perhaps that was appropriate given our goal of going sub-stationary.

I waited with the other members of the Harvard Six at the marquee's hot pink entrance, where the taut PVC surfaces caught the reflections of the advancing desert sun. My colleagues were still not talking to one another – or to me – which made the wait even more uncomfortable than it already was on account of the heat. It was a relief when the motorcade pulled up and our visitors spilled out.

Emmanuel Porphyrin was prominent. He emerged from a Mercedes Benz coupe wearing an exquisite biscuit-colored suit, the skin of his forehead gleaming under the glaring sun like a photovoltaic cell. We had invited journalists, including two television crews, and some prize-winning science students from a high school in Reno. There were high-ranking diplomats from the European Union, Japan, Qatar, and Brazil, teams of scientific observers from some of the leading journals, delegates from the American Academy of Sciences, and representatives from various physics departments across the nation. Most significant though, from my perspective, were the officeholders from our American funding bodies.

The first of these to step from his vehicle was Dr Irving Gurgler, Secretary of the Department of Energy. With four official advisers in tow, he emerged from his immense Cadillac Escalade, mopping his face with a checked handkerchief. His elephant-gray suit already looked damp. He was a thin, unsmiling person with a reputation for taking life very seriously. Under his administration, the Department of Energy had been threatened periodically with billions of dollars of funding cuts. Not one, of course, had ever materialized, but Irving Gurgler had consistently sheltered the Ooala Project from the damaging instability often inflicted upon public initiatives by rumors of impending cutbacks.

"Hell, it's hot here!" he said, shaking my hand somewhat damply.

"Yes, it's over a hundred today," I replied.

"Still – an exceptional day for American science. We're counting on you, Duronimus!" He looked like he might pat me on the back but then changed his mind. "I'm getting out of this heat," he said, and he and his cadre of advisers disappeared inside the tent.

Next, there was Wilberforce Avery, the Nevada Senator. He was a handsome and muscular individual, whose downy blond hair made him look far younger than his sixty years. His father and grandfather had both been senators before him and the family was widely admired. They had all been peerless exponents of modern American federalism, ensuring that three generations of taxes raised on the citizens of other states had seeped into Nevadan pockets, like gold dust through the cracks of a limestone escarpment. Exiting his vehicle, he touched his lapel pin to make sure it was on straight and then surveyed the crowd. Like most politicians, he was only truly at ease when he was working a room, glad-handing voters, or standing with a microphone in front of a camera. Still, he looked genuinely pleased to see me, smiling broadly as he shook my hand.

"Well, are we all ready for it?" he asked.

"As ready as we'll ever be," I replied.

"I'm sure it's going to be a great day for Nevada," he said, gripping my arm reassuringly before moving on to explore the tent.

After Senator Avery, there were many others. Denis Doberman, special adviser to the President, arrived. Like Gurgler, he'd apparently come from Washington without checking the weather forecast; he was dressed in a black double-breasted suit. I observed the droplets of perspiration forming in the whiskers of his beard, and a pink flush rising in his round cheeks, all the way up to his vitreous eyes.

"The President passes on his personal apologies. He wishes you all the very best for today," he said, pressing my hand.

"Thank you," I replied. "That's very touching. I am honored."

"Not at all. The honor is all ours," he said benevolently. "We know how important today is."

The last person I must mention was Walt Martin, from DARPMA. He emerged from a small, gray Hyundai sedan, polishing his spectacles. He was sensibly attired in a pair of navy blue pants and a simple khaki shirt with the DARPMA logo on the chest. He sidled up just after I'd ushered a group of school children into the marquee.

"You'd better not stuff this up," he said quietly.

"I wouldn't worry about that, Walt," I replied confidently.

"Well, if anything goes wrong, you'll find that I wasn't here," he said.

His strange remark stuck in my head but there was much to be getting on with, and many more dignitaries to greet. The only important absentee was Nevada's Governor, who was dealing with a particularly pressing corruption scandal in Reno, but he'd sent an entourage. I made sure to pay each government attendee my respects, conveying my personal gratitude for their presence. For although I've never admired the life of a government official, the fact was that these people had come through with the bulk of our funding and nothing we'd achieved would have been possible without them. So I gave them all my very warmest welcome. I even patted a few backs myself as I followed the last of our visitors inside.

Our glorious pink marquee was supposed to be air-conditioned, but just to be on the safe side we had diverted all power from the Array for Inducing Electricity from Accumulated Sand in order to ensure that the Ooala Reactor had more than enough of the energy needed for our experiment. As a consequence, it was very warm under the tent. Champagne and beer ensured that our sweltering visitors mingled with hundreds of sweating scientists in a mood of jubilant expectation – although the other members of the Harvard Six remained scowling and testy, which I found very off-putting.

In the middle of our venue, we had erected a display to explain the Ooala Reactor to non-specialists. It covered the fundamentals: How much did the Ooala Reactor cost? What is a particle decelerator? How many negatronium particles fit on the top of a pin? And so on. We also had a much larger display presenting many of the spin-off technologies that had emerged as we built our reactor. Lewis had laminated a poster on the life cycle of the putty mole and its role in transforming farms across California. Millicent had installed a series of giant panels about the Array for Inducing Electricity from Accumulated Sand.

There were some physical objects on display too. There was a spot where our guests could trial a couple of "restaurant tables that never wobble" or the "Parker clasp for tying shoelaces automatically", which had also arisen out of Millicent's work. In addition, a dozen graduate students were handing out pink golf balls. The intention was that every delegate would go home with his or her very own SuperOrbit™ vibration-free golf ball. These were balls that incorporated unique Ooala materials. The idea was to convey a sense that we were on the cusp of something truly transformational, although we discovered later that the balls were non-regulation so anyone who used them in a game had to forfeit.

At a pre-designated time, everyone gathered to the right of these displays and I marshaled the official party onto a small dais. It was here that we embarked upon our formal presentations. It should have been a wonderful, positive moment. But glancing across at the other members of the Harvard Six, I was struck once again by how miserable they looked. Of course I can't say whether the tensions were evident to others. Nobody present knew my colleagues as I did and thankfully, if the policymakers noticed, they were too professional to show it.

Senator Avery called the Ooala Project a "grand, visionary initiative" and described how we had "generated two thousand hi-tech jobs in a part of Nevada previously populated only by heat-resistant lizards". Irving Gurgler called it "a flagship initiative" of the Department of Energy. He praised our "commitment to freedom" and our "breathtaking scientific ambition". Denis Doberman was even more grandiose, having the ability to namedrop the President of the United States of America. "The President wishes he could have been here," he announced in a thin, high-pitched voice. "He hopes that someday, future generations will remember that the American people went sub-stationary first, under his watch."

Afterwards, we fielded questions from journalists. Naturally they asked nothing contentious; journalists have tremendous faith in science, coupled with a fear of asking stupid questions. They all appreciated that this was not a discussion about the federal budget, or healthcare, or gun control, or abortion. It was a chance to write about the American can-do spirit, the triumph of human ingenuity over the forces of ignorance and darkness. And if the science made their editor's eyes glaze over, they'd been instructed to make us into a human-interest piece. The closest we got to a challenging question came from a young, slightly nervous print reporter from Reno.

"Ah ... who's going to benefit from this billion-dollar investment?" he asked.

"Who's going to benefit?" I repeated, by way of clarification.

"Yes," he responded, notepad open. "I mean, if you go sub-stationary, you know, in addition to all those spin-off technologies you've been telling us about."

He seemed to have a very superficial appreciation of the nature of government-funded research. The US had long since abandoned prescriptive designations along these lines. Outcomes of public research were widely acknowledged to be unpredictable and often intangible. Typically, the purported beneficiaries were neither the individuals funding the work, nor those performing it. Understanding who would benefit from public research before it had actually happened was therefore profoundly difficult, if not impossible. Having said this, I was not surprised by the question. What did surprise me was Irving Gurgler stepping forward to answer it.

"Who are the beneficiaries?" he confirmed, clearing his throat.

"Yes, who will benefit from all this?" said the young man, meekly.

Irving Gurgler smiled and adopted a cadence such as a teacher might use when clarifying an argument already understood by the class and written clearly in large letters on the blackboard, but which must be repeated for the slow boy.

"Well, in this case, I would say it's mankind itself; it's the whole of humanity that benefits," he drawled, chuckling slightly as if it was the darnedest thing. "And I wouldn't say this about too many research projects, let me tell you."

The young journalist nodded quietly and transcribed the words onto his pad. Then, he looked up again and tentatively raised his hand. "Um ..." he began, his Adam's apple bulging in biological alarm.

"Yes?"

"I don't mean to labor the point ..."

"That's alright," said Irving Gurgler, adopting a kindly expression.

"But can you tell me in what way?"

"In what way what?" asked Irving Gurgler.

"In what way exactly will the whole of humanity benefit?" asked the journalist.

"Oh, well ... yes, of course ... perhaps Duronimus ... Dr Karlof can answer that," Irving Gurgler said, turning encouragingly in my direction.

I nodded at Gurgler reassuringly. I was conscious that this was an important moment, but an odd feeling of inadequacy afflicted me. I felt distracted by the angry glaring of my colleagues, which seemed only to have intensified as the presentations went on. I was also conscious that this was a question we'd become very adept at answering during our fundraising phase. But having made those arguments and having acquired those funds, it had become necessary to focus our attention on the technical challenges inherent in building the Ooala Reactor – not the why, but the how. Indeed, it seemed like suddenly I'd forgotten why we were doing any of this in the first place. But I shook myself, looked across at Amelia who was slightly apart from the others, took a deep breath, and then began.

"In our world, nature is sovereign. We live by its laws. We are born, we survive, and we die entirely on its terms," I said, stumbling slightly over my words. "The history of our species is often portrayed as a series of battles. It's presented as a catalog of man's ideas and technologies competing, of men and of societies pitted in opposition to one another, and of our organizations, our institutions, and our nations all vying for supremacy." I gazed around the room. I felt their deepening interest, their curiosity, and this gave me confidence.

"But there's a bigger contest than the struggle of man against man," I continued. "I remind you of the eternal struggle between man and nature. If we succeed today, if we can go sub-stationary, then we will be doing something that nobody in the history of the universe has ever imagined possible. We will be setting a precedent that opens up a profound new paradigm. We will be enabling a fundamental transformation – a complete reset – in man's relationship with the universe."

I paused and looked back at Gurgler then at Amelia. They were both beaming but the joyful brilliance of Amelia's smile thrilled me to the marrow, and a frisson of energy cascaded down my spine. I turned back to the crowd and to the Harvard Six, who looked almost like they were warming up.

"If we are right, and I hope we are right, then our work today will transform everything," I said. "In due course, it will mean new ways to avoid disease and natural disasters. It could mean new ways to live, using transformational technologies that even we can hardly imagine. But most important of all is the principle that will be established.

Today, we shall try to demonstrate that humanity can countermand what nature decrees. Surely, there is no greater service that science could provide."

I finished with a crescendo, and the crowd broke into applause. I have never felt so honored as I did at that moment. Amelia's eyes shone with elation, and even the other members of the Harvard Six had stopped looking quite so dour. I gestured to them, on the spur of the moment.

"And these are the people who will have made it happen – my leadership team!" I said.

I introduced them one by one, starting with Jack, and each got a round of applause. Then we posed for a series of commemorative photographs. Amelia had arranged with the photographers that the untidiest of our group were to be coaxed into the back row or pushed to the edges and then cropped out later. She gave me a signal once this was finished, then I waved casually to the crowd and led the official party off the dais and back outside. Somehow, we had made it through the public relations component of our launch. Now it was time for the real work to be done.

CHAPTER XXV

GOING SUB-STATIONARY

We left the marquee and made our way in the bright sun through Sarcobatus Springs to the building we termed the "dressing station". On either side of us, several hundred staff and reporters crowded along the path – smiling, applauding, and giving us the thumbs-up. We were a small group: the Harvard Six, plus Amelia, Senator Avery, Emmanuel Porphyrin, Denis Doberman, and Irving Gurgler. Walt Martin from DARPMA had declined, explaining that he wasn't good with heights and that large machinery made him nervous. We walked in single file, somber and unspeaking, like astronauts striding across the launch gantry about to enter their rocket.

The dressing station was where everyone entering the facility could be showered and dressed in skin-tight vibration-free fabrics in order to minimize air movement within the reactor. Our garments had been made to measure and dyed fluorescent pink to maximize visibility and thus minimize the chances of accidental interpersonal collisions. Once attired, we were sprayed, one by one, with a thin film of mephitic vinegar. The intention was to create an "odor zone" – an expanded personal space – which might further discourage interpersonal physical contact. Then we climbed a ladder to the departure platform, and entered the small cabin attached to the white balloon that was to ferry us over to the reactor.

This balloon was tethered to a cable that joined the dressing station at Sarcobatus Springs (our point of departure) to the landing bay at the top of the Ooala Reactor Site (our destination). It was an odd feeling, to be sitting all together in that little cabin. The mood was formal, on account of the dignitaries. Bureaucrats are not usually invited to witness experiments and perhaps they were feeling a little sheepish in their unusual attire. I think everyone was relieved there'd be no more photographs. There was a moment of unsteady laughter as the balloon took to the sky. I still sensed the persistent tensions between the others, but also a mounting excitement. I could only hope that the residual animosities would dissipate as we approached the reactor and as my colleagues recalled the magnitude of what we were about to do.

As the balloon set us down at the landing bay, I had a powerful sensation of the world suspended. Apart from our distinguished guests, we'd all been here hundreds of times before, but we'd never arrived knowing that we were about to put our facility to the ultimate test. One by one, we disembarked and it seemed to me that we were entering another world – or arriving, perhaps, in a dimension of this world that had not been visited before. I wondered if this was how Darwin had felt in the Galapagos Islands, or Galileo when he first turned his telescope toward the moon.

A senior postdoctoral researcher was waiting for us at the landing bay. He was a heavyset fellow with thick glasses and long skinny legs. Dressed in the same fabric as the rest of us, he looked like a plucked flamingo. Yet what he lacked in physical dignity, he made up for in enthusiasm. After he assisted our dignitaries onto the levitating platform for our descent 300 feet beneath the surface to the inner section of the reactor, he grinned at us from behind the safety rail.

"Ooala forever!" he called.

"Ooala!" we called back.

At my nod, Colin pressed a button with his thumb and we commenced our descent. On the way down, Senator Avery smiled at me very warmly and then made a remark that I found strangely moving.

"You know, Duronimus, few politicians ever personally experience the consequences of their decisions. It's a great privilege to have been asked here and to have this chance to see something actually happening with my own eyes."

"I absolutely concur with that sentiment," Irving Gurgler agreed. "The same is true not just for politicians. It applies for policymakers more generally – myself included."

"You'd better believe it," Denis Doberman drawled. He leaned toward me conspiratorially. "It was a nice touch to get us involved."

I responded that it seemed a natural course of action because of the tremendous support they'd given us over the years.

"We'll all remember where we were today," murmured Emmanuel Porphyrin.

It wasn't long before we reached the bottom. There, at the entrance to the reactor's inner section, another younger man in fluorescent pink vibration-free garb greeted us. He was one of my PhD students, Eric Choi – a friendly Korean with a floppy mop of ink-black hair. Like his colleague up at the surface, he was extremely excited to see us.

"Ready, sir?" he asked, looking across at me eagerly.

"All set, Eric," I replied.

He opened a door for us. It was the sort of door you might find in a submarine; a small metal ringed structure with a large rubber seal. This was the entrance to the facility's core.

"Ooala forever!" said Eric.

"Thanks," I replied.

Then we stepped through, and with a soft sucking sound, like gorillas kissing, Eric sealed the door behind us.

To reach the primary control chamber, we now had to pass through three compartments. These were the so-called "green", "orange", and "red" zones, about which our visitors had received extensive briefing notes so they would experience no surprises along the way. We were now in the green zone, so called because the walls were painted a faint eucalypt green. This was where our systems established the air temperature and pressure for the accessible perimeter of the reactor, and where larger particulates were filtered.

"So this is the green zone," said Irving Gurgler, looking learnedly around the compartment.

"Oh yes, the green zone!" said Senator Avery, also sounding immensely knowledgeable.

I nodded.

"Yes, I see – the green walls," murmured Denis Doberman, coming in behind us and, like the others, adopting a tone of immense satisfaction, as if nothing could be more pleasing than to have discovered that the "green zone" was in fact painted green.

Once everyone was in the compartment and the door behind us was sealed, we opened the facing portal and moved through to the next chamber. This was a slightly larger compartment with additional filtration capacity, where a sequence of orange-colored anti-vibrational louvers helped to segregate motion in the exterior from the inner core.

"And I suppose this is the orange zone," said Wilberforce Avery, stepping inside.

"Yes," I said.

"It certainly looks very orange!" said Denis Doberman, moving up beside us and studying the anti-vibrational louvers approvingly.

We took a moment to steady ourselves, and to ensure that our passage through to the next section could be made quietly and efficiently.

"The next room is the red zone," I said for the benefit of our visitors. "Complete silence is now required. But if you must speak, please whisper." I made eye contact with our visitors one by one to confirm they'd understood.

When we were ready and the door behind us was sealed, Jack activated a hatch, not much larger than a small window, and in single file we stepped over its lower ledge. The chamber on the other side was painted pink. This final compartment – the "red zone" – was where the air was filtered most intensively, and pressure, temperature and humidity were most carefully regulated. The small door at the end of this room was painted scarlet and led directly to the primary control room for the deceleration chamber.

"*The red zone!*" whispered Denis Doberman.

I signaled for him to shut up.

"*Oops. Sorry!*" he whispered in reply.

It annoyed me that these policy people couldn't help but announce the colors of every room they visited. But stating the obvious and repeating everything ad nauseam has always been the modus operandi of those involved in public life, so I kept my feelings to myself. The same could not be said of my colleagues. I had noticed Colin lowering his eyelids, as our guests demonstrated their powers of observation. I had also observed Rubin's disparaging gaze while Denis Doberman was studying the anti-vibrational louvers in the orange zone. These were only momentary things, fleeting signals of little importance, and they were partly offset by Jack's generally sycophantic demeanor. He, at least, was a fawning toady in the presence of any person of influence. But I did wonder, as I depressurized the red door, whether it had been a mistake to ask Irving Gurgler, Wilberforce Avery, Emmanuel Porphyrin, and Denis Doberman to attend the inauguration of our reactor, especially given the sour attitudes of my scientific colleagues.

We streamed through, and I sealed the door behind us. We were now in the primary control compartment. The ceiling here was painted soft beige to promote harmony and calm, but all around us the walls were built up with instrumentation and data panels. It must have looked extremely impressive to the outsiders. Levitating stools were positioned at equidistant points about the room. I gestured for everybody to sit. Straight ahead of us was a narrow viewing window, and it was in this direction that we all turned. The window provided a view of the reaction chamber: we could clearly observe the front end and cone-shaped nozzle of the picoslumberous decelerometer as well as, about a foot away, the central golden auricle and sphere of adamant crystal nestled within it.

"*Ready?*" I whispered.

Everyone nodded nervously. I reached over and took Irving Gurgler's right hand on one side, and Wilberforce Avery's left hand on the other, and guided them together under the holographic initiation beam that served as our starter switch. We had arrived at a pivotal moment in history. They say that the world stops for no man, but we were now poised, for the first time, to make one small part of the world completely still.

We initiated the reactor.

It goes without saying that observing a scientific experiment is not usually an interesting pastime. If you enjoy football, or trips to the theater, or an occasional visit to the circus, then watching a scientific apparatus in action will usually seem very dull by comparison. In terms of basic excitement, capacity to divert the mind, or pure entertainment value, there is little by way of positive comment that can be made about most scientific activities, and our initial experience within the Ooala Reactor was entirely consistent with this precept.

We studied our instrumentation very carefully and peered resolutely through the window as the facility's slothotrophic pumps began to suck energy from the deceleration chamber. Then we stared for a long while at the golden auricle, right in the center of everything, while our laxtorpid monotronic decompressors slowly reconfigured the electromagnetic field around it. We gazed patiently with ashen faces while our esocavitated deventilating paracelsian lasers focused their invisible beams directly upon the adamant crystal.

"*What's happening?*" Irving Gurgler whispered.

"*Shhhh*," I said, quietly.

Nothing was happening – at least nothing visible to the unaided eye. This was only the preparatory phase. There was nothing to see but the steady flow of numbers on our control screens, each one quantifying some critical aspect – the falling temperature, the plummeting pressure, the declining Gibbs free energy of our target, and so forth. For the benefit of our guests, I pointed at one of the data loggers. It showed that all vibrations were tracking inexorably downwards. Silently, diligently we watched those numbers as they fell.

Within minutes we had moved into what we called the *dead state*. This was the moment when our target approached the temperature of zero Kelvin, the moment when our experiment could move into its decisive phase. But it was also a period where we might run into some undesirable quantum effects. I found myself holding my breath. Everything indicated that the reactor was working exactly as we had hoped, but one couldn't be sure until it actually happened.

Slowly, I turned the holographic dial that controlled the picoslumberous decelerometer. It was a moment of intense excitement. I noted a line of sweat on Amelia's lip. I experienced an oddly skittish feeling. Was this it? Was this the culmination of all those years of work? As the picoslumberous decelerometer engaged, we wished we could pull our chairs closer to scrutinize events through the viewing port. Negatronium particles are invisible to the human eye, but we all knew they were there, streaming out in a concentrated rush to collide with the adamant crystal. It was just a matter of time now, or so we hoped.

But we were mistaken. Time passed and absolutely nothing happened, or more precisely, things kept happening.

All evidence suggested that we had failed even to reach the stationary state. Our outputs flat-lined, the adamant crystal kept levitating within its magnetic field, suspended in mid-air within the golden auricle – black and unchanging. It wasn't long before I sensed some fidgeting from Avery and Gurgler. Behind me I also discerned a growing anxiety from Colin, Lewis, Rubin, Millicent and Jack – fear of failure.

"*The background vibration is too high*," whispered Colin.

"It seems to me there is too much tension in the air," I said, my voice subdued. I looked again at the data logger. We'd flat-lined at an energy level just in excess of what was required to reach the stationary point, but now our anxiety was raising the vibration level again.

"White jacket vibration," warned Lewis.

The situation was starting to look desperate, especially given the potential for a negative feedback loop in which an escalating negative emotional response would rapidly become a self-fulfilling prophecy. Fortunately, to the right of our viewing window there was a small poster placed there by Lewis. It read:

Remember! Keep Calm.
This chamber will register your emotional state.

I pointed urgently at this sign, looking around to make sure everyone saw me. What I observed was not reassuring. The veneer of eagerness our visiting dignitaries had brought to the facility had worn thin. They were good men. They'd been supportive. They were essential to us. But these were people shaped by bureaucratic duty. They weren't risk-takers and their perception that our experiment was failing was beginning to worry their nerves.

As for my scientific colleagues – they were even worse. Those tensions that had been growing for months now seemed to be ripening, like orchard fruit about to fall off the tree. I caught Jack swearing under his breath. I saw Millicent and Lewis exchange a poisonous glance. Rubin and Colin both seemed very glum. My colleagues were anticipating failure; they were giving up. Only Amelia looked as though she retained faith in what we were doing. She alone looked across at me, smiling encouragingly.

"Okay, everybody – I want you to take a slow, deep breath. We can do this," I said, very, very quietly. I breathed in and exhaled at a long, drawn tempo, but not everybody followed. *"Come on,"* I whispered as urgently as I dared, *"we need to calm ourselves."*

So we breathed together, slowly and steadily, in the nose and out the mouth a number of times, and the vibration tracker showed a slight decrease in activity, but it wasn't enough. I looked around at my colleagues and guests. Why had I brought so many of them down here? Colin and Rubin had been useful in interpreting some data, and in adjusting some minor system settings in real time; and of course it was appropriate to have some independent people to witness our results, but there's no virtue in being inclusive when it leads to a fiasco. I cursed my open and embracing personality. No other scientist would have risked including representatives of his funding bodies for such a pivotal experiment. I wanted to kick myself, but I couldn't for fear of stimulating further vibrations. Then a strangely reckless, seductive thought occurred to me.

"Brace yourselves," I murmured, still in an undertone.

"What are you going to do?" hissed Rubin.

"I'm going to increase the negatronium load," I replied softly.

"*But won't they leak through the window?*" Rubin snapped back, pointing at the viewing port.

"Yes," I said. "That's what I'm hoping."

"*But is it safe?*" asked Millicent, her voice scarcely more than a breath.

"It's our only chance," I said, shrugging.

My intention was to flood the chamber in the hope that some negatronium particles would seep through the glass screen into the control room. It seemed to me that most of the people here needed a dose of negatronium to dampen their emotional states.

Cautiously, I turned the holographic dial past eleven, ramping up the picoslumberous decelerometer's discharge rate. To the naked eye of course, nothing changed, but less than a minute later, we felt it: a sensation of dull stupidity, a terror of movement and change, a desire for quiet, and a grim, oppressive apathy. It was not dissimilar to the feeling one gets following pre-anesthetic sedation.

Under the influence of the negatronium, I found my thoughts slowing. Physical motion of any kind became tremendously difficult. At some point though, I realized that if I kept increasing our load, we risked paralysis or worse, and that I should lower the flow rate at once. My capacities were drained. It took all the energy I could muster just to shift the fingers on my right hand. With Herculean effort, however, I did so. Slowly, I brought the flow of negatronium particles down to an intermediate concentration. The rate of discharge was no longer quite so overpowering, but still pitched at a level above what I'd maintained at the outset. At this point, I felt so apathetic that I couldn't even turn my head to see the others. I assumed they were all right but I didn't really care. Vibration levels were trending downwards again. This was all that mattered. Stupefied by the effects of negatronium absorption, I sat slumped in my stool watching the adamant crystal.

We sat in that numb state for what felt like hours – although our data subsequently showed that it took six minutes. The negatronium distorted our sense of time – but it was not a bad feeling. At that moment, I felt there was nothing I'd rather be doing than watching that small crystal ball. My mind, my whole being, felt blissfully vacant.

And then it happened. The data on our control panel indicated that the adamant crystal was stationary. Yet measurements relating to the activity from our picoslumberous decelerometer showed that the crystal was continuing to absorb negatronium. Then, just like that, the crystal itself spontaneously disappeared.

There was a gasp – if one can use the word for a collective inhalation of breath in slow motion. For my part, I'm certain that my eyes and mouth were both wide open, though how I managed to move any muscles defies explanation given my physical torpor. But then, just as suddenly, there it was again. The crystal reappeared! It was astonishing. Later, we would learn from our instruments that this disappearance took less than half a second, although at the time we experienced it as a much longer period. The important thing is that we'd done it. For half a second, the crystal had entered the sub-stationary regime. For the first 500 milliseconds in human history, we had defied reality.

Overwhelmed, I slowly reached out to initiate the shutdown sequence, reducing the negatronium load. Then slowly, methodically, I powered down our peripheral instrumentation. No one spoke. For a moment, we could barely move. But there was a slowly mounting sense of triumph in the room. We'd really done it! I turned slowly to the others; I caught the proud smiles on the faces of my colleagues; I saw the lazy amazement in the eyes of our eminent guests; and then my own jubilation gave way to concern. I suddenly realized that Amelia had vanished.

"Where is Amelia?" I asked, forcing myself to speak.

Nobody knew. They looked back at me in numb silence. It was a terrible silence: a stunned and fearful astonishment. It seemed that while everybody had been gazing at the adamant crystal, Amelia had disappeared, and unlike what happened with the adamant, her dematerialization appeared to be permanent.

CHAPTER XXVI

UNDER STRATEGIC REVIEW

They shut us down as soon as we filed the missing persons report. First the state police shut us down while they conducted their enquiries, then the federal police, and then we were shut down again while Harvard University, the National Science Foundation, the Department of Energy, the Office of Science and Technology Policy, the Environmental Protection Agency, and the State Department all conducted their own, more thorough scientific reviews.

"Are we stationary enough for you now?" Rubin quipped.

The state police found nothing. Nobody at the reactor site had seen Amelia leave. More to the point, there was only one door to the control room, and it had remained shut throughout the entire deceleration process. We could verify this because every portal opening was logged electronically. Absolutely no one had passed through that door and there was simply no other way out. The fact that none of us had seen Amelia disappear was irrelevant. When it happened we were all in a negatronium stupor and besides, everyone's attention was concentrated upon the deceleration chamber and the adamant crystal.

The federal police were flummoxed. At first they assumed that one of us was hiding something; that it was a publicity stunt; that there must be another way out or that someone had hacked into the reactor's database. But they could find no supporting evidence and the consistency of our testimonies left little possibility of doubt. Everything indicated that Amelia had vanished during the course of our experiment, sometime after I had intensified the output from the picoslumberous decelerometer.

Finally, Amelia's disappearance was categorized as a "laboratory accident". Her family in Wyoming had been notified and were assured that every conceivable action was being pursued in order to understand what had happened and establish where exactly she'd gone. Yet unexpected circumstances and a frustrating bureaucratic preoccupation with safety and probity restrained us from doing this in any rigorous manner.

In the days immediately afterwards, we were all desperately, preternaturally tired due to the residual impact of the negatronium exposure. With the best intentions in the world, I tried to write up our findings. I truly believed that we'd succeeded in circumventing something fundamental about nature – on which score, I must confess, part of me was euphoric. But I was also frantic with worry about Amelia and determined to find a rational explanation for her disappearance. Yet I couldn't think straight. We found we needed to sleep several extra hours each day. Furthermore, as a safety measure stipulated by the Office of Public Health Preparedness and Response within the National Centers for Disease Control and Prevention, we were forced to undertake daily medical testing, which proved extremely tiresome and time-consuming.

With all this going on, I had enormous trouble writing. I simply couldn't organize my thoughts. Meanwhile, back in Washington the rumor mill churned. A couple of days after the police cleared out, Jack came to my cabin. He didn't look good. He'd lost weight and he had dark rings under his eyes.

"Bad news, Duronimus," he said.

"What have you heard?"

He lowered his chin, and studied me ominously. "I've heard they're planning a major review," he said.

Then he explained that a contact in the White House Office of Science and Technology Policy had called to ask whether I'd been romantically involved with Amelia, and whether I had been secretly spending time in Las Vegas, and did I have any debts? After hearing this, I redoubled my efforts to contact Denis Doberman, Irving Gurgler, and Walt Martin. I'd been trying for days, wanting to know exactly where we stood. I also hoped to get the reactor up and running again, not least to try to figure out what had happened. No one was returning my calls.

Jack's contact was right. Immediately after their return to Washington, Gurgler and Doberman had referred our activities to the National Post Project Reporting Office, a joint initiative of the National Science Foundation and the Office of Science and Technology Policy. Furthermore, in an example of uncharacteristic bureaucratic efficiency, they'd liaised with officials from six other federal departments, along with Porphyrin at Harvard, announcing within days the establishment of the Ooala Project Outcomes and Ethics Committee – a panel of international experts. Their brief was to visit the site, interview us, evaluate what had happened, both scientifically and in relation to Amelia's disappearance, and formulate a series of recommendations with regards to the Ooala Project's future. The official word from both Washington and Harvard was that, pending the results of this review, the reactor would remain closed.

The man appointed to chair this committee was Sir Terrence Shaft, director of the Cambridge Centre for Impossibility, an initiative in mathematical physics funded by the United Kingdom's National Lottery Commission. A familiar figure in scientific circles, he had the lank white hair that was in those days obligatory at Trinity College, where he was a Fellow, and he had the smug, crooked grin that's been a hallmark of Fellows of the Royal Society of London since the days of Sir Christopher Wren. I knew him only in passing from interactions at international conferences, but in the scientific world you don't need to know someone well to be apprised of their nature: Sir Terrence was encumbered with one of the most obstreperous and cantankerous minds in the whole global community of scholars.

There was little prospect either that the other members of the Outcomes and Ethics Committee would counterbalance Sir Terrence's tendencies, for in their own ways they all shared his reputation for intellectual pugnacity. First, there was the blond and zestful Professor Susan Paddock. An energetic British woman with enormous buckteeth, she was celebrated as the first woman to be appointed President of the Loyal Institution, one of the oldest scientific establishments in Europe; an organization that had been inaugurated by Louis XIV in 1687, and which still maintained its original premises in Paris on the tiny Île Saint-Louis in the middle of the Seine. A staunch wearer of pearls and advocate of scientific traditions (indeed, a woman more interested in communicating knowledge than in advancing it), we knew to expect a savage critique from her.

Then there was Professor Maarten Haarsplitsing, former director of the National Science Foundation, a specialist in structural molecular biology, and a winner of the Lasker Prize for his work on neurogenesis in starfish. A sincere, severely conservative Christian, he saw himself as an upholder of the intellectual tradition of Sir Isaac Newton and Martin Luther. Aside from his various directorships, he now worked as a lay preacher in Atlanta's Baptist community, promoting the idea that the laws of nature proved the existence of God. According to Haarsplitsing's fusion of science and theology, the laws of nature were the contemporary equivalent of Moses's tablets. I do not think any of us relished the prospect of a discussion with him. Frankly, his inclusion was a slap in the face.

Lastly, rounding out the committee was Morris Schlub, Dean of Philosophy at the University of California, Berkeley. Schlub was not actually a scientist, but he fashioned himself as an expert in medical and professional ethics, having written extensively about human experimentation. He was also highly regarded among an older, thoughtful demographic for his regular contributions to *The Good Life*, a program about philosophy in the contemporary world, regularly broadcast on National Public Radio. Schlub's airwave admonitions implied that he was a man of moderation, conciliation and sense. In reality, though, his huge beer belly and bloodshot eyes suggested a rather healthy appetite for good living. His sharp nose was unmistakably that of a provocateur, not a conciliator. It seemed to me that no sane researcher would, of his own volition, consent to submit his life's work to this man's evaluation. Dean Schlub was a jerk.

Collectively, the committee knew nothing about what we'd been doing. Their backgrounds were inappropriate, their personalities antagonistic, and their technical expertise irrelevant. I did not object formally to this arrangement, for such is convention. It is well known that ignorant, glowering committee members tend to ask stupid questions, and stupid questions are the nuts and bolts of any scientific review. However, I admit I was apprehensive about the direction their review would take – a concern that proved well founded.

In advance of their arrival, as is true in most formal review processes, the committee requested documentation on everything we'd done. They wanted information on the project's history, organizational structure and management practices, the formal checks and balances we used in decision-making, the relationships between individuals, and our internal communications practices. They also asked for a list of every scientific publication we'd produced over the previous three years, and wanted the names and contact details of twenty external experts in each of our fields – all in addition to my own scientific summary and personal account of our fateful experiment.

Assembling this material was not easy. Exhaustion frequently overwhelmed me and I received little assistance from the other members of the Harvard Six. I focused mostly on what might have happened to Amelia. I missed her terribly. Over and over again, I replayed in my mind those final moments in the control chamber. I thought about her entering the room in her pink, vibration-free garment, her hair carefully pinned behind her ears, her moist lips curled into an expectant smile. I remembered her helping Irving Gurgler into place before she took up her position behind me to the left, on her own levitating chair. I also recollected her shortly afterwards, perched eagerly, knees drawn together, eyes glued to the adamant crystal. There was no obvious indication of anything unusual. I could think of no sign or clue as to what might have happened.

So I tried to puzzle things out in a different way. I reworked our scientific proofs. Had we misunderstood the significance of the negatronium function? Was a decimal point in the wrong place somewhere? But I could find no error. I speculated, too, about various conspiracy theories. Had she been kidnapped and murdered? Was she a spy or saboteur? Or was it some trick my colleagues were up to? None of this seemed credible either. And why had Amelia vanished but no one else? What made her different?

Weariness and dejection were still with me when I had my first interview with the review committee in a small, poorly air-conditioned seminar room at Sarcobatus Springs. The setup was fairly traditional. Committee members were seated behind two tables that had been joined together on a raised platform. A few feet away, at ground level, stood a small, solitary plastic chair, to which Sir Terrence gestured me. They made me wait for several minutes while they poured sparkling water into glasses and busied themselves with their papers. I had no option but to watch. Being the director of a multi-billion-dollar international project counted for nothing. Eventually, Sir Terrence looked up and scrutinized a wooden floorboard about three feet to my right: it is a Cambridge tradition never to look at a person directly.

"We are having some trouble," he said at last, his British accent hinting at hidden depths of perspicacity.

"Yes?" I replied.

"Yes," he said, then abruptly stopped. "That is to say ..." he started again. "That is to say ..." he continued, nodding thoughtfully, "how are we to know in all this," he gestured at the papers piled up before them, "that you really have done what you've said you've done?"

"I'm sorry, but I don't follow you," I replied.

"Well –" he began, then suddenly interrupted himself and turned to the others. "You don't mind if I ask this, do you?" he said.

"Oh no!" and "Please!" and "Go ahead!" they replied.

"Well then," he said, turning back to me, "let us take this Ooala Reactor. Did you really build it?"

"Of course," I said.

"Yes," Sir Terrence murmured contemplatively. "Yes, well you would say that. But how ..." the word hung in the air like a wasp about to dive, its stinger primed. Sir Terrence cleared his throat and we all waited for him. "But how ..." he continued gravely, "but how do we know? How do we know you really did build it? How do we know we can believe you?"

"Well there it is – just look out the window," I replied, pointing outside.

"Oh, well, yes!" he scoffed. "You may well have built something."

"Yes, of course you've built something," said Paddock briskly.

"None of us would deny that!" chuckled Haarsplitsing, almost affably.

"But it doesn't mean you built what you thought, does it?" said Sir Terrence.

"Or that it's done what you thought it would. I am thinking here of your claims with respect to the adamant crystal," drawled Schlub, his bloodshot eyes feasting on my confusion.

I must say I found their expressions of omniscience profoundly irritating. Evidently they'd all sat on a great many evaluation panels. They were very experienced in seeming to own a much greater knowledge and understanding than they possessed in actuality. At the same time, I felt that they were seeking to trivialize and belittle what the Ooala Project had achieved. It also struck me as curious that they did not introduce our discussion with any reference to Amelia, since this was clearly the most worrying aspect of our case. I was keenly aware, however, that if I showed any aggression or sarcasm, I would then be painted as uncooperative and irrational, so I resisted the impulse to lash out.

"Well, we clearly built something," I said, keeping a steady tone. "I don't think you can deny that. And it clearly did something. In fact, one part of what it did was, more or less, just what we expected."

Sir Terrence shot a glance at Professor Paddock.

"Really?" he asked.

I happened to have the piece of adamant crystal in my pocket. I'd taken it from the reactor as soon as the police had unsealed it as a crime scene, and I held it up now, to accentuate its extraordinary purity. Then I got up off my chair and handed it to Sir Terrence so that he could feel its remarkable hardness, its density, and then pass it round for the other committee members to feel it too. Difficult concepts and challenging facts are easiest to accept when you can grasp them in your hand.

"We all saw this. We all watched this crystal disappear," I said, as calmly as I could. "It was there one moment, perfectly still and perfectly obvious to us all, and then it vanished. We saw it happen!"

"So why is it here now?" asked Professor Paddock, fingering the crystal suspiciously.

"It came back," I replied.

There was a moment's silence.

"Very convenient, wouldn't you say? It sounds like a magician's trick," Haarsplitsing muttered to Sir Terrence, who nodded profusely.

There was an uncomfortable pause. I had the strong impression that the members of this group disliked me.

After tapping one of the papers in front of him, Sir Terrence leaned forward slightly. "Do you know ..." he began, then paused and turned unexpectedly to Schlub, the expert on ethics. For a minute they whispered together like rats.

"You do know, I assume," he continued, "that some of your colleagues are not so sure – not so adamant shall we say – that the crystal disappeared?"

This was a significant blow.

"Who?" I asked, horrified.

They named Jack Gasket and Millicent Parker, adding that Irving Gurgler and Denis Doberman had both signed statements to the effect that they weren't sure of what they'd seen. I could understand, of course, that government bureaucrats might not be willing to admit what had happened. Compelled by their profession to spend much of their lives sitting on fences, it's their job to equivocate. But Jack Gasket! And Millicent Parker! Their denials were a personal and professional betrayal.

"To be honest, given your extreme exposure to negatronium radiation, we're not convinced that any of you can be sure of what you saw," Professor Haarsplitsing stated matter-of-factly.

"But I'm not asking you just to believe what others saw," I countered somewhat indignantly.

Tragically, we'd had a camera set up in the control room, but in the excitement of the occasion Jack Gasket, whose responsibility it was, had forgotten to switch it on. However, there was plenty of other instrumentation, which had generated a wealth of data to confirm what we'd seen. I gestured to the review documents.

"We're not basing our judgment solely upon human observation," I assured them. "Our detectors picked it up. It's all recorded there in the documentation accompanying my reports. All the instrumental evidence confirms our experience. The facts speak for themselves; the object simply wasn't there."

"Not necessarily," said Professor Haarsplitsing.

"Really?" I asked, surprised by his certainty. "So what's your explanation?"

"Experimental error," he shot back.

"A mistake!" proclaimed Paddock and her pearls shook with conviction.

"Or fraud," said Dean Schlub, slyly.

I stood up, thinking to walk out. Enough was enough. It's hard for anyone to face disbelief, but for a scientist there is no more abhorrent charge than that of fraud.

"Well what about Amelia then?" I asked. I would give them one more chance.

"Amelia?" said Sir Terrence.

"Yes, how do you explain Amelia's disappearance?"

Sir Terrence looked at his colleagues blankly and Schlub leaned across to his ear.

"He means this woman – Amelia what's-her-name – the one who disappeared."

"Oh yes – what about her?" asked Sir Terrence returning his attention to me.

"Well, surely you accept that she has disappeared?"

"To tell you the truth, we're not entirely sure," retorted Professor Paddock.

"Well, where is she then?" I demanded.

"We were rather hoping you might tell us that," said Haarsplitsing knowingly.

"Where she is, you mean?"

"Yes."

"But I don't know where she is. None of us know. That's the point. She's vanished!"

I realized that I was speaking with excessive stridency. There was a moment's silence. Once again, I sensed their disbelief. Schlub rolled his red eyes. Somebody sighed. I felt hollow and weary.

"So let's get this straight," said Paddock, suddenly sitting up. "This woman interests me. She disappeared when the crystal disappeared – or thereabouts?"

"Yes."

"And she never came back?"

"Correct."

"And you have no explanation for this?"

"No – not yet at any rate."

"So she's just vanished – ah – miraculously?"

"Yes, but I'm sure there is an explanation."

"Only you don't know it."

"No – not yet at any rate."

"Handy, isn't it?" she reflected, turning smugly to the others.

It was pitiful. I had not swung the argument, but I felt the issue was not being treated fairly. Sir Terrence sighed and ran his hand through his soft white hair and I think he might have felt a measure of sympathy but he was out of patience.

"Professor Karlof, what you purport to have done is Impossible – Quite Impossible," he said. "This woman's disappearance is also Impossible. The only thing here that surprises me is that you genuinely seem to believe it. Anyway, that will be all for now. We'll interview you again later this week."

And that was that. I left the room convinced that the Ooala Project was not going to get a fair hearing. Next, the committee would interview Jack, Millicent, Rubin, Colin and Lewis. I expected nothing positive from them. Jack and Millicent had already betrayed me – and the truth. Just to make things even worse, as I left I overheard Schlub musing to the others.

"Come on. We've seen this sort of thing before: magic shows, rabbits in hats, sawing girls in half," he chuckled. "She disappears and then miraculously she'll reappear at some point. How he did it though ... that's what I'd love to know!"

From then on I didn't hold even a microgram of hope that something constructive would arise from these proceedings. If I was worried when the Outcomes and Ethics Committee was first announced, now I was terrified. Over the next week I had other careful discussions with the committee, but I never got through to them. I don't think they believed a word I said. A severe censuring seemed inevitable.

CHAPTER XXVII

PERSONA NON GRATA

Two weeks later I was in Boston, being ushered into Emmanuel Porphyrin's presidential office. For the first time in my life, the Harvard homunculus didn't rise to greet me, but leered unpleasantly over his prodigious mahogany desk. I was clearly persona non grata.

"Duronimus, you have disappointed me," he said in a sad voice.

"I am sorry to hear that," I answered.

He quietly picked up a small plastic folder. "Do you know what this is?" he asked.

"The findings of the Outcomes and Ethics Committee?" I guessed.

"Yes," he replied, "that is precisely what it is, and let me tell you, it's the most damning document of its kind I have read since ... well, never mind."

He looked at me glumly; his eyes doleful like those of a basset hound.

"May I read it?" I asked, discovering that I was nervous and that a hard lump, like a little nut, had suddenly formed in my esophagus.

"No," he replied, "I don't think we'll be letting anyone read this."

He opened a small drawer at the side of his desk and theatrically tossed the folder inside, slamming the drawer shut. Then, for what seemed like an eternity, he cleared his throat. "But I can tell you what it says," he added.

I nodded wearily and he shot me an unhappy smile.

"On the project itself," he commenced, "they have questioned the value in investing billions of dollars just to watch something purportedly disappear and reappear again, and they have queried in no uncertain terms whether trying to transcend reality is in fact a legitimate goal for a scientific project."

"That's ridiculous –"

"Excuse me, Duronimus, I'm not asking for your opinion," he interjected.

He looked at me sternly for a moment. "With respect to the results," he continued, "you'll be pleased to hear that the committee had some positive observations to make about the Array for Inducing Electricity from Accumulated Sand and, naturally, about the unearthing of *Neurotrichus porphyrin*. In other respects, though, they are extremely skeptical. They question whether the picoslumberous decelerometer can be considered a legitimate scientific instrument. They state that the purported disappearance of the adamant crystal contravenes the laws of physics –"

"But that's precisely what we were trying to do!" I exclaimed, unable to contain myself.

"Yes, Duronimus, but they don't believe you did it," he snapped back. "And they strongly dispute the circumstances leading to the disappearance of your chief operations officer. On almost every issue they impugn both your evidence and your motives."

"But how can they say this?" I stammered. "There is no empirical justification for –"

"Duronimus, please!" he said, cutting me off again. "I'm not finished. I think you ought to know that the committee also made a number of remarks about your style of leadership."

My heart sank. Few things are more damaging to a person's scientific reputation than being personally criticized in the findings of a formal review. For an instant I experienced the force of gravity more acutely than usual. My limbs became leaden and my eyelids seemed like heavy stones. I felt powerless and angry.

"On your role as director," Emmanuel Porphyrin continued, "the committee has questioned whether you spent too much time doing research instead of managing the project. They've raised grave concerns about your management style and about your capacity to adhere to health and safety regulations. Perhaps most severe of all, they hold that you, and you alone, must be held responsible for the decision to flood the reactor with negatronium particles, an act which produced no scientific value, while jeopardizing the lives of everybody present in that room – myself included."

He ended with a shake of the head, making a few disapproving tut-tut noises with his tongue. "Duronimus," he observed gravely, "what I've just told you is the consensus opinion of four very eminent assessors."

"May I speak in my defense?" I asked.

"No," he said, flatly. "I don't think there's any turning back from this. The Ooala Reactor will be shut down indefinitely, and you'll stand down as its director."

Then he stood up and indulged me with his sudden goblin's grin. He gestured me to the door. "Any questions?" he asked.

There was only one.

"Who's taking over the leadership down in Nevada?" I asked, assuming that he would need somebody to do this, even if it was only to administer the shutdown and the future sale of the Ooala Project's assets.

"Oh, yes. I've invited Jack Gasket to fill that role. He seems like a safe pair of hands," he said.

Jack Gasket! It was the cruelest blow.

I flew back to Nevada. Obviously I deeply regretted the loss of my position, the closure of the Ooala Reactor, my exclusion from the Harvard Six, and Jack's elevation as director in my stead. I felt like a mountain climber who'd reached a lofty summit, only to find himself propelled by his companions down into a sulfurous volcanic crater. But there was no point brooding; it was more important to discover what had happened to Amelia. Her disappearance still made no sense to me. I refused to see it as a trick, as the Outcomes and Ethics Committee had apparently done, for she was the one person I'd felt certain I could trust.

I got back to Sarcobatus Springs early evening on a Friday. There weren't many people about. Most researchers were on extended leave. Others no doubt had shot through to Las Vegas for the weekend. An insouciant breeze swept up the Nevada dirt, whirling it in little eddies and vortexes along the twilit paths and up against the sides of the fiberglass huts. Our little village seemed sad and deserted; I had a melancholic sense of how things would be when the Ooala Project was formally closed.

I drifted up the main street past where we'd all stood with so much fanfare inside that marquee only weeks before. It had long since been packed up and put away. Who knew where? Amelia hadn't been here to oversee the dismantling. I felt a great desolation in the dusty barrenness of this quiet, nostalgic spot. For the first time, I felt the inextinguishable pain of regret. I glanced guiltily at Amelia's cabin, still cordoned off with police barricade tape. I knew that if no one believed that Amelia's disappearance was real, nobody would give any serious consideration to finding her again.

I hurried to my cabin, intending to organize my effects. But after a few minutes there was a knock at the door. It was Colin.

"I saw that your lights were on," he said.

"Yes," I replied, steadying my voice with some effort. "I'm back, but I won't be staying more than a day or two."

I told him about my meeting with Porphyrin.

"But that's ridiculous!" he snorted, and I was surprised to see that he genuinely meant it.

We pulled a couple of chairs outside the cabin and sat slumped, gloomily sipping rye whiskey and chomping raw peanuts. Colin asked me how I was feeling, but I was too morose to answer, whereupon he proceeded to tell me about the despair he'd experienced some decades previously, when he'd been unable to find a partner to commercialize the Oblique Oscillating Polarizing Sensor.

"I became profoundly, clinically depressed," he said.

Then, with tedious attention to detail, he laid out the symptoms of his experience: how he'd put on weight, lost his wife, and how he'd been brought back from the brink by conducting a geological survey of the Lena River Basin in northeast Siberia. But I was only half-listening.

"You know there's only one explanation," I said suddenly, interrupting him.

"What's that?" he asked.

"That Amelia went sub-stationary too," I said.

He looked at me doubtfully.

"Of course. We've all wondered about that," he muttered, "but why her and not the rest of us?"

"Perhaps she was more susceptible than the rest of us," I said.

"Yes ... but why?" Colin asked, grabbing another handful of peanuts.

This was the key. If one assumed Amelia's disappearance was a consequence of extreme exposure to negatronium, why was no one else in the room also affected? Colin stretched back on his little wooden chair and stared out at the night sky. For a moment, neither of us spoke. I studied him. Sitting there, he seemed just right – in his natural state with his flannel shirt and old jeans. He had the air of a man who'd spent a lifetime sitting on porches. Maybe my future held some porch sitting too, I pondered. Then I realized, with an acute sense of urgency, that this might be my last time in this place – and my last chance to track down Amelia.

"Come on, let's think it through," I said, with mounting urgency. "Let's consider everyone present."

"Okay," Colin said.

"How would you categorize all of us – you know, the Harvard Six?" I began.

"All Harvard scientists," observed Colin.

"And how would you categorize Gurgler, Avery and Doberman?" I went on.

"All from Washington – bureaucrats," Colin noted sagely.

"And what about Porphyrin?"

"A university administrator. Top of the heap."

"Yes – and Amelia?"

"Same as Emmanuel Porphyrin but ... lower level."

We looked at each other. No distinguishing features there.

"Okay," I said, "so that's no use. It must be something else."

"What about the fact that she's a woman?" asked Colin suddenly, speaking quickly, with excitement.

He rocked forward in his chair, as if he really thought this might be it.

"But Millicent's a woman too," I said. "Isn't she?"

"Oh, yes," said Colin. "I keep forgetting."

He chuckled slightly, but I didn't join in. I was in no mood for laughing. Besides, I felt an interesting idea forming at the back of my head, but it wouldn't quite crystallize. I looked out across Sarcobatus Flat in the direction of the reactor.

"What else do we know?" I mused, as much to myself as to Colin.

"Well ..." said Colin shyly, "you knew her much better than I did."

Then it came to me, an idea of such simplicity that I wondered why it had not crossed my mind before. I clutched one of Colin's broad shoulders.

"Do you remember how happy she was that day?"

"I suppose ..." he replied.

"But, Colin, that tells us something. The reactor – we know it was so sensitive it could register human emotions ..."

"Yes, that's true," he said, still perplexed.

"So think what that means!" My hands gesticulated upwards in excitement. "If our reactor could register human emotion, then why couldn't a negatronium particle do the same?"

Colin was looking at me strangely.

"Don't you remember the day it happened?" I asked. "Don't you remember how happy she was? And how negative the rest of you were? You must remember!"

"Well, yes ... certainly the others ... but surely I wasn't negative!"

"Yes you were!" I said, triumphantly. "You were in a terrible frame of mind. All of us were. Don't you remember the tension between you and Rubin, Millicent, Lewis and ..." Somehow I couldn't bring myself to mention Jack's name. "And think of the others," I continued. "Given the bureaucratic nature of their lives, Gurgler, Avery, Doberman and Porphyrin all strike me as somewhat negative people."

"Yes, I'd agree with that," Colin said, nodding slowly. "But wasn't Amelia on the bureaucratic side too?"

"Not in a bad way," I said, feeling slightly self-conscious.

Colin bent to refill our glasses.

"So what if negatronium particles are particularly attracted to positive people?" I speculated. "Think what that implies, because at that decisive moment when I increased the decelerometer's output, Amelia was unquestionably the happiest person in that room."

Colin was looking at me intently. "Perhaps she was in love," he murmured.

"No, no –" I stared at him awkwardly. "It was purely excitement, I'm sure of it. The realization of a dream ..." I turned away and looked out at the road. Colin's unexpected observation had made me uncomfortable. "Let's not speculate," I said. "Let's just look at the facts."

"Okay," Colin said. He cleared his throat and shifted quietly in his chair. "So you mean the negatronium particles channeled around the rest of us and selectively targeted Amelia?" he said.

I shrugged. "It's a hypothesis."

"But do you really think it's possible?"

"There's only one way to find out," I said. "We need to replicate the experiment."

I stood up and pointed down the hill toward the dressing station. "Are you coming or not?" I asked.

CHAPTER XXVIII

RIGHT SAID FRED

We gulped back our drinks and made our way to the dressing station. Colin seemed nervous but I felt only exhilaration. Nobody was around to stop us. Lewis was away in Riverside, California, peddling his beloved moles. Millicent was in Silicon Valley trying to raise venture capital for a large-scale induction array to be built behind Lawrence Livermore. Snowbird Rubin had flown back to Boston to get away from the heat. That only left Jack, but there was no reason for him to be anywhere near the reactor tonight. He was probably off somewhere celebrating his promotion.

Standing under the shadow of the concrete block that served as the dressing station's entrance, I fumbled for a moment, then pulled out my electronic access card and held it up to the reading device. But nothing happened. The door remained locked.

"*Here, let me try mine,*" whispered Colin.

He held out his card but it didn't unlock the door either. Clearly, we'd both been electronically barred.

"Porphyrin must have done this," I hissed.

"Or Jack," muttered Colin.

"Come on then, let's try Frederick Fust," I said.

As quickly as we could, we jogged up the dirt road to the security hut at the other end of Sarcobatus Springs.

Neither of us was a runner. I worried that someone might hear us panting and gasping and come out to investigate, but the cabins we passed were either empty or their occupants were absorbed in their own affairs.

Nobody interrupted us.

Frederick's hut was dark inside, with only the light of a flickering television faintly visible through the window. I knocked gently at the door, but there was no answer so I knocked again, louder this time. There was still no response.

"Hello ... Frederick ... Fred ... Security?" I called out. There was nothing but silence. I turned to Colin. "I don't think anyone's in," I observed. I put my hand on the door handle and tried to twist it, without success. "It's locked," I said.

Colin pointed to a window beside the door. It was partially open. "You might get in there," he remarked.

He stepped up on the porch beside me, and together we put our hands under the wooden frame of the window. It was stiff, but with a little exertion we managed to wrench it open – just wide enough for me to squeeze through. I wriggled in, head first, and landed on a small desk, which seemed to be covered with various papers, keys, and plastic containers. As I shuffled forward, some of the material clattered onto the floor. Slowly and cautiously, I managed to bring my feet down and around. Unsteady, and panting slightly with the effort, I stood up. But just as I did so, the light in the room came on.

Standing in the doorway and facing me was Frederick Fust. He was wearing striped undershorts, with an empty pigskin holster thrown across one shoulder. In his left hand, he clutched a large television remote control, and in his right hand he held a gun. "Don't move!" he commanded, and instinctively I raised my hands.

"Frederick –" I began.

"Who are you? What the hell do you think you're doing?" He sounded cross.

He peered at me, eyes puffy with sleep. Evidently he couldn't see much without his glasses and even now he was only just waking up. He squinted.

"Frederick, it's Duronimus –" I said.

"Professor Karlof?" He spoke haltingly, suspicious, frightened, not quite sure whether to believe me.

"Frederick, it's an emergency," I explained. "We did knock, but there was no answer. I thought you were out. We need your help. It's important."

We were now less than two feet apart. He stared intently at my face. It made me uncomfortable to be so close, but I didn't want to make any sudden moves. Then he recognized me. He stepped backward quickly, deftly holstering his revolver and fiddling with his television remote. "Excuse me, Professor, I was asleep," he said. "Do you mind if I just ..." He indicated the doorway behind him and I nodded him through.

As he disappeared, I took the opportunity to turn and open the front door for Colin. For about a minute, we heard Frederick shifting clumsily around in the other room. When he re-emerged, there was a thick pair of glasses balanced upon the bridge of his nose. A shabby dressing gown was thrown on his shoulders and a pair of old tartan slippers graced his feet.

"Sorry about that," he said. "Oh, hello, Professor Capstone too!"

"Hi Fred," said Colin smiling. "We're sorry for waking you."

"Yes," I agreed. "But I'm afraid we really need your help."

Frederick straightened his back proudly. "No problem at all," he said, trying to look alert. "What's up?"

"This has stopped working," I said, holding up my security card.

"Mine too," added Colin.

"Yes ... well, that's to be expected, isn't it?" Frederick observed, with remarkable forthrightness.

Colin and I looked at him blankly.

"What do you mean?" I asked.

Frederick's fingers fidgeted slightly inside the pockets of his dressing gown.

"Well," he said, shrugging, "Professor Gasket asked me to cancel all card access to the facility – all except for mine and his."

"When?"

"Yesterday."

"I see," I said dryly.

"He says he's the director now," Frederick observed, by way of justification.

There was a moment's awkward pause.

"Fred, we need to get into the reactor again," I said as firmly as I dared. "It may be our last chance to find Amelia. Is there any chance you can help us? Can you reactivate our cards?"

Frederick Fust looked down at his feet. "Yes ... I mean, no ... no, I'm sorry," he said. "Technically, Professor Gasket is my boss now. I have to do what he says."

"I see," I said grimly.

"Tell you what, though ..." Frederick said. "I can't give you a new card ..." He was speaking slowly as if thinking aloud, "but who's to say I shouldn't come along and let you into the place myself? I've never been inside, you know. I wouldn't mind a closer look while I can."

He smiled and my heart went out to him. It was clear that he didn't like Jack Gasket any more than I did. "Oh, thank you, Frederick!" I said.

He opened a drawer in the desk I'd just clambered over, and pulled out a security access card on a loop of black ribbon and hung it around his neck. Then he led us out through his front door into the night.

We hurried back down to the dressing station. As far as I could tell, we'd passed undetected. At the entrance, Frederick used his card and the door slid open. Now we were inside. Frederick followed us up the ramp as we made our way to the men's changing area. Colin and I searched the lockers for our pink suits, changing once we'd found them. I gave Jack's suit to Frederick. It was too long and made certain parts of his body appear extremely floppy, but he did not complain.

We climbed the ladder to the departure bay, coming out beside the cabin of the transport balloon. Floating in the night sky above us, the white balloon looked like a gigantic deflated moon. With the press of a button, the cabin door slid open. I initiated the system and we sat back in silence while the vehicle slowly slumped along toward the reactor. We had just enough hot air to make it but there was always a possibility that someone over at Sarcobatus Springs would see the balloon moving. Indeed, if I experienced any moment of awful concern about being seen, it was now; but looking back through the window at the little collection of huts behind us, we saw nobody.

All was still and quiet at the landing bay. Colin banged his foot on the lip of the cabin door as he dismounted and cursed under his breath. I told him to keep quiet and he rolled his eyes good-humoredly at me. There was another security panel here, but Frederick waved his plastic card again and the doors slid open. Briskly, the three of us made our way through and onto the levitating platform.

"*Are you absolutely sure about this?*" Colin whispered.

"Yes," I replied.

He pressed the button and we began our descent to the reactor core. At the bottom everything was dark until the lights snapped on, the sensors having detected our presence. Once more Frederick used his security access card and the door to the inner section of the reactor swung open smoothly with its familiar shlpping kiss.

"*Are we all okay?*" I whispered, looking at Frederick.

He nodded. Suddenly it occurred to me that if I were to go sub-stationary and disappear like Amelia, then there'd be some merit in having another witness present.

"We're about to fire up the reactor. Do you want to come with us?" I asked.

"Is it safe?" Frederick replied. "You know – for non-experts."

I smiled regretfully, and shook my head, thinking of Amelia. "There are no guarantees," I admitted.

Frederick looked doubtful then glanced at Colin. His eyes seemed to ask Colin if I was being serious. Colin nodded gravely and Frederick took a deep breath. "Okay then," he said, undeterred, "I'll come."

I nodded grimly. "You'll find it's interesting in here, but there's one thing you need to know," I told him. "Inside the control room, we all need to stay as quiet and still as possible."

"And no matter how oppressive you find it, breathe deeply and remain calm," added Colin.

We stepped through the door and sealed it shut behind us. It felt good to be down there again at the heart of the reactor. I glanced at Frederick. He seemed curious but relaxed. I gave him the thumbs-up.

We passed through the green zone, the orange zone, and into the red zone. Not a word was said by any of us. Then we were in. It struck me how little had changed since that fateful day. I switched on the baseline instrumentation. The deceleration chamber looked just as it had the day we went sub-stationary; the only difference was that there was no little sphere of adamant crystal resting in the golden auricle. I'd left this in the pocket of my trousers, back in the dressing station. Not that it mattered. Slowly we seated ourselves on the levitating stools. It took Frederick a moment to adjust to being up in mid-air, but he managed to hold himself still and I saw, with some delight, that he seemed to think it was fun. Colin sat beside me at the main panel and we began to check that everything was in order.

"*All set?*" I whispered, and Colin nodded nervously.

Insofar as it was possible, it was important that we replicate the procedure we'd followed on the day Amelia had vanished. I reached out and moved my hand to the holographic initiation beam. We watched as the slothotrophic pumps began gradually to suck energy from the chamber. We looked on as the monotronic decompressors slowly and indiscernibly reconfigured the electromagnetic field. We waited while our paracelsian lasers focused their invisible beams through the heart of the golden auricle.

We monitored the data panels, steeling ourselves as the energy levels in the deceleration chamber dropped. In the absence of the emotional tensions that had beset us last time, we transitioned to the dead zone relatively smoothly. As we moved into the stationary regime, I signaled to Colin. He got up and took my chair, and I sat on Amelia's stool. We had to wait a moment for the system to re-equilibrate, but energy levels within the chamber soon continued their downward trajectory. This was it! On a gentle nod from me, Colin reached out and turned the holographic dial controlling the picoslumberous decelerometer.

Whatever happens, you must stay calm and positive, I told myself.

It took only a second before I felt the impact of the negatronium radiation: that sensation of dull stupidity, the terror of movement, desire for quiet, and the grim, oppressive apathy. But I forced myself to smile. I thought of heartening things: the beach outside Tirana I used to visit as a child; of the day I learned I'd been admitted to MIT; of the smile of my first doctoral student when she finally grasped the Lorentz transformation. I was determined to remain positive, to attract as much negatronium radiation as I could. But the feelings of oppression grew. I turned my thoughts to Amelia: to her rusty brown hair and green eyes, her peculiar fashion sense, her loyal smile, and her kindness.

The dullness and the deadening of nerves was now worse than anything I'd ever experienced. I had a vague sense of Colin swallowing – it seemed to take hours for him to swallow – and then Colin was staring at me in horror. Now Frederick Fust caught my eye: he was shimmering slightly. I saw Colin trying to reach for the dial but he was unable to move. Nothing seemed real anymore. Then I was aware that Frederick was becoming less and less perceptible. For a moment he became translucent, and then he vanished completely. I felt a wave of indescribable nausea and disgust. Everything about me became very small and hateful. I felt bombarded by negativity, powerless, detached from the world. Then there was nothing but strange, echoing dreams.

CHAPTER XXIX

A THEORY OF NOTHING

I awoke in a small bed with light blue curtains drawn around it. My first thought was that I was in hospital, but not the Sunrise Hospital in Las Vegas. I could hear voices, but I couldn't make out what was being said. I felt extremely weak. I closed my eyes and tried to remember what had happened. By concentrating, I could recall only Colin's horrified stare. Then the curtains parted, and there, of all people, stood Walt Martin, our program manager from DARPMA.

"Walt?" I said, aghast.

"Hello, Duronimus. How are you feeling?" he replied, smiling.

"Where am I?" I moaned. I tried to raise myself up in the bed, but I was too weak.

"Don't," he said. "You need to rest."

He said something else but I was suddenly too tired to listen. I felt myself losing consciousness. The feeling reminded me, for a delicious moment, of a lecture on the cosmological constant that I'd attended years before as an undergraduate. Then I slipped back into deep, impregnable sleep.

The second time I woke, I felt slightly stronger. Walt Martin was standing by my bed and I became aware of someone behind him in a wheelchair. Her skin was pale, here eyes were watery, and her head lolled unsteadily to one side, but my breath choked to see her – it was Amelia. She seemed to be speaking but I couldn't make it out.

Walt leaned over beside me. "We found her," he said.

"Can you hear me, Duronimus?" Amelia asked, weeping softly.

I tried to turn my body toward them but my limbs were numb. I tried to ask Amelia if she was all right, but the words wouldn't form in my mouth.

Then Walt turned to her. He looked thinner than I remembered. "We don't want to wear him out," he said gently.

Amelia nodded, but she didn't take her eyes off me.

Walt placed a hand on my shoulder. "Everyone's going to be fine. But you mustn't talk. You're still too tired," he said, and once again I was overcome by intense fatigue.

This time I experienced a deeper and more beneficial sleep. When I woke next, I felt much stronger, more like my old self. Around my bed, the plastic vanity curtains were already drawn and I could see that I was in a small, white, windowless room. I noticed the intravenous drip in the back of my hand, and the trolley beside my bed with the bag of saline suspended from it. Behind me, there were two large life-support machines, and in one corner there was a sink and a cupboard. There was also a man standing by the door in a dark blue uniform with a white belt and white shoes. He left as soon as he noticed I was awake, and returned a few minutes later with Walt. This time, there was no sign of Amelia.

"Feeling any better?" Walt asked, beaming.

"Better," I croaked.

"Good. I'll get the nurse to bring you something solid to eat but first I want to explain a few things," he said.

"Amelia …?" I asked.

"She's sleeping."

His voice was subdued as he went over what had happened. Amelia and I had been asleep for the best part of a year. She'd woken just a few days before me and was recovering well. We were now being housed in a secure facility under the US Department of the Treasury's Research and Special Projects building in Washington D.C., though he was initially reluctant to say why. He explained that our condition had perplexed the minds of the finest physicians in the nation and that the US Army's Survivability and Lethality Directorate had itself spent several million dollars running a barrage of tests on mice, pigs, and even a couple of human volunteers, looking for novel ways to revive us.

As to the others, Frederick Fust had succumbed to the impact of extreme negatronium exposure too, but he had woken from his coma far sooner than I, albeit with acute amnesia, and was now recuperating in a government sleep-disorder clinic in Sacramento. Walt also set my mind at ease about Colin, assuring me that he had survived our experiment, was in good health, and had returned to his old teaching duties at Harvard. But this was all the information I could absorb before drowsiness overcame me again.

Over the next week, Walt and Amelia visited often, and my periods of slumber gradually contracted. It was hard at first to stay awake, but the two of them helped me a great deal – especially Amelia. She looked so weak and frail, but the fire still burned in her eyes and as I lay there, fragile and exhausted, she would reach out and clasp my hand in hers, and each time I felt that this alone was worth staying awake for. I took courage, too, in her own recovery, for I sensed that she was getting stronger every day.

During this time, Walt told me his version of what had happened when we disappeared from inside the Ooala Reactor. He broached the subject as soon as I was clear-headed enough to sustain a proper conversation. I remember him sitting on the end of my bed and studying me pensively, as if observing a laboratory rat that had just undergone a flawed experiment.

"Do you have any idea where we found you?" he asked.

I shook my head.

"Or where you were when you entered the sub-stationary regime?"

"No," I said, ruefully, "I was unconscious the whole time."

"It doesn't surprise me."

He paused and gazed at me with curiosity and concern.

"What happened, Walt?" I asked with sudden trepidation. "Where were we?"

"To tell you the truth, we're not entirely sure," he said quickly. "Perhaps we'll never know for certain, but according to our best calculations ..." His voice trailed off, and he peered at me quizzically. "Duronimus, this may be hard to take, but we are of the opinion that you weren't anywhere at all."

I breathed deeply.

"Yes," he went on with great solemnity. "According to our models, you were literally nowhere ... for an instant, we think you actually ceased to exist."

I gasped. In science, there are theories about everything: matter, energy, space, and time. But this was something else entirely. To understand it would require nothing short of a theory of nothing. This was even more extraordinary than wave-particle duality, or Gödel's incompleteness theorem.

"But of course the universe couldn't tolerate your non-existence for long – conservation of energy and all that," Walt continued. "We estimate that you were gone for a minute, tops. But an absence like this creates some sort of deficiency of matter or energy. We think it's this that sucked you back."

"Back into existence?" I muttered. It was like the old myths – a hero returning from the underworld.

"Yes. Absolutely," Walt said. "The only thing is … where do you reenter? You have to pop up somewhere. But there's no reason for you to come back at the same point you started from. Time's moved on. Nothing's in quite the same place it was when you left. You probably could've ended up anywhere."

"But we didn't … did we?" I asked, nervously.

"Well, no …" He coughed and seemed embarrassed. "Truth is, you all reappeared in Fresno."

"Fresno?"

"Yes … Fresno, California. Interestingly, it's about the same latitude as the Ooala Reactor. We think that when you disappeared, the world kept spinning without you. So, naturally, when you came back … there you were!"

For a moment I could not speak. It seemed apposite that a particle derived from the void should convey us back to the void, but I was nonetheless surprised – there were so many momentous implications. What if we could stay nowhere for longer? Did this mean we could now probe beyond the bounds of our cosmos? And what were the implications for high-speed transportation? Our experiment had inadvertently demonstrated, albeit at great cost, the teleportation of three living, if comatose, persons. This was unprecedented. Admittedly, we had rematerialized in a strange place, and in no fit state to survive without intensive care, but I pondered the enduring truth that no technological development is ever straightforward. Indeed, it struck me, as I lay prostrate and weak upon my stainless-steel hospital bed, that Amelia and I – and perhaps even Frederick – might one day be hailed like the Wright brothers and Yuri Gagarin. And I understood in that instant how Archimedes must have felt when he ran naked and dripping wet through the streets of Syracuse; only in my incapacitated state, I found that I was barely able to lift my head and talk, let alone run about and scream "Eureka!"

One thing troubled me, however. For it seemed obvious that if our absence really had lasted just a few minutes, then Walt or someone must have known about Amelia's reemergence, even as I sweated things out back in Nevada. I thought of the agonizing worry that we had all endured following Amelia's disappearance, of the unjust verdict issued by the Ooala Outcomes and Ethics Committee, and of the year of my life I had just lost, asleep in a subterranean Washington bunker. It seemed to me that all this might have been avoided, if only I had known in time – if only someone had told me – that Amelia had been discovered and that our experiment had proved successful after all.

"But, Walt," I said, in a sudden flash of anger, "who found Amelia? And when? And why didn't they tell us?"

He sighed and shook his head regretfully. He explained that Amelia had materialized on a desk in the library of the Federal courthouse in Fresno, prompting the court librarian to notify the records clerk, who in turn phoned the chief clerk of the court, who immediately contacted the Federal Bureau of Investigation. As Walt proudly elaborated, it was a testament to the efficiency of the chain of command that Amelia was receiving medical assistance within just two hours of her unexpected materialization.

Initially, they'd rushed her to a secure clinic in south Fresno, where she was stabilized but remained in a coma. But discovering that Amelia's pink vibration-resistant suit had "Property of the Ooala Project" stitched into the collar, the federal agents had contacted their counterparts in the Department of Defense, who in turn notified Walt as he stepped off his flight back from Nevada.

"When I heard the news, it was the proudest moment of my professional career," he said wistfully. "It was the first time I could unequivocally say that I had backed the right horse."

"But why wasn't I told, Walt?" I cried out, despairingly. "Why didn't you tell me that you'd found her?"

"I couldn't tell you," he replied softly. "By the time I was informed, Amelia had been put on a plane and was being brought in here. The wheels were already in motion. I was instructed to wait. The Department of the Treasury was taking over."

"The Department of the Treasury?" I asked, remembering what Walt had said earlier about being in D.C., under the Treasury's Research and Special Projects building.

He nodded and I saw that his face was glowing with excitement. "Yes, that's why you're here," he said. "You might be surprised to learn, Duronimus, that the Department of the Treasury has its own particular interest in the laws of nature."

I felt a shiver of apprehension.

"They'd been monitoring you for years," he murmured. "They didn't like the idea of people failing to conform to natural laws. Can you imagine trying to run the Inland Revenue Service in a society where people can make things just disappear?"

I admitted that this was a ramification of our work I'd never considered.

"But that's only the beginning," he went on. "When Amelia showed up in Fresno, they realized something much more important –"

"What's that?"

He looked at me closely then leaned forward with a conspiratorial air. "It is something that extends upon your achievement, which they're now implementing, even as we speak, in this very facility. But one thing at a time. You must understand that they insist upon total, unremitting secrecy. I was instructed that nobody should know what had happened – not even you. I couldn't tell anyone about Amelia and I haven't been able to tell anyone about you either."

"So what about Colin then?" I asked. "Didn't he speak out after I disappeared?"

"He tried. He wrote to us all – to me, Irving Gurgler, and Denis Doberman, as well as to various others, even the President of the National Academies. He was sure he'd sent you sub-stationary but nobody believed him. The official view is that he was a victim of another of your frauds. Harvard threatened disciplinary proceedings. He was given six weeks leave, and now I believe he's back at work."

For a moment, I stared morosely at the white synthetic blanket on my bed. My feelings were torn between indignation and an insatiable curiosity. "Please tell me, Walt," I pleaded. "What are they up to? Why such secrecy?"

He smiled, congenially. "It is the culmination of everything you have strived for, Duronimus. But I can't tell you more. The Treasury people wish to show you themselves."

CHAPTER XXX

STRANG AND DURM

For some days we were effectively imprisoned in the facility, but I didn't mind at first since everything was laid out for our recuperation. Military physiotherapists took us through exercises designed to get us walking again. Men in the navy blue uniform and white shoes brought us meals at regular intervals. We also benefited from adjacent rooms. As our mobility improved, Amelia and I slowly made our way back and forth, encouraging one another in our efforts. We reminisced about Sarcobatus Springs and the rest of the Harvard Six, and speculated about the interest we'd excited within Treasury.

When I was too tired for anything else, I stared at a crack in the ceiling above my bed, quietly contemplating everything that had happened. Sometimes I would run through the equations relating to the negatronium particle; at other times I would try to recollect what it had been like in the sub-stationary state; and I often wondered what we might have missed that Treasury was now pursuing. Then one morning, as Amelia and I breakfasted, Walt arrived with a fresh set of clothes and shoes for us both.

"Please put these on," he said. "They've asked to see you upstairs."

"What? Nothing pink?" Amelia joked.

When we were ready, he took us down a stale and empty corridor to an elevator. We went up one floor, emerging in a simple, carpeted foyer. There was a frosted-glass door in front of us, which opened automatically. To our right, a security agent was seated at a small desk. He looked up as we entered, and nodded at Walt as we passed. Then, rounding a simple plasterboard wall with a couple of leafy indoor plants arranged against it, we found ourselves in a huge open plan room.

To my surprise there was no laboratory and no technical equipment. There was no evidence of scientific activity. On the contrary, we found ourselves standing at the edge of a communal workspace such as one might expect in a large accounting firm, or insurance company. There were about two hundred people present, all dressed in suits, peering at screens.

"Who are these people?" I asked Walt.

"One or two are army guys," he said, "but the rest are Treasury modelers."

"Modelers? But don't you have any laboratories here?" I asked.

"No," said Walt. "The Treasury people know that scientific experimentation is difficult, dangerous, and expensive – and for their purposes they consider it quite unnecessary. This is the way they do things here, through simulation. They just run endless simulations. All that counts for them is what they model. I believe it saves a lot of money," he explained.

He led us quickly off to the side, into a glass-walled meeting room. There was a long beech table in the middle with green leather chairs around it, a whiteboard in one corner, and a bench with a hot-water urn and tea-making facilities.

Two men in gray suits were adding milk to their cups, their backs to the door. They turned when they heard us enter and we all shook hands. One was quite short and had a close-cropped beard. His eyes were bright and beady. He introduced himself as Robin Strang, the Chief Econometrician to the Department of the Treasury. The other, Julius Durm, was Treasury's Director of Economic Modeling and Computer Applications. He was heavier set and clean-shaven with thick silver hair. He held his chin high, like a connoisseur, and wore rectangular, rimless spectacles.

You can always guarantee some surety of opinion from those who make their living by prognosticating, but there was something especially self-assured about these two. We sat down and they began with a few hurried pleasantries. They asked whether our medical facilities were adequate.

"I'm afraid it's rather spartan down there," said Robin Strang, "but you'll understand that budgets are very tight at present."

"Budgets are always tight," Julius Durm agreed, "but we learn to make do."

"True. Very true," Strang said, looking over at Walt, who nodded hastily.

I glanced beyond the glass wall at all the modelers hunched over their screens. From the scale of the operation it was clear that this notion of "making do" was a relative term.

"Well, let's get on with business," Strang said, directing his attention to me. "I assume Walt told you that we have an interest in your work?"

"Yes – and I am intrigued about your work too," I added.

Strang extended an eerie smile. "Do you know what the primary job of a Treasury official is?" he asked.

I shrugged.

"Well, let me tell you," he said. "As Treasury officials, our main duty is to keep politicians and our colleagues in other government departments connected to reality. Government officials are like children. They want everything and they want it now, and they want it without proper consideration of feasibility or cost. Our primary job, therefore, is to keep these instincts under control."

I nodded.

"But it's an uphill battle, isn't it, Julius?" he said.

"They should all learn to make do!" said Durm, his voice a stiff, mechanical staccato. "They always aspire for more than they can afford."

"Which brings me to our secondary function, Professor Karlof," Strang continued. "When our political masters lose connection to reality, it's still our job to give what help we can. After all, we live in a democracy. No matter how stupid their ideas, or how restricted our capacity to pay for them, we must manage the government finances in order to provide our political masters with the resources they need."

"And how do you do that?" Amelia asked.

"Oh, we have a simple solution. Tell me, are you both familiar with the concept of the perpetual motion machine – a machine that produces more energy than it consumes?"

"Naturally!" I replied.

"Yes, of course you are. How silly of me! You're one of the world's authorities on the subject, aren't you?" He placed his hands restlessly on the table in front of him. "Well perhaps you don't realize, Professor Karlof," he said, leaning forward, "that for many years we've had such a machine available to us here at the Treasury."

I caught my breath. Amelia and I looked at one another in alarm. Robin Strang was evidently a man of intelligence but I'd always imagined that the Treasury was a fairly mundane instrumentality. Surely these prosaic number crunchers had not also found a way to circumvent the laws of nature.

"But what are you saying?" I cried.

"What I'm saying," said Robin Strang, "is that while a perpetual motion machine may be impossible according to the laws of thermodynamics, the laws of finance are a completely different kettle of fish. Long ago, we invented the first truly effective way to disconnect America from reality. It's called the national debt."

I looked at Amelia and raised my eyebrows in disbelief.

"Yes, Professor Karlof," Strang declared triumphantly, "you're not the first person to study the problem of reality. What we've shown, through the practical application of simple economic principles, is that if Americans cannot have free energy, they can at least have free money. Public debt is our equivalent of a perpetual motion machine." He stared at me through unblinking eyes. "Have you never considered this before?" he asked. "When the reality of government financing fails to meet the expectations of policymakers, Treasury naturally dips into the public debt."

"It enables nearly everything a society could want and at virtually no cost," Durm clarified.

"But don't you have to pay it back?" I asked.

"At this time – Not if you're America!" Strang scoffed. "But we didn't call you up here to gloat. My point is that we too have an interest in understanding the limits of what's possible –"

"And what's impossible," added Durm.

"Yes, quite!" Strang confirmed, before turning back to me. "We have always regarded your work very seriously, Professor Karlof. Why do you think we funded you over all those years?"

There was a pause while Robin Strang stood up.

"But that was only the beginning," he resumed. "There's another reason we are interested in your work. You see, we have a problem ..."

"A problem?" I asked, involuntary excitement welling up in my throat.

"Yes –"

He nodded to Durm, who also stood and walked to the wall at the end of the room. From the bench beside the hot-water urn, he picked up a small remote control. With a heightened air of expectation, he pressed a button and the entire wall began to slide away. It opened onto a room so vast that I couldn't see its end. It was filled with row upon row of blinking computer hard drives.

"This is Node A of the Prodigious Rose Garden Supercomputer," said Durm grandly. "It is the dominant source of all economic and social analysis conducted within the United States Treasury."

I stood up, awestruck.

"Please come in," added Strang.

They ushered us through the opening. The room was very long and wide, and at some point the hard drives gave way to a series of interconnected colored pipes, which extended up and down from the floor to the ceiling. This was where we stopped. It was dimly lit and there was a faint hum in the background. I could make out that the floor was transparent with a jumble of electronics packed beneath it. Someone explained that we were standing in just one of an array of sixty-four such platforms. Then for a second, there was an eerie silence and I realized that Strang's fierce, impatient eyes were watching me closely.

"We have brought you here to give you a sense of the scale of the computational power we have at our disposal," he began, and I remember thinking how well they had succeeded, at least in this respect, for it really was an awe-inspiring location, an impressive monument to human ingenuity.

"Right now we are standing in the middle of the most powerful computer on Earth," he continued. "The models we run on it are the most sophisticated representations of reality ever devised. And yet –" He paused a moment to wet his lips. "And yet even with all this," he went on, "we still can't tell you what the price of petroleum will be five days from now. We can't predict next year's tax revenues. Nor can we forecast who will win the next presidential election."

"But these are hard problems," I noted sympathetically. "Maybe you just need a bigger computer."

Julius Durm and Robin Strang both shook their heads dolefully. "We used to believe that," said Strang. "Hence all of this –"

He gestured all around us and once again I took in the low-ceilinged room that seemed to go on forever, with its shiny glass floor and embedded electronics, and with its great, chaotic mess of colored pipes twisting in all directions.

"We used to think that bigger computers would enable us to overcome these problems. But it's not enough. The world's just too complicated to model accurately," Durm added, shaking his head forlornly.

"Yes, there are fundamental constraints on what we can calculate," continued Strang. "Reality is essentially bewildering. For which reason, we have reached a fairly obvious conclusion ..."

"And what is that?" I asked.

"Well, obviously we need a simpler world!"

I looked at him in astonishment. Was this the same person, I wondered, who'd declared only minutes earlier that his principal duty was to keep others connected to reality? I thought I saw an evangelical gleam in Strang's piercing brown eyes.

"We've always known that our greatest constraint lies not with us, nor with our tools, but with the world itself," he said, in a surprisingly matter-of-fact way.

"If the world were simpler, our models would work just fine," added Durm soberly.

"We never imagined, though, that anybody would discover a capability for making such an extraordinary thing happen," mused Strang. "Then you came along!"

"Me?"

"Yes," said Strang. "By teleporting Amelia to Fresno you revealed that the laws of nature are far more compliant than anyone had imagined, and you opened up an unexpected possibility. We realized that if *you* could break a few laws – well then, surely *we* could simplify them."

Beside me, Amelia squeezed my arm. I looked from Strang to Durm and back again. This was extraordinary.

"After your controversial experiment," Strang went on, "we considered all the possibilities. Walt here wanted to create a national repository of negatronium for military purposes. There were others in Washington who proposed turning the Ooala Reactor into some sort of communications and transportation hub," he scoffed. "We assessed a great many ludicrous notions. But in the end, one proposition emerged that was infinitely more interesting and advantageous!"

Strang reached out suddenly and patted Amelia's shoulder. "Tell us, Amelia, what do you remember most about your exposure to negatronium?" he asked.

I recalled the visceral heaviness that had encompassed me as the negatronium seeped in.

"The emotions," she said, without hesitation.

"Precisely!" Strang declared, and he released his grip on Amelia and stepped closer to me.

"From every test we've ever performed, from every model we've run, and from your own personal experiences," he said excitedly, "we have come to the realization that the negatronium particle represents not a physical force, but an emotional one. Professor Karlof, do you grasp what this implies?"

My heart was thumping. Had we overlooked something so obvious in our analysis? "Are you saying," I offered hesitantly, "that the negatronium particle affords a mechanism for crossing the boundary between the physical and the psychological?"

"Yes," said Strang. "We believe it's proof that the cosmos, nature – whatever we want to call it – has psychological as well as physical forces. But that is not all ..."

He took a step backward and suddenly looked around him, as if to check no one was eavesdropping.

"There's something even more important," he said with exhilaration. "Just think what this implies. We've known, ever since Newton, that for every force there is an equal and opposite force. If nature can exert such a strong emotional impact upon us, then why shouldn't our emotions be able to impact upon nature?"

It was an enthralling idea, but his argument was flawed. "Humans have been emoting for hundreds of thousands of years, and with little, if any, effect upon the nature of the universe," I observed dryly.

"Yes, yes," said Strang impatiently. "But our capacity to generate emotional fields has been limited by the scale of human populations. To have any effect, we would need to convince a certain threshold of people to feel a particular way about a particular aspect of the world – a threshold that's never been reached before."

"The world has simply been too small and too diverse," enjoined Durm fiercely. "The entire global population only exceeded a billion people two hundred years ago, and ever since then it's been fragmented into too many different cultures and communities."

"Now, though, everything has changed," added Strang. "For the first time in history we have access to a globalized community of many billions of people, all interconnected with modern communications technologies. No one's really thought about this issue before. In the past, humans have projected their emotions toward one another. People en masse have not been terribly emotional about the laws of nature. It's usually considered common sense to accept the laws just as they are."

He looked at me as if to check I'd followed his arguments, so I nodded. In truth, I was stunned. Their proposition seemed to be that if they could only make enough people feel a certain way about the universe, then they could shake the very foundations of nature. What they were suggesting did sound vaguely plausible, although it still seemed highly unlikely. It's one thing to get people to pretend they feel a certain way about something, but quite another for their feelings to be real.

"But you can't force people to feel something," I interceded. "How are you going to project human sentiment on a mass scale? How are you going to guarantee their emotions are authentic?"

"Oh, that's easy enough for the bulk of them," said Strang. "We may not be scientists, but we are experts in the psychology of crowds. One thing we do know is how to stimulate real emotions driven by genuine beliefs on a collective scale. We can generate massive emotional fields, no problem."

"Really?"

"Oh, it's the easiest thing in the world," he said, boasting now.

"But how?"

"Well," said Strang, "what's the one thing that nearly everyone trusts implicitly?"

"God?" I asked.

"No. Something here on earth – something that we can control," he said.

"The Federal Reserve Bank?" I hazarded.

"Don't be stupid!" he went on, impatiently. "I am talking about the one thing that we all place perfect faith in."

"The President of the United States?" asked Amelia.

"No! Of course not! At any one time at least fifty per cent of Americans think he's an idiot."

"What then?" I asked.

Robin Strang looked at me with exasperation. "You are standing in the middle of one," he said.

He was talking about the computer!

"Haven't you noticed?" barked Strang. "People will believe anything at all, so long as it is calculated by a computer and, in our experience, the more powerful the computer, the more likely people are to believe it."

He waved his hand and my eyes were drawn again to the scale of the space in which we were standing.

"This immense calculating instrument, which we have assembled here in Washington – the Node A of the Prodigious Rose Garden Supercomputer – is already the equivalent of the Delphic Oracle," he said. "On certain social and market-related themes, we already exploit its power to create self-fulfilling prophecies. What we come up with here, people tend to believe; then they go out and act in a way that makes it true."

"But only sometimes," said Durm, regretfully.

"Yes," went on Strang, "that's our great problem. The approach works where perceptions actually are reality. But we want to see whether we can reach the threshold beyond which collective emotions about our world can start to transform the world itself. We want to exploit your new paradigm in order to change – to simplify – the physical facts of reality."

He reached this climax with an air of exaltation. It was a profound and unexpected notion: first, to speculate that human emotional forces could actually impact upon the natural world; and second, to take the supercomputer and invert its use – employing it not to calculate but to persuade. My mind reeled.

Then suddenly Amelia stepped forward. "But what does all this have to do with us and the Ooala Reactor?" she demanded. "And why was it so important to keep everything secret?"

Robin Strang's dark eyes flitted this way and that, restless as froghopper nymphs in a jar. I noticed the slight flash of his teeth. "Unfortunately, there was one impediment to our plan," he said, and turning on his heels he led the way across the transparent, glassy platform in the direction of the far wall.

Surprised by this abrupt movement, the rest of us followed in silence.

CHAPTER XXXI

THE CONTAINMENT MODEL

We came to a small door. Strang opened it and we followed him in and along a dark passage, until we approached a set of double doors with DANGER and NO ENTRY and NO PACEMAKERS written in bright orange letters. Durm pressed a button on the wall and the doors swung open, revealing a small foyer. Opposite us there was another door, but this one was different. It had a seal around it, similar to those airtight hatches one sees on submarines. It also had a huge wheel on its face, which Robin Strang turned enthusiastically until, with a gentle hissing sound, it swung open and at once a dazzling light shone out from the other side.

He gestured for us to walk through. At first, I could make out nothing specific, but when my eyes adjusted I saw that we had stepped onto a metal platform with a gleaming white painted safety rail extending all around it. Looking outwards, I realized that we were on the edge of a very large cylindrical cavity. Everything was white and brilliantly lit. The chamber itself was maybe fifty feet wide. The base was perhaps two or three stories below, and I noticed that there were people in white protective suits walking about down there. They seemed to be cleaning its surfaces until they gleamed. Then I looked upwards. The ceiling extended so far above us that I could scarcely make it out.

"Hold on!" Strang commanded.

I clutched the railing beside me. Durm prodded a control pad, and the platform slowly began to ascend. As we went up, I recalled the Ooala Reactor and the various devices we had installed in order to access our reaction chamber. I glanced at Amelia and felt a sudden pang of fear.

Then the platform shuddered to a halt. One by one, we stepped inside a compartment built into the wall at the top of the cylinder. Julius Durm was last off. At the entrance, he turned and pulled a lever at another console, and the platform from which we'd just disembarked folded snugly into the wall behind, sealing us in.

The outside of the chamber was a floor-to-ceiling window. Beyond it, one took in the vast cylindrical cavity with its long, curved walls. It really was a startling piece of engineering. Turning inwards, however, I experienced an even greater surprise: the compartment we'd just entered was an exact copy of the reaction chamber at the heart of the Ooala Reactor in Nevada! And there in the center of the room was my very own picoslumberous decelerometer. Its nozzle was sealed into the window, pointing out into the cylinder beyond, but everything was otherwise just as it had been that last day I'd seen it. I looked at Walt in astonishment and he smiled happily, like a parent indulging a child with an especially sought-after gift. I couldn't help myself. I walked over and reached out to touch it tenderly.

"We requisitioned it and had it shipped here," said Strang, gently. "As you can see, we've had the whole setup replicated more or less as it was down in Nevada."

"But why?" I asked.

All three men looked at me, eyes wide with barely contained excitement.

Strang cleared his throat. "The picoslumberous decelerometer is the defining instrument of our time," he exclaimed. "It's the dream of anyone who wants to make a real difference in the world. But I'll let Julius explain."

"Ah yes!" Julius Durm surveyed the room as if it were his own personal dominion. "It's like this. We told you about our models. To be convincing a model doesn't need to be right, it merely needs to be plausible – and we don't have any trouble generating powerful and highly persuasive models. You saw our room full of modelers?"

Amelia and I both nodded.

"Even as we speak," he stated forcefully, "our people are putting together a number of excellent models, showing any number of things about the world: not as it is, obviously, but as we would prefer it to be. Yet to advance any of these models on a universal scale – to advance any new belief about the world – we need one more thing."

He looked at Strang, who nodded him on.

"You see," Durm continued, "we've found that not everyone believes what they are told, even by a supercomputer. And it doesn't seem to matter how plausible an idea is, how persuasive, there's always a minority who will resist it."

"The truculent minority!" interjected Strang, his eyes flashing.

"Yes," Durm observed morbidly. "In every population there's a minority who'll never listen. We think it is something fundamental to human nature, statistical even. Naturally, we've tried to bring these people round. We've tried assembling a community of reputable scientists to sanction our prophecies, drawing upon the credibility of allies like you – you know, people who share our goals, people who can validate the ideas that we want to put forward."

"Doesn't work!" snapped Strang. "Third-party endorsements don't work!"

"No," said Durm, shaking his head. "None of it does any good. In fact, in some ways it makes things worse, because there are always people who will go out of their way to believe the opposite of what any expert tells them. There are always people who can smell a rat!"

"And that's where your negatronium comes in," announced Strang.

"Yes ..." murmured Durm, ominously. He stroked the side of the picoslumberous decelerometer. "This is for them!" he declared.

Strang took a step toward us and lowered his head confidentially. "You see," he said, "while you've demonstrated that high doses of negatronium can send a person into a sub-stationary state, we've discovered something else."

"And what is that?" I asked.

"We've found that in extremely low doses, negatronium has a different effect – it slows people down."

I thought of the sluggishness we'd all experienced when I flooded the control chamber of the Ooala Reactor, and I remembered Colin desperately trying to turn the holographic dial, but being unable to move. "That's not exactly a revelation to me," I said.

Strang shook his head. "I'm not talking about slowing people down physically," he corrected me. "I'm talking about the impact that an extremely low dose of negatronium, absorbed over a long period of time, can have on people's minds. We've found that low doses can make people more ... pliable."

It was not an implausible idea. I recollected the profound sense of apathy that we'd all experienced. But I did not like where this was heading. I glanced at Walt, but he was focused upon Strang and the decelerometer. Beside me, though, Amelia squeezed my hand. She seemed extremely anxious.

"It's simple really," Strang was saying. "At high dose, this stuff will send a person sub-stationary. At a moderate dose, it will slow you down physically. But at very low doses you just become ever so slightly more compliant. It's almost imperceptible."

"I see. And you think you can use this to change the attitudes of the American population? You want to use this on ... on the truculent minority?" I asked.

"Oh no! Not just on them," said Strang, strutting to the edge of the compartment and looking out into the space contained within that giant cylinder. "Our plan is to de-energize the atmosphere of the entire earth with negatronium." He turned his head and pointed upwards. "Look. The top of the cylinder can open," he explained.

Then he nodded at Durm to press another button, and the ceiling began to move apart. Here was sky. I heard Amelia gasp. It was the first time we had seen the sky in over a year. For a moment, I held my breath and couldn't take my eyes off that pure, sweet blue.

"Our plan is to fire up your picoslumberous decelerometer, fill this giant cylinder and then send a continuous stream of negatronium up through that opening."

Strang turned and pointed to the rear of the compartment and I noticed a series of valves in the back wall.

"These are connected, via introspective tubing, to a number of high-volume anacranial canisters stored below us," he explained. "We've enlisted hundreds of dedicated volunteers from across the public service, and collected an unprecedented volume of empty space – a process that's ongoing. We add to the stockpile every day."

Then he gestured back toward the window. "This vast structure below us is the containment cylinder. It's designed to stop negatronium flowing downwards into the rest of our facility. But it's more than that." He pointed at the cylinder's sides. "We've applied a negatively charged emulsion to these walls, and there's a synthetic resin on this window as well, both proven to repel negatronium. The same technology protects us here in this building. And behind these walls we have an array of superconducting magnets. Once we've filled the containment cylinder, these will be used to create a turbulent flux that will fling the negatronium upwards into the atmosphere!" He flung his hands skywards as he spoke. "This will enable widespread dispersal across North America," Strang stated matter-of-factly.

"And into other countries too. Ideally, we want to dose the entire planetary atmosphere," added Durm.

"At which point people everywhere will find it easier to believe your models ..." I interjected. "Are you serious?"

"Absolutely! And all because of you!" declared Strang, clapping me on the back.

I felt my heart galloping in my chest. "So when do you start?" I asked.

Strang tapped the side of the picoslumberous decelerometer. "In a few days ... we've had some small problems, but we're nearly there. We're hoping you and Amelia will join us for the occasion."

I didn't know what to say. Scientific ambition is a powerful ember and, once lit, it's not easily extinguished.

We returned to our rooms exhausted, but I was filled with feverish elation, flattered that my brainchild was being put to use, yet terrified that I was losing control of the consequences. At the commencement of any truly original scientific endeavor, it's difficult to predict what one is likely to discover; and having discovered something, it's impossible to forecast exactly how one's discovery will be used.

I looked back upon our arduous quest to repudiate the laws of nature. I marveled at how far we'd come since that night when Amelia took me up to Sandra Hidecock's office. I considered how incredulous I would have been if someone had told me back then where all this would lead. Never could I have anticipated what these economists had revealed. I contemplated their ideas with a horrible fascination.

Even before Sandra Hidecock's death, it had long been clear to me that the world is excessively complicated and messy. This was partly why I'd become a scientist in the first place – to make sense of the complexity, to find order in the mess. The notion that we could not only transcend the laws of nature but also simplify them according to humanity's needs and aspirations was highly appealing. It stirred me to think it was suddenly feasible to replace the questions "What is nature?" and "Can we get around it?" with the much more empowering query, "So what would we like nature to be?"

On the other hand, I was very concerned about the implications for the scientific community – the community in which I'd spent my entire adult life. In the world I'd grown up with, physics had been the master of all sciences and experimental observation had been the essential mechanism for advancement in any discipline. The scientific enterprise had been a pursuit of truths, benchmarked against the rigorous and unyielding facts of reality. Under Strang and Durm's new paradigm, however, the scientific enterprise would be recast as a political game: a game in which computers would be used to create imaginary but plausible projections about the world – projections selected according to somebody's reason or benefit or whim, and designed in order to stimulate maximum public support. In such a world, perhaps the fields of economics and politics would rise triumphant and surpass physics at the pinnacle of intellectual enquiry. It seemed obvious too that computer simulation rather than empirical observation would become the dominant methodology of our age.

Thankfully, Amelia woke me up to the gravity of the situation.

"So what do you think, Duronimus?" she asked, slipping into my room and sitting beside me on the bed. "Is this what you'd hoped for? Do you think we can all be free at last – truly free from the laws of nature?"

"Well, yes ..." I replied, with a tingle of jubilation.

She frowned and glanced over her shoulder to check that no one was at the door.

"But surely you must be worried. Doesn't it trouble you, this idea of everyone being dulled down and persuaded to think the same thing? I mean, what about freedom of thought?"

"Well, I suppose that in this new world some people will have to renounce it," I said, but even as I spoke them the words tasted wrong in my mouth. "But only with respect to certain scientific topics," I hastened to clarify.

Then I stopped because there was something haughty in her eyes. I hadn't seen that wintery, withering expression since the day we first met, when she'd berated me for being a scientist.

"You mean you of all people would stand against freedom of thought?" she exclaimed coldly.

"Well, they're only planning to slightly restrict it," I reasoned. "That's the trade-off and it's only a very low dose of negatronium; just enough to make people slightly more compliant, to take the edge off ..."

My words trailed off. Amelia shook her head and her eyes refused to meet mine.

"But Amelia, most people don't exercise their own thoughts anyway! They never have and never will. They think what they have already been told. If we sacrifice freedom of thought ... well, we won't exactly be losing something that most people would miss."

She turned away from me.

"As far as I'm concerned, freedom from nature's constraints is a dubious achievement if it comes at such a cost," she replied. She gazed ferociously at a light fitting above us, her pale green irises shimmering with determination.

"Amelia, I understand your concern, but let's look at the positives –"

"I'm sorry, Duronimus!" She suddenly shifted her head and looked me straight in the eyes. "I've woken from the deepest, longest sleep of my life, into a nightmare. If there is a trade-off to be made, I don't want to be part of it, and nor should you!"

"But think of the good we could do. We could end poverty, eradicate homelessness, cure cancer, stop war. Amelia – we could lessen the world's suffering."

She pursed her lips and shook her head, determined not to hear me. "Do you know what Sandra Hidecock used to say when she was my doctoral supervisor? She said that the scientific worldview destroys spontaneity, spirituality and the transcendent. She detested the totalizing control of the scientific paradigm. She always said she objected to a world that is reduced purely to the rational."

"Yes," I said, "that sounds like her."

Amelia smiled wanly. "Well, what if Sandra was wrong?" she asked.

"Wrong?"

"Yes! What if we actually need the laws of nature? What if they are part of our defense against human tyranny? What if anyone who abandons the concept of objective truth pays a price? What if we actually need people who want to test things with their own eyes?"

"Or throw themselves out of office windows?" I countered, enjoying the argument now.

"Better to jump than be thrown out by a bunch of economists!"

In her excitement, Amelia seemed more beautiful than I had ever known her. She was animated, her face was flushed, her eyes were enlarged and her pupils were unusually dilated.

"And anyway," she went on, "who chooses the Law under this new model? Is it you? These economists? Strang and Durm? And who chooses *them*?"

Of course, I too felt very uncomfortable about this. No doubt the vast cohort of computer modelers was capable of stimulating very specific attitudes about the universe among a significant proportion of the world's population, and I was certain that Strang and Durm would deploy this capability whether I helped them or not. In the long run though, these choices would fall to whichever members of the intellectual class had the greatest power to shape public sentiment. I gave Amelia the following explanation.

"It will be the intellectual class – our class! Our children's class! The intellectual community will quickly adapt. They will learn to create knowledge rather than merely discover it. It is Plato's dream: the rule of the philosopher kings."

"Absolutely," she snapped and rolled her eyes. "But it'll be the most manipulative, not the most intelligent or the wisest whose choices will prevail. And in my view, a tyranny of scholars is no less reprehensible than any other tyranny."

She took a deep breath. "I would not bring a child into such a world!" she said quietly. "I understand exactly how intellectuals think. Intellectuals have never held much regard for the ordinary person, and if we give them the sort of power you describe, they'll never truly represent anyone's interests but their own."

"Worse still," she went on, "they will enact their dreams at the expense of the rest of us. It'll be the fate of ordinary people like me and my family back in Cheyenne simply to become instruments of their projects."

She was right of course. But then this has always been the case, I explained. How else were the pyramids constructed; the Great Wall of China; the Taj Mahal?

"One last thought," I continued. "If it's going to happen anyway, there's no disadvantage in being on the inside. Even if things go horrendously wrong, nobody will ever be held accountable. Intellectuals are almost never held accountable for the consequences of their ideas."

"Unless that's the reason they want us involved, Duronimus. Maybe they're looking for a scapegoat in case it all goes wrong?"

I looked into Amelia's imploring eyes. There was something lovely about her formidable moral sensibility. I admired her humanity. It was difficult to resist the passionate and instinctive nature of her opposition. But in the end, it was those green eyes that swayed me.

"You are absolutely right, Amelia," I said, and leaned forward to kiss her mouth. And although it caught her by surprise, she responded instinctively without considering Newton's third law, the enduring truth that had already been discussed that day – namely that for every action there must be an equal and opposite reaction.

CHAPTER XXXII

DO YOU FEEL LUCKY, PICO?

That evening I told Walt that we wanted to leave as soon as possible and that we wouldn't be staying to watch the implementation of Strang and Durm's plans. He tried to talk me out of it, but I stood my ground. By now I was very much in Amelia's camp and I felt that the sooner we extracted ourselves the better. I told him that we'd had enough of grand experiments. Walt shook his head sorrowfully.

"I'm disappointed," he said. "We were hoping you'd be here when they filled the containment cylinder."

"I know – and we're very grateful," I explained, "but you don't need us, and we'd like to start our lives afresh, if we can."

We were standing in Amelia's room. She was leaning gently against my arm.

Walt scratched the back of his neck thoughtfully. "Okay," he said, "so when do you think you'll be ready?"

I turned to Amelia.

"Tonight. Right now, if you're game!" she replied.

"And what about your recuperation?" Walt asked.

"We'll manage," I said.

He looked at us and shrugged. "I won't try to argue with you, but I can't think of another scientist in the world who would turn down this opportunity."

He went to the door, but I stopped him as he got there.

"There's just one other thing, Walt ... Can I talk to you?"

"Yes."

We stepped into the corridor, leaving Amelia behind in the room, and I lowered my voice. "Walt, I'd like to visit the picoslumberous decelerometer one last time," I said.

His eyes narrowed suspiciously.

"Why?" he asked.

"I'll likely never see it again. Amelia feels differently. But between you and me, I'm proud of what we've achieved," I said, simply enough.

"Oh – so it's like that," he replied with a grin. "I'll see what I can do. Wait here."

Minutes later, he came to collect me. This time we went by a different route, bypassing the Treasury supercomputer. It turned out there was a dedicated elevator, which carried us directly up to the roof. From here, we could see the whole of Washington majestically spread out around us. It was an extraordinary spectacle made all the more dazzling by the city lights – those glittering pinpricks of human ingenuity. I began to have second thoughts about my decision, but the feeling passed.

To one side of us the view was blocked by a vast structure with curved walls, which I surmised was the containment cylinder. Moving around its circumference, we came to a door marked DANGER and NO ENTRY. Walt unlocked it with a metal key, then switched on a light and we walked through into the cubicle beyond. Directly opposite us there was another steel portal with an airtight seal and a metal wheel on its face, like a marine hatch. Walt opened it and we stepped through. Once again, we were in the compartment containing the picoslumberous decelerometer.

The Treasury engineers had been at work. Tools were scattered about the room and there were several boxes of spare parts arranged on portable shelving beside the decelerometer. I walked carefully around the device, studying their progress. They were almost finished. I ran a hand along the outside of the centrifugal cogitator, the component responsible for compressing voids at high volume and triggering the process that led to the formation of the negatronium.

Walt looked at me quizzically.

"It's an amazing invention, isn't it?" I stammered.

"What?"

"This – this beautiful machine!"

I reached casually into a box to pick up a handful of stopcocks, letting them run through my fingers before returning my gaze to the decelerometer. I felt like a virtuoso violinist gazing at his next Stradivarius. Yet I also had an intense impulse to pick up a spanner and break it all apart.

"Walt, do you know man's deepest fear?" I asked suddenly.

He shrugged. "Death? Pain?" he hazarded.

"No, it's the fear of a life without meaning, fear of emptiness, fear of the void."

As I spoke I ran a hand casually along the decelerometer's nozzle.

"Yet here, with this wondrous device, humanity has mastered the void," I continued. "Walt, we've learned to harness the power of emptiness, and you, Strang and Durm will soon exploit this power –"

"Absolutely!" Walt agreed.

"Yes, but for what?" I asked.

Walt looked at me steadily. "For simplicity ... to simplify things ... to create simplicity. Isn't that what we all want?"

"That's right!" I felt nearly overwhelmed with excitement. "That's precisely what we all want. Simplicity! But what is the simplest thing in the universe?"

"I don't know ..." Walt took a stab, "Death?"

"The simplest thing in the universe is a void," I replied, all the time continuing to run my hand under the side of the decelerometer.

Where the nozzle joined the body of the apparatus there was a small interstitial cavity. I inserted a finger into this hole, and pulled out a tiny flow-back valve. I do not believe Walt noticed.

"Come on," I said, abruptly. "Time to pack."

"Okay," Walt muttered, an element of disappointment in his voice.

Maybe he'd hoped I'd change my mind about staying and even working with DARPMA or the Treasury. As I followed him to the door, I slipped the flow-back valve into my mouth and swallowed it. At the doorway, I turned my head and took a final look backward. It was the last time I would ever see the picoslumberous decelerometer.

Back in my room, Durm was waiting for us with Amelia and four security guys. There was no sign anywhere of Strang. Everybody seemed very grave, except for Durm who looked awkward and disappointed. As we entered, he stepped toward us stiffly.

"So you're going?" he asked, with a veneer of affability. I nodded solemnly.

"And there's nothing we can do to change your mind?" There was a twinge of bafflement in his voice.

I shook my head.

"We are truly disappointed," he said, blinking at me through his rectangular, rimless glasses. "We'd hoped to work with you. In a funny way, we felt we owed you the opportunity." He frowned uncomfortably. "You know you will be affected by the negatronium – once we release it into the atmosphere?"

"We'll make the best of it," Amelia said.

"They've lived through much worse than anything we can do," Walt added.

"Yes … well, never mind," Durm replied, gazing past us abstractedly. "Of course, we do have some formalities to attend to. You must know that this facility is secret. We were going to have you sign a confidentiality agreement, but we decided that this would be counterproductive – tantamount to an admission that you were here. But if you ever say anything, either privately or in the media, then …" he coughed slightly, "we will weave a net around you and yours as only Treasury can."

As he said this, he glowered and I felt the warmth drain from my face.

"So now I'm going to give you just two verbal instructions," he continued. "First, you must realize that we will deny any knowledge of your appearance in Fresno."

He gazed at us in turn and Amelia and I both gulped and nodded.

"Second," he continued, "you should know that we will also deny any claim you make in relation to the year you have spent here in this facility."

We nodded again.

"Right then!" he said, and he signaled to the four men in uniform.

Within an instant, two of them surged forward and grabbed Amelia. I tried to keep them off her, but the other two were now grasping me – around the neck and the ankles. Within a moment I was on the floor. Somehow through the melee that ensued, I caught a glimpse of Durm. His fixed, unblinking stare conveyed no emotion; and in that strange moment of violence and powerlessness, I felt certain I was making the right decision.

Then I saw handkerchiefs in the hands of our captors. I struggled as they raised one to Amelia's face. For an instant she looked directly at me, an immeasurable beauty in the courage of her swooning expression. Then they smothered her nose and mouth and I saw her body go limp. I struggled on, but to no avail. Another handkerchief was pushed onto my face. A powerful, encompassing smell that I recognized as halomethane or maybe halogenated ether suffused me and I lost consciousness.

When I awoke, it was night and someone was stroking the hair behind my ears. I felt groggy and dazed. I saw Amelia's darkened, upside-down face. I was lying with my head in her lap. I felt sand under my hands and body – coarse, warm sand and the smell of the sea.

"Where are we?" I asked.

"I don't know," she said. "Seems coastal. Maybe Oregon."

CHAPTER XXXIII

UNINTENDED CONSEQUENCES

When I was a professor at Harvard, I used to believe that knowledge is power without the corruption. Now I am not so sure. The viciousness of our eviction from the Treasury Containment Facility was a clear warning that we should stay quiet and out of sight, and I suppose, at some level, this is what we've done. We've built a home for ourselves, far from the world's intellectual affairs, in a small town. It doesn't matter where. I now run a general store. Amelia is a schoolteacher. We've found a sanctuary of sorts here, a temporary shelter from the long shadows of our past, and there are times when we manage to lay aside the fears that haunt us.

It's sometimes said that rural people are narrow-minded. But in Oregon we've met with an openness and freedom of spirit that would be unimaginable at any university or research establishment. The local community is composed of simple folk who experience the world with their five senses just as it is, not as they imagine or desire it to be with their intellect. Untouched by concerns beyond their common fold, the people here never seem to give a moment's thought to their own significance in the grand scheme of things, or to the importance of their contribution to society at large, or to the enduring value of their ideas. They live not for the future or the greater glory of humankind, but in the present and for those nearest and dearest.

In such company, I've learned a great deal. I've discovered the good that exists in a great many activities I would once have considered trivial. I have also stumbled across new pleasures: the joy of laughing with a neighbor, the satisfaction of helping someone mend a fence, and the many rewards that come from training as a volunteer firefighter. As to my new profession, I have been surprised at how much gratification there is in tidily stacked shelves, in selling soda bottles, milk, eggs, and bread. Exerting myself as a grocer, obviously I can have no profound impact upon the world, but there's a curious pleasure in helping people acquire what they need in a convenient and cost-effective manner. I am reminded nearly every day of the fundamental decency of human nature when it's applied in person, rather than in the abstract.

Amelia and I have thus taken on a new kind of existence. But we both know that this simple, ordinary life is only a temporary hiatus. Having bypassed the laws of nature, and having seeded in the minds of some of the most powerful people on earth a mechanism for modifying the cosmos according to their own desires, we are acutely aware that our world could change in an instant. As Amelia often reminds me, there will always be those who are attracted to mass movements, and the justification for shaping collective consciousness now has a scientific basis. Worse still, we might not even be aware that it is happening.

Of our old friends and colleagues, only Colin and Rubin know where we are now. Given my tarnished reputation following the Ooala Outcomes and Ethics Review, and with Harvard continuing to perpetuate the lie that my work was fraudulent, I was reluctant to communicate with any of them. But finally I did write. I wanted to tell Colin the rest of my story and I approached Rubin too, hoping for a rapprochement of sorts. In our initial exchange of letters, Colin had mentioned that Rubin's marriage to Millicent had ended badly, and I wanted to express my sympathies.

Together they came to visit us in Oregon. Colin had lost weight, and Rubin too seemed even more diminutive than I'd remembered. But in other respects they hadn't changed. They brought us quickly up to date on life back at Harvard: how Jack Gasket had been appointed Provost; how Lewis Winterbottom had been made President of the American Academy of Science; and how Millicent Parker had left to join a venture capital firm based in Austin, Texas. Then, over dinner, we told them our story – about our teleportation to Fresno, our year asleep, those strange meetings with Robin Strang and Julius Durm, and our uncomfortable mode of departure from the bunker underneath Treasury.

As I came to the end of my account, Colin looked up from his dessert. "There's just one thing I don't understand," he said.

"What's that?" I asked.

He leaned back slightly in his chair and gestured upwards with his huge hands. "Well, it doesn't seem to have worked, does it? I mean, from everything you've said, shouldn't we now be immersed in an atmosphere laced with negatronium?"

"Maybe we are!" I replied. I exchanged a glance with Amelia, who gave a nod of encouragement. "But there is reason to hope," I added, smiling.

I rose from the table and opened a drawer in the small cabinet we kept at one end of our dining room. I pulled out some news clippings I'd printed at the public library, and passed them around. "You'll see here that Amelia, Fred and I are not the only ones who have been sub-stationary," I explained with a smile.

There were several disparate reports, which I'd sourced from local newspapers of various towns in West Virginia. They conveyed a consistent tale. On a single day, about a week after our own enforced departure from Washington, two security agents in blue uniforms and white shoes, as well as half a dozen or so Treasury officials, had been discovered in a comatose state in a peat bog in the Monongahela National Forest, West Virginia – roughly the same latitude as Washington D.C.

Local news outlets had reported these stories, but to my knowledge they'd failed to attract national media attention. I suppose people are discovered unconscious all the time in America. One account, however, did gain more attention than the others: a report from the *Washington Post* about a former Chief Econometrician for the Department of the Treasury, who'd been discovered separately from the others, unconscious on a sidewalk outside a brothel in the nearby town of Elkins. Fueled by his wife's outspoken insistence that he would never dream of visiting such an establishment, and by the mysterious failure of the West Virginian health authorities to identify a cause for his condition, it seemed that for a day at least, Robin Strang became a figure of minor national scandal.

"But how did all this happen?" Rubin asked.

I reached into my pocket and pulled out the tiny back-flow valve that I'd surreptitiously slipped from the nozzle of the picoslumberous decelerometer.

"What's that?" asked Colin.

I held it up for them both to see. "Something I removed from our decelerometer the last time I saw it," I said.

"And what does it do?" asked Rubin.

I handed it to him. "Simple really," I replied. "It directs the negatronium out through the nozzle of the decelerometer. Without it, instead of filling the containment cylinder, a proportion of any negatronium funneled through the device would leak back into the control compartment."

I found myself gleefully clasping my hands together at the thought of what must have happened next. "My guess is that they fired it up and found themselves flooded with so much negatronium they weren't able to switch it off. It could be that the picoslumberous decelerometer itself went sub-stationary. Though if it did, who knows where it might have rematerialized, or whether the Department of the Treasury – or anyone else for that matter – has managed to build a new one."

"And if it didn't go sub-stationary?" Colin asked.

"Well, I guess if it kept ticking over up there, the negatronium particles could still be flowing out to this day. But not in the way intended," I said. "They'd be flowing out, all over the District of Columbia."

Colin chuckled.

"It'd serve them right!" he said.

After dinner, we went outside and sat around a campfire, drinking vodka and peering up at the stars. The air was fresh but not too cold, and the fire was mesmerizing – even to three scientists who could describe all the main reaction pathways involved in the combustion of wood. For a while we sat in silence. There was nothing more to say about what had happened to Amelia and me, but we hadn't yet spoken of the future.

"The big question now is whether someone else might succeed where Treasury failed," I mused.

"And what we can do to protect ourselves," said Amelia, the light and shadows of the fire flickering across her face.

"Oh, I'd be relaxed on that score," Rubin said suddenly.

"Why's that?" Amelia asked, her perceptive eyes turning quietly toward him.

"Well, for their scheme to work, it would have to mean that the truth is ultimately just a matter of majority opinion," Rubin said, indignantly. "No one at Harvard would ever agree to that, no matter how much negatronium you pumped into us."

"Yes, can you imagine?" added Colin. "The faculty at Harvard accepting that their ideas should be judged by popularity rather than merit ... and that unity of opinion is more important than independence of thought!" He threw his hands in the air, as if to accentuate his incredulity.

Then Rubin reached across and tapped me on the knee. "Your Treasury friends would have to convince us to write papers and give seminars in which nobody ever asked for evidence," he said, grinning. "We'd have to accept that it's reasonable to judge the legitimacy of our results by how many Nobel Laureates spoke on our behalf, or how many learned organizations endorsed our ideas, or whether a majority of Fellows of the American Academies were supportive!"

It was clear that he also regarded the concept as thoroughly idiotic.

"Actually, Rubin, it would be worse than that," murmured Colin. "Think of our teaching programs.

Lectures would simply become forums for inculcating belief. Instead of showing our students how to think for themselves, we'd have to persuade them simply to believe whatever they were told."

"No, no, Colin! You've got one thing wrong," Rubin exclaimed. "More likely, we'd have the students themselves telling the faculty what is the acceptable majority view. So there wouldn't be any lectures. That is the eventual outcome when truth is selected not by rigorous standards, but by popular demand."

He looked up sharply, a glow of passion in his intelligent eyes. "I think most people in universities would be very resistant to these ideas, Duronimus, no matter how much negatronium there was in the atmosphere," he suggested. "I mean – can you name a single university anywhere in America where the idea of solidarity, community consensus, and speaking with one voice would ever be touted as a valid alternative to the ideal of objective truth and free enquiry?"

"I don't know," I said.

I really wanted to believe him. I wanted so much to share their optimism, but I wasn't sure. I was tired, and for some days my limbs had seemed weak, my mind listless. Beside me, I felt Amelia reach out and clasp my hand. I saw that she too lacked the confidence of the others. But neither of us felt like arguing the point.

"I suppose you're right," I said.

"Of course we're right –" Colin muttered.

"We're Harvard professors!" Rubin exclaimed.

We laughed again, and the conversation moved onto other themes. We reminisced about our early meetings at Harvard, about brainstorming in the Old Arlington, and about the living arrangements at Sarcobatus Springs. Colin and Rubin spoke about the latest developments in their old fields of geophysics and cosmology. They asked us questions about life in Oregon. And they reminded me of something I'd long since forgotten: how good it is to spend time with those who are happy simply to uncover a truth about the world, and who are not also enthralled by the desperate urge to change it.

We talked long into the night. It was all very normal and reassuring. I believe we were all grateful of the chance to see one another again. But for my own account, a sense of fear remained.

The next morning I woke at dawn, feeling curiously depressed. Slowly and carefully, I let myself out of the cabin and walked up a dirt track through the forested hill behind our home. My legs were heavy and the air was hazy. I felt tired and I found myself moving more slowly than usual. At the top, I stopped and gazed at the valley below – at the green fields, the scattered woodlands, and the quaint farmers' cottages. It was a beautiful vista, but that morning it had no impact on me. I suddenly felt unendurably sad. Indeed, when Amelia found me some time later, the first thing she did was to reach up and touch my cheeks. They were wet from weeping.

"What's wrong?" she asked.

I couldn't answer. The words stuck in my throat. But I remember what I was thinking. In the nineteenth century, the great physicist, Nikola Tesla said, "One day, man will connect his apparatus to the very wheelwork of the universe; and the very forces that motivate the planets in their orbits and cause them to rotate will rotate to his own machinery."

It seems to me that by tapping into the void within and harnessing the power of the negatronium particle, we had brought humanity very close to Tesla's moment – that

Robin Strang and Julius Durm would have reached it, in fact, had Amelia and I not thwarted their ambitions and that, although they did not ultimately succeed, it is only a matter of time before someone else will.

THE END